Praise for the E

"A thoroughly entertaining series debut, with enjoyable yet realistic characters and enough plot twists—and dead ends—to appeal from beginning to end."

—*Booklist*, starred review, on *Booked 4 Murder*

"Filled with clues that make you go 'Huh?' and a list of potential subjects that range from the charming to the witty to the intense. Readers root for Phee as she goes up against a killer who may not stop until Phee is taken out well before her time. Enjoy this laugh-out-loud funny mystery that will make you scream for the authors to get busy on the next one."

—*Suspense Magazine* on *Molded 4 Murder*

"Engaging characters and a stirring mystery kept me captivated from the first page to the last."

—Dollycas, Amazon Vine Voice, on *Divide and Concord*

"Well-crafted sleuth, enjoyable supporting characters. This is a series not to be missed."

—*Cozy Cat Reviews* on *Death, Dismay and Rosé*

"A sparkling addition to the Wine Trail Mystery series. A toast to protagonist Norrie and Two Witches Winery, where the characters shine and the mystery flows. This novel is a perfect blend of suspense and fun!"

—Carlene O'Neil, author of the Cypress Cove Mysteries, on *Chardonnayed to Rest*

Books by J. C. Eaton

The Wine Trail Mysteries

A Riesling to Die
Chardonnayed to Rest
Pinot Red or Dead?
Sauvigone for Good
Divide and Concord
Death, Dismay and Rosé
From Port to Rigor Morte
Mischief, Murder and Merlot
Caught in the Traminette

The Sophie Kimball Mysteries

Booked 4 Murder
Ditched 4 Murder
Staged 4 Murder
Botched 4 Murder
Molded 4 Murder
Dressed Up 4 Murder
Broadcast 4 Murder
Saddled Up 4 Murder
Grilled 4 Murder
Strike Out 4 Murder
Revved Up 4 Murder

The Marcie Rayner Mysteries

Murder in the Crooked Eye Brewery
Murder at the Mystery Castle
Murder at Classy Kitchens

The Charcuterie Shop Mysteries

Laid Out to Rest
Sliced, Diced and Dead

Revved Up *4* Murder

J. C. Eaton

Revved Up 4 Murder
J. C. Eaton

Cover design and illustration by Dar Albert, Wicked Smart Designs

Beyond the Page Books
are published by
Beyond the Page Publishing
www.beyondthepagepub.com

ISBN: 978-1-960511-52-2

ACKNOWLEDGMENTS

We owe so many thanks and appreciation to the folks who gave generously of their time and expertise to ensure *Revved Up 4 Murder* would keep our readers laughing and guessing whodunit.

Thank you, Regina Kotokowski in Sun City West, Arizona, and Susan Schwartz in Coorparoo, Australia, for scrutinizing our manuscript and catching everything from scene inconsistencies to logistics and pesky grammar mistakes. You are both godsends!

To Larry Finkelstein and Gale Leach, thank you for keeping our technology running and everything else you've done related to our book. You're incredible!

And to the following members of the Sun City West Automobile Restoration Club, we are certainly in your debt. Not only did you walk us through that amazing garage, but you taught us so much about automobile restoration. This book could not have been penned without you. Kudos to: Pete Bowman, Evelyn Burrier, Paul Burrier, Don Holman, Dan Kahl, and Tom Jones.

Of course, none of this would have been possible without our tireless and wonderful agent, Dawn Dowdle, from Blue Ridge Literary Agency, who passed too soon. We were so blessed. And she will be so missed.

To our editor, Bill Harris, and the phenomenal staff at Beyond the Page Publishing, we are genuinely appreciative of all you do.

Finally, we thank you, our readers, for bringing our acerbic and quirky characters into your lives!

To Evelyn and Paul Burrier, who gave us the idea to stage a murder in their favorite place—The Sun City West Automotive Restoration Garage. We were mesmerized the first time you mentioned it!

CHAPTER 1

Office of Sophie Kimball
Williams Investigations
Glendale, Arizona

No sooner did I slip off my lightweight fall sweater and boot up my computer when I heard Augusta. For an office secretary, she sounded more like a longshoreman at times. "Pick up the phone, Phee! It's your mother. I transferred the call as soon as I recognized her voice."

"I'm on it, Augusta!"

"Good! I don't think she or one of her friends found a dead body like the last time because she's not that frantic."

Wonderful. That means she's about to invite me to one of their brunches. Or worse.

"Thanks. This should make my day."

Sure enough, my mother was as chipper as all get-up-and-go. "Wonderful news! The book club ladies and Herb's pinochle crew will be celebrating at the new Boyer's Bakery in Sun City this Saturday. Everyone wants you to join us."

No. Everyone wants me to get indigestion.

"Um, what exactly are you celebrating? Usually, the guys go to Curley's Bar."

"Not this time. Oh, don't get me wrong. They'll probably order a pitcher later on in the evening, but we all decided to have breakfast at Boyer's."

"You still didn't tell me the reason for this joyous occasion."

"Wayne's car was selected to be next at the Sun City West Automotive Restoration Club. They'll be restoring that old eyesore of his. The 1965 Ford Mustang that he bought at an auto auction last year. His name finally came up on the November list. If that's not cause for celebration, who knows what is!"

I tried to be enthusiastic and not snarky. "Terrific news. Not sure I can make it. I—"

"You're off work that morning. And besides, their raspberry cobbler and double fudge brownies are spectacular."

"I'll see what I can do." *Or not.*

"Okay, let me know. Hang on a minute, Streetman and Essie want to say hi!"

Before I could object, I heard my mother call out to the dog and cat.

"Say hello to your sister." Then a soft meow and what sounded like a half yowl, half bark.

"Give them my regards, too, Mom. Gotta run. Catch you later." And before she could respond, the phone was back in the cradle.

"I heard that!" Augusta called out. "Did she make you speak to the pets?"

I stepped into the outer office and smiled. "No, only listen. I hung up before she had the chance."

"Couldn't help but overhear you. Your mother's friends are celebrating the fact that an old car is getting restored? Isn't that kind of, well, odd?"

"In their circle, not at all! Last month they celebrated Myrna Mittleson losing five pounds. They all went to the Homey Hut for their pie special, where Myrna, I'm sure, gained those five pounds back plus a few more. She ordered ice cream to go with it."

"Unbelievable."

"That's nothing. In the past few months, they've celebrated Louise spotting an eagles' nest near the dog park, Cecilia making a meat loaf that didn't taste or resemble a brick, and Kenny finally getting a spare when he bowled."

"Got to admit, they give retirement a whole new meaning in Sun City West."

I sauntered to the Keurig machine and popped in a dark roast K-Cup. "Yeah, I have to agree. It's not at all what I expected when I moved out here a few years ago. But then again, there were plenty of warning signs."

I'm Sophie Kimball Gregory, better known as Phee, bookkeeper/accountant for Williams Investigations in Glendale, Arizona. I was first dragged into the "Valley of the Sun" on a wild-goose chase for my mother when I was working in accounts receivable for the police department in Mankato, Minnesota. She and her book club ladies were convinced a cursed novel was killing them off. Don't ask. I flew out here on a whim and vowed I'd never return. Ha! That was before my good friend Detective Nate Williams retired and opened an investigative agency not far from my mother's community. With an endless amount of persuasion, he convinced me to take a year's leave and help him with the business end of things.

As it turned out, my sojourn to the Southwest resulted in a permanent move and a reconnection with detective Marshall Gregory, who, like me, left the Mankato Police Department to work with Nate. One thing led to another and before I knew it, I was Mrs. Sophie Kimball Gregory. Who says book curses don't lead to romance?

"Think your mother will bring the dog to the bakery?"

"As long as Vera Bradley keeps making bigger and bigger tote bags, she will. Ugh. The dog. I try not to think about Streetman. At least the cat's not as neurotic as that chiweenie. And I swear, that dog picks up a new neurosis each day. Now it's certain fabrics he doesn't like. Barks or tears at them."

Augusta chuckled. "That's the trouble with little dogs. They have a Napoleon complex. Give me a Rottweiler or a Doberman any day of the week."

"Who's getting a dog?" Nate asked. He stepped out of his office and made a beeline for the coffee machine. As he plunked the lid over the K-Cup he looked at Augusta.

"Not me, Mr. Williams. Grew up on a dairy farm. Don't need to be reminded."

I shook my head. "We always have to babysit for my mother's darlings. That's enough to scare anyone away from four-legged friends."

"Speaking of scaring away, we picked up a doozy of a case. In fact, that's where Marshall is right now. Seems a priceless artifact from the Phoenix Art Museum was discovered missing early this morning. It's an eighteenth-century wooden doll said to have a cipher built into it. If anyone smashes the doll, the treasure inside it will be destroyed. The cipher has to be solved to unlock and release the treasure. Go figure."

I took a sip of my coffee and furrowed my brow. "Yeesh. That *is* a doozy. Of all things. A treasure trapped inside a doll. I thought those museums had state-of-the-art security systems."

"They do." Nate retrieved his cup and took a gulp. "Unfortunately, the doll is on loan to the Phoenix Unity Council for its upcoming cultural celebration and is no longer in the museum. Too bad they didn't request something else. Like a nice handkerchief. Good thing that event is a few weeks from now."

Augusta cocked her head. "I don't understand why they didn't call the police department. Not that you and Mr. Gregory aren't top-notch, but you come with a fee."

Nate laughed. "The actual jurisdiction where the doll was last seen was outside city limits so the Maricopa County Sheriff's Office got the call."

"Uh-oh." I tried not to roll my eyes. "Don't tell me it's a Bowman and Ranston thing?"

"With all the pomp, circumstance and fanfare that go with it." By now, Nate had finished his coffee and started making a second cup.

"Which one is the one who looks like a grizzly bear?" Augusta tried to keep a straight face. "I get him mixed up with the short guy who could pass for a Sonoran Desert toad."

Nate choked on his coffee and all but spat it out. "You didn't hear this from me. The shorter detective is Ranston. The larger, taller one is Bowman. And let's keep this conversation to ourselves."

I nodded. "I take it their office is mired under so we were asked to consult."

"Short answer—yes. It's part of our continuing contract with the sheriff's office. At least we're not dealing with loonies, kidnapping, or murder."

Yet.

"The museum and the sheriff's office want to keep this as low-profile as possible so don't expect any media coverage. Museum employees are under a gag order as well. We also touched base with the museum's insurance company. It's one we've dealt with before so we'll be sharing information and conferring as needed. They seem to be comfortable with the arrangement. At least for now."

"Too bad we can't put my mother and that book club of hers on a gag order. Not to mention the pinochle guys. And by the way, Wayne's old 1965 Ford Mustang is going to be restored. Right now that's the big news."

Nate grabbed his coffee cup and started for his office. "Good. Anything to keep that crew from getting embroiled in their usual quagmires. Hmm, funny that a car restoration would be cause for excitement."

"Not excitement," Augusta said. "More like a reason to eat out."

"*That*, and a reason to keep the rumor train running on track. And don't worry, I'm not about to breathe a word about that doll to anyone. Last thing I need is for those women to insist we unlock the treasure. Next thing you know, she and her entourage will be camped out at my mother's place, poring over information on decoding puzzles. By the way, what's the story behind that thing? Just in case."

Nate reached in his pocket and pulled out a crumbled piece of paper. "Got the gist from Bowman. The handmade wooden doll was carved from a tree in Virginia where a notorious thief was hung in 1790. The thief supposedly carved the doll and hid a priceless treasure in it. Ironic, huh? The doll was given as a gift to the daughter of a plantation owner but after three days, the little girl died from a mysterious illness."

Augusta shrugged. "Doesn't sound that unusual. Back in those days people succumbed to all sorts of diseases."

Nate looked up from the piece of paper. "Hold on. There's more. Once the girl was buried in the family cemetery, members of her family began hearing her voice and, even stranger, noticed the doll had moved from the girl's bedroom to the butler's pantry."

"That's easy," I said and laughed. "The butler did it."

"There was no butler and the doll didn't remain in the pantry. Long story short, the family believed the girl's spirit was trapped inside the doll, along with the treasure."

"Then what?" Augusta gave her bouffant hair a few pats and widened her eyes.

"According to Bowman's notes, the mother passed away the following month as a result of a fall down the stairs. And the girl's father was killed when he was thrown from his horse."

"A whole lot of coincidence if you ask me."

"I agree with Phee," Augusta said. "And a whole lot of hooey."

Nate flattened the note and put it back in his pocket. "Hooey or not, that doll created a whirlwind of public interest and somehow accrued value. It was rediscovered after the Civil War and remained in the possession of one Germaine Webb, a descendant of that family."

"Don't tell me she died from some bizarre circumstance." I took another sip of coffee, this time a larger gulp.

"Yep." Nate's smile grew wide. "Germaine was bitten by a spider in the late 1930s and never recovered. The doll went into the possession of a local museum and from there, grew in notoriety until it was purchased by an art museum in New York and later the Phoenix Art Museum. According to Bowman, 'If we don't find the darn thing, it will be blamed for every death and accident in the valley.'"

"Better tell your husband to work fast," Augusta said.

I nodded and retreated to my office, coffee cup in hand. As I pulled up the monthly expense spreadsheet on my computer, I was hit with the most awful realization regarding the Phoenix Unity Council. I narrowly avoided knocking over my coffee and raced back to Augusta's desk.

"Shh! Not a word, but Nate and Marshall's investigation is in deep, deep trouble."

"Huh? So soon? You were gone less than ten minutes."

"Not a word." I moved closer and leaned over. "I remembered something. Something awful."

Augusta's eyes got wide as I continued. "Cecilia Flanagan and Louise Munson from the book club are *on* that council. It didn't dawn on me at first but as soon as I sat at my desk and went to work on a spreadsheet, I remembered. Holy cow! This is awful. They're bound to know about the missing doll. The missing 'trapped soul inside of it' doll that kills off anyone who comes in close contact with it. If we thought the book curse was bad, this will make it look like child's play. And once word gets out to my mother, there'll be no telling what's next."

"Just keep your fingers crossed that Wayne's car restoration takes center stage."

"Ugh. Looks like I'd better go to that breakfast at Boyer's after all. Someone's got to keep that news about the doll under wraps."

"I thought they were under a gag order."

"The museum employees, not the members of the unity council. Good heavens! Even if they were, do you honestly think Cecilia and Louise could keep their mouths shut? A gag order wouldn't mean anything to them."

"Look on the bright side. It's not a homicide. Not yet anyway. Only a missing doll. With a dead soul inside."

"Thanks, Augusta. That's very encouraging. I'll think of that when I pull back the covers and try to go to sleep tonight."

She smiled and winked. "Anytime."

CHAPTER 2

Four days later, on a colder than usual day, I figured I'd better hightail it over to Boyer's Bakery for the car restoration celebration. In actuality, any excuse for my mother and her friends to fill up on chocolate croissants, fudge bars, assorted decadent muffins, and cookies too numerous to mention. Nate and Marshall were convening with Bowman and Ranston on the doll case and I wanted to steer as far away from it as possible. Unfortunately, Cecilia and Louise saw to it that I didn't.

When I arrived at the lovely little bakery on Bell Road, my mother, Myrna, Lucinda, and Shirley were already seated. I ambled over to the large table filled with assorted sweets and looked around. "Hi! Where's everyone else?"

Myrna put a finger to her lips. "We arranged to meet here a half hour earlier than the men. That way we can schmooze before they get here and start yammering about cars."

"What about Cecilia and Louise?"

"Turn around," my mother said. "They're right behind you."

Sure enough, before I could utter another word, Cecilia rushed over and pulled out a chair. She unbuttoned the top two buttons of her black cardigan, then rebuttoned one of them. "We're not supposed to say anything. Right, Louise?"

I knew that in less than five seconds, the Maricopa County doll investigation would be spread like hair lice.

"Lordy, what now?" Shirley asked. She set her cup of tea in the small saucer and looked up.

"Worse than that book curse a few years back," Louise said.

Myrna tilted her head toward Louise. "I'm always prepared for this sort of thing. Curses, hexes, murderers, lunatics, you name it. I bought a new Screamer. Not only does it have a penetrating siren, but it comes with a strobe light. You can temporarily blind your attacker and pierce his or her eardrums at the same time. I'll give you ladies the purchase link on Amazon."

"What aren't you *not* supposed to say?" Shirley asked Cecilia.

"The thing that's worse than the book curse. But no one's supposed to know."

I jumped in immediately. "Let's keep it that way. Look! Here come Herb and Wayne."

"Rats," my mother said. "Those two are the worst gossipers. They can't keep anything to themselves. The only one worse is my sister, Ina, and she and Louis are in Palm Springs for some sort of a wellness retreat."

"Hey, ladies! What's good on the menu?" Herb asked. "Are those fruit-filled croissants I spy at your table?" He reached for one and my mother tapped his hand. "That one has my name on it, you'll have to buy your own."

Herb muttered to himself and meandered to the bakery case while Wayne pulled up a chair but stopped before he sat. "I'd better put in my order for a ham and cheese sandwich before the rest of the crew gets here. Meantime, take a look at this beauty."

He handed his cell phone to Louise and walked to the counter.

"Some beauty," she said. "What do you think, Harriet?"

My mother eyeballed the photo and shrugged. "Maybe with a new paint job and those dents fixed. Unless the guts—Is that what you call the insides?—are really rotted out."

"It's going to be totally overhauled from what Wayne said." Shirley sipped her tea and glanced at the photo. "They've got all sorts of car fanatics working at that restoration shop, along with the work the pinochle crew will do. By the time they finish, Wayne's Mustang will be worth a fortune."

"And it'll cost him a fortune, too."

Just then, Kenny, Kevin and Bill walked in and nearly collided with Herb, who was on his way back to the table with a large platter of cookies and sweet rolls.

"What happened to your diet?" Myrna asked him.

"I'm incorporating it into my baseball team exercise. The more I exercise, the more calories I need."

I did a mental eye roll and stood. "I suppose I should order something. Looks like they've got plenty of breakfast choices."

"Or chocolate delicacies and cupcakes. I'll join you, Phee. I wanted to try their mixed berry cake." Myrna stood and thundered to the counter before I was out of my seat.

Ten minutes later, with enough sugary treats on the table as well as my veggie omelet, the conversation resumed. Never mind that people spoke with mouthfuls of food or paused to swallow in between tidbits of valuable news. I listened with full attention for fear the subject of the missing doll with the trapped soul would somehow weave its way into a long-winded discourse about carburetors or alternators. Sadly, I wasn't wrong.

"That gem of a find will turn heads come this spring," Wayne announced. "Even getting a match-up paint for the original color—Nassau Blue Metallic."

"Do they take the insides out and start all over?" Lucinda asked as Wayne bit into a large four-cheese muffin.

"They access the engine and go from there. Sometimes all a car needs is a tune-up, but in Wayne's case, it will need to be resurrected." Then Bill laughed.

Shirley reached for a small applesauce cookie and cocked her head. "You mean *restored*."

"Nope," Bill was adamant. "Resurrected. Like from the dead."

"Oh, goodness," Cecilia blurted out. "That's just like the priceless doll with the trapped soul and treasure inside. The one that was stolen from the Phoenix Art Museum."

The men furrowed their brows and looked at each other. Then the questions sprang up like weeds after a good rain.

"What doll?"

"What treasure?"

"What did you mean by 'trapped soul'?"

"When did you hear about a theft?"

"How much is it worth?"

"Is there a finders reward?"

"It's an art artifact," I announced in a loud voice. "An artifact. You know how those things come with legends and folklore." Then I faced Wayne. "Tell us, Wayne. Are you going to have the original parts put back into the car?"

"Well, in all honesty—"

"Don't anyone say a word about that doll," Cecilia said. "No one is supposed to know."

Kevin rubbed his chin and squinted. "If no one is supposed to know, how come you do?"

"It was on loan to the Phoenix Unity Council for cultural week. Part of a major exhibit. And for your information, Louise and I are both on the unity council."

"More like the 'Misplaced Council.' And how come it wasn't on the news?"

"No one is supposed to know."

"Guess that kernel of corn popped, huh?"

Popped, burnt, spilled . . . You name it.

"Look, everyone," I said. "This can't go any further. That doll is worth a small fortune and the investigation is under wraps."

"Oh my gosh!" My mother sat bolt upright and leaned toward me. "Williams Investigations is handling the case. I'm right, aren't I? Why didn't you tell me, Phee? A doll with a trapped soul inside of it? *And* a treasure?" Then she spun her head around to Cecilia and Louise. And faster than that girl in the *Exorcist*, I might add. "And why didn't one of you tell me?"

"We wanted to, Harriet," Louise answered. "But we were told in no uncertain terms not to breathe a word of it or it will compromise the investigation. It's a very delicate matter. You know, a doll that harbors a fortune inside of it, not to mention a lost soul."

"If that isn't the most ridiculous poppycock I've ever heard, I don't know what is." Bill latched on to a bear claw and finished half of it in one bite.

"Yep. Bunch of malarky if you ask me. Now, about my car. The first thing we're going to do when it gets to the shop is—"

"How did a lost soul get inside the thing?" Lucinda brushed the long blondish gray hairs from her brow and fixed her eyes on Cecilia.

"I'm not sure. But I can tell you, that doll was responsible for more than one death. Not including the person whose soul is inside of it."

"Oh Lordy!" Shirley clasped her hands together and took a deep breath. "Tell me, Cecilia, were you or Louise anywhere near that evil thing?"

The ladies shook their heads and Shirley let out her breath. "That's good."

"So," Wayne went on, "as I was saying, the first thing they'll do at the club is to look under the hood, where they'll find the—"

"The history behind the doll. We need to know what it was." Myrna wiped some cobbler crumbs from the sides of her lips. "All of us need to be prepared. Just in case."

"In case of what?" Kevin asked. "What do you think's going to happen? The doll will make an appearance at one of your houses? Give me a call and I'll collect the reward."

"That's not funny. These things are to be taken seriously." Shirley poured herself another cup of tea from the delicate teapot that was centered in the middle of the table.

"Not as serious as the Sun City West Buy-Sale-Trade event this spring." Wayne reached for the sugar bowl and moved it closer to him. "If all goes well, I intend to put that car on the market and reap the enjoyment of pocketing my own fortune."

"Good luck with that," Myrna said. "Who's going to pay a fortune for a restored car?"

Suddenly it was a cacophony of male voices.

"Historic value."

"Sentimental value."

"A sixties legend."

And finally, from Herb, "Barrett-Jackson, that's who."

The women looked at each other with blank faces.

"Don't tell me you've never heard of Barrett-Jackson," Wayne said.

"Does he live in Sun City West?" Cecilia rebuttoned her top button and proceeded to take a bite of a cinnamon roll.

Wayne threw his hands in the air and shouted, "Good grief! It's the largest car auction company in the state. Televised everywhere! And for your information, those cars go for millions."

"Like that doll," Louise whispered to Cecilia.

"The whole table heard you, Louise," Kenny said. Then he looked at Wayne. "Say, maybe you should be on the lookout for that doll and give it to Betsy Sprig."

I turned to my mother. "Who's Betsy Sprig?"

Before she could answer, Wayne beat her to it. "The infamous nitpicker who's on the automotive restoration club board. Getting any paperwork through is a nightmare with her as secretary."

"That *has* to be the same Betsy Sprig who worked the bingo games a few years ago. She terrorized everyone."

"You're right, Harriet," Lucinda said. "I mean, how many Betsy Sprigs can there be?"

Then Lucinda gave Wayne a nudge. "Is your Betsy Sprig a tall, thin woman with gray roots?"

"Gray what?"

"Hair roots, Wayne. You know, gray hair in dire need of a touch-up."

Wayne shrugged. "I didn't look that closely at her when I filed my paperwork for the club. All I can tell you is that she scowled the entire time. Now, back to my Mustang. I was darn lucky to get called up next. That car of mine is a real treasure and I'm sure collectors will want—"

"That doll! Maybe a collector stole it," Myrna said. Then she furrowed her brow and rubbed her chin. "If I were a detective, I'd be rummaging through Craigslist and eBay. Let them know, Phee. They can thank me later."

I gulped and tried not to grimace. "Wonderful idea. I'll pass it on."

"Hey," Bill laughed, "maybe when they find it, Wayne can take it out for a spin in his car."

"Not funny! Not that I believe for a minute in that whack-a-doodle nonsense, but if that thing does show up, my car will be the last place it sets foot in. Along with Betsy Sprig."

I smiled. "Good to know."

Then my mother took the last raspberry cobbler and broke a piece off. "For Wayne's sake, we should all look into Betsy Sprig."

"Huh? Why?" I all but jumped out of my seat.

"People with ill wills shouldn't be allowed in auto repair shops. Last night I watched the thriller movie, *The Maniacal Mechanic*, on Turner Classic TV. Need I say more?" Then she steepled her hands and made eye contact with Wayne. "Lots of ways to sabotage a car."

For a moment, we were all speechless. I leaned toward Wayne, and when my mother wasn't looking, twirled my index finger. He gave me a wink and I was sure all would be right with the world. But what did I know? That car restoration was about to change everything.

CHAPTER 3

"Well, the cat's out of the bag as far as your investigation goes," I told Marshall that afternoon as we munched on leftover salad before it wilted.

"What do you mean? Nate and I have been working on that case all day. At noon, when Augusta left, we interviewed some of the museum employees. No one mentioned anything."

"You didn't interview the unity council. Namely the two biggest rumormongers this side of the Mississippi."

"Myrna and Lucinda?"

I shook my head. "Good try. Cecilia and Louise. Both of them are on that council and they just couldn't keep their mouths shut. Now the entire book club knows, plus Herb and that pinochle crew of his."

Marshall removed a dried piece of lettuce from his fork, put a hand to his cheek and shook his head.

"I tried to do damage control," I said, "but you have no idea how difficult it was to segue from a priceless doll to Wayne's pricy car restoration."

"I'm sure you did your best. Are the women off the rails about the story behind the doll?"

"Off the rails? They're off the train and running. But that's not all. Seems Wayne's car restoration comes with a caveat no one expected."

"Huh?"

"A woman by the name of Betsy Sprig who's the secretary for the auto restoration club. According to Wayne and a few others, Betsy is one heck of a bossy know-it-all who makes everyone's lives miserable. And to make matters worse, she's filling in for the president of the club because he and his wife are on a cruise. Apparently, the club doesn't have a vice president."

"I see. Why doesn't the club elect someone else as secretary?"

"Probably because no one wants to do all the work involved."

"No matter. Maybe everyone will be so preoccupied with Wayne's new project, they won't pay much attention to our doll investigation."

"Fat chance. Especially when it comes to things that hint at another realm."

"Let's pray the news doesn't get to social media, because once it surfaces on Facebook or Instagram, we might as well invite every TV anchor over for coffee and chitchat."

"I don't think social media is a worry. The men can barely manage their cell phones and the women would rather tie up the phone lines than text or post things. In fact, the only one fairly conversant with those things is

Shirley and she's mainly on Pinterest with all her cute teddy bears and pet clothing."

"Let's hope it remains that way."

• • •

It didn't. A week later I got a call from my girlfriend and pool companion, Lyndy. She heard about the doll from someone in her medical billing office and they heard about it from their beautician.

"Her beautician?" All of a sudden my voice was shrill and one step away from rivaling Augusta's.

"I know. I know. Might as well put it on a public announcement."

"You haven't seen it on any of the news channels, have you?"

"Not yet."

"Marshall and I keep tuning in and holding our breath but I doubt this is going to stay under wraps much longer."

"It hasn't reached my looney aunt in Sun City West so maybe that's a good thing. Hey, want to brave it and swim one afternoon when you get home from work? The pool temperature is eighty-eight and if we run fast, we can get into the locker room before we turn into ice cubes."

"I'm game. Let's touch base in a day or so."

When the call ended, my stomach did flips. Gossip at the beauty parlor rises exponentially at rates not even seen by mathematicians. I only hoped Nate and Marshall could work faster.

Meanwhile, work on Wayne's car moved at a decent rate. He was bound and determined to get a hefty price at that buy-sell-trade event in the spring and made it a point to work on his Mustang most every night. According to my mother, Bill and Kevin were helping with the restoration along with the Turk sisters, Darleen and Aimee, two single women who were retired airplane mechanics.

I didn't expect to be included in Wayne's project, but I should have known better. He phoned me shortly after my conversation with Lyndy and invited me to help him decide which material to use on the car cushions.

"I need a woman's opinion," he said. "Should I use leather, vinyl or fabric? I have samples from an upholstery shop in Peoria and I have to decide. The book club ladies are coming over but between you and me, I question their taste."

I question everything about them.

"Uh, what about your pinochle crew?"

"I don't even think they look at the seat cushions. Unless someone drops a donut or something on them and they need to find it."

"Okay, when and what time?"

"Tuesday evening at seven. The shop will be open until nine so that will give us plenty of time."

Two hours to pick a material? Shoot me now.

"I doubt we'll need all that time. Marshall and I will grab a bite after work and drive over. Um, my mother isn't coming with the dog, is she?"

"If Harriet could have that chiweenie permanently attached to her, she would. Don't even ask. All I want is for the tote bag manufacturers to start making stronger mesh. For a little guy with little teeth, Streetman can chew through anything."

Visions of the dog ducking under cars and getting covered with oil raced through my head. "Yeesh."

"Meanwhile, we're working under the hood. Ordered a new timing belt, engine valves, and water pump gasket for starters. I'll probably need a new camshaft pulley but I'm not sure, then again—"

I walked across the room and rang my doorbell, a trick I learned from my aunt Ina. "Someone's at the door, Wayne. Got to get it. See you on Tuesday."

If I thought the book club ladies rambled on, it was nothing compared to Wayne describing car parts. I crossed my fingers that we wouldn't get stuck for two hours as he rendered a decision on the seat cushions.

• • •

Luck must have been smiling at us because news of the doll hadn't made it to the news media by Tuesday evening. It did, however, manage to infiltrate every conversation my mother had with anyone and everyone who would listen.

"Don't keep that thing going, Mom," I said when she phoned me Tuesday afternoon. "It's the last thing Nate and Marshall need. They're up to their necks already with interviews and on-site visits."

"The public has a right to be forewarned."

"Not by the gossip klatch. And forewarned about what? Some wacky old legend? All that matters is that the doll is worth a fortune and needs to be found. Listen, I have to get back to work. We'll see you tonight at the auto club garage." *With or without the dog.*

She mumbled something and the call ended.

Marshall and I had taken one car to work, making it easier for us to stop by Smashburger and from there to Sun City West, without having to make an extra stop on the way home to retrieve the other vehicle. The usual lineup of Buicks belonging to the book club ladies took up the parking spaces in front of the garage. I braced myself for a barrage of questions the minute we went inside but thankfully, everyone was preoccupied offering advice to Wayne.

"You don't want to go with fabric," Shirley said. "It gets dirty and it's difficult to clean. Pick vinyl or leather."

"Not leather!" Cecilia gasped. "It's from cows. Live animals."

"They're not live anymore." Bill rolled his eyes. "Besides, you eat hamburgers, don't you?"

Myrna elbowed her way closer to the Mustang. "That's different. It's a food. We need food to survive."

Marshall patted Wayne on the shoulder and laughed. "Glad this is your decision, buddy, and not mine."

I looked around the garage as the crew continued talking. A few women were at the workbenches, two in close proximity chatting as they cleaned what appeared to be small car parts. A man appeared to be straightening out some paint cans that were on a shelf while the other woman sorted nuts and bolts. Only three other cars were in the garage, including a rather large sedan with a tarp draped over it so I couldn't see the make, let alone the model.

In the far corner near one of the few windows, a stout dark-haired man and a pencil-thin woman with a tight bun appeared to be having an argument. Although it was impossible to tell for sure, considering how loud the book club ladies and the men were. Still, the couple's gestures spelled out "verbal altercation." My eyes shifted back and forth from the loud couple to the even louder book club ladies and company. Then Wayne gestured to everyone and whispered, "That's Betsy Sprig over there. Looks like she's duking it out with Holt Kavanaugh. He's the club treasurer."

Everyone quieted down for a split second and the conversation between Holt and Betsy broke through the momentary stillness.

"You've got a screw loose, lady! This is a rec center club, not a business. Why on earth would we need to hire an auditor at club expense to scrutinize our books? The accounts and disclosures go through *their* auditors."

"We had a two-dollar-and-seventy-five-cent discrepancy last month."

"Oh, for heaven's sake! If it'll make you feel any better, here's five bucks. Count the extra two dollars and twenty-five cents as a donation."

I watched as he opened his wallet and handed her the money.

"That's bribery! Outright bribery! This isn't over."

With that, Betsy grabbed a jacket from one of the pegs on the wall, put it on, and stormed out of the garage without acknowledging anyone in her path, including all of us and the Turk sisters. Then Wayne spoke. "When I said she was cranky, I meant it."

Cranky? That woman made Miranda Priestly from *The Devil Wears Prada* look like Mother Goose!

"Probably all show," Herb said.

Then Holt walked past us and turned to Herb. "Be careful. That's one show all of us should miss."

CHAPTER 4

The Turk sisters ambled over to us once they were done at the workbench. Only two other women remained and were fixated on whatever they were doing.

"Don't mind Betsy. She's been like that since the Carter administration," the shorter of the sisters said. "I'm Aimee, this is my sister Darleen. You can tell us apart because I've got the blue streaks in my hair."

"Yeah," Darleen added, "and I'll keep my brunette color. And as far as Betsy is concerned, I'm in and out of here if she's around. Don't need all that aggravation. Even if she *is* a thorough club secretary. Got into it last year over some missing lug nuts. Lug nuts! Can you believe it? She pretty much accused me of pocketing them. I wanted to strangle her right there and then."

Aimee nudged her sister. "Good grief, Darleen, let it go. You bring up those lug nuts every chance you get."

Wayne stifled a laugh while the rest of us stood in silence. "So, what are you working on?" he asked.

Aimee pointed to our left. "See that cute little red Volkswagen Beetle over there? It needs a new engine. Good thing Darleen and I know how to swap it out. Not the first time we did a Subaru engine conversion into a VW. Got a terrific deal on a Subaru EJ257. Great horsepower and a really compact engine that fits the bill. Not everyone's familiar with the process seeing as the engine is in the rear of the car and pulling it out takes quite of bit of maneuvering, but we've done it before so it shouldn't pose too much of a problem. Not like restoring the whole shebang!" She eyeballed Wayne's car and winced.

"Yep," he said. "That's why I'm glad I came up next on the list. Don't want anything to jinx that. I'm hoping to really make out at the buy-sell-trade event."

"As long as you stay in Betsy's good graces, it shouldn't be a problem."

"Did you hear that, Wayne?" my mother asked. "Don't do anything stupid. From what I've seen and heard, that woman could suck the life out of someone without even trying."

"Just like that priceless doll with the treasure and the soul trapped in it," Myrna added.

I barely opened my mouth to respond but it was too late.

"What doll? What soul? What are you folks talking about?" Darleen's jaw all but dropped.

And then, like a water main break, the book club ladies spilled out the "keep-it-under-wraps-not-to-be-disclosed" information. Marshall and I did all we could to redirect the conversation but it was futile. Within five minutes, Darleen and Aimee Turk were privy to every detail involving that priceless wooden treasure, lost soul notwithstanding.

"It's useless," I whispered to Marshall. "Might as well post it on Facebook."

"Don't worry. I'm sure someone already has."

When we left the auto restoration garage that evening, it was as if we stepped off the centrifugal force wheel at a county fair.

"My head is spinning," I said as I got into the car.

"Every fiber in my body is on edge." Marshall turned on the ignition and headed out of the parking lot. "I give it exactly one hour and news of that doll will have reached Australia."

"It was bound to happen. Just downplay it if anyone asks you."

"What do you make out of that argument between Betsy and the club treasurer? Holt Kavanaugh, right?"

"Uh-huh. She had a bone to pick and he was on the defensive for sure."

"Do you think she was on to something?" He reached over and raised the car's thermostat.

"Hard to say. She strikes me as one of those people who can find fault with a sunny day."

"At least Darleen and Aimee seemed nice. Wayne's going to be working around that crew for quite a while."

"Wayne, Bill, and Kevin, according to what I heard. Like the Three Musketeers."

"More like the Three Stooges if you want to know."

We both burst out laughing as Marshall headed south on RH Johnson Boulevard toward Bell Road.

"I don't know about you, but I wouldn't mind stopping at Starbucks. I'm wide awake so one more cup of coffee isn't going to make a difference."

"Good, because I had the same idea."

We pulled into the Starbucks on Bell and Del Webb boulevards and were surprised to see so many seniors chatting in small clusters.

"Must be one or more of the Sun City clubs finished their meeting," I said.

We placed our orders and grabbed part of a bench between two full tables. As we waited to hear them call our names for the drinks, I caught the drift of a conversation and poked Marshall. Then, I lifted my head in the direction of the conversation. He immediately turned his.

A woman with a blue and green scarf around her head held up her phone. "Phoebe sent me a text. She just got off the phone with her sister. Someone stole a priceless doll from the Phoenix Art Museum. And that's not all! It's supposed to have someone's soul trapped in it! And lots of money! Lots and lots of money. Or gold. Or diamonds."

The four other women seated next to her fired off questions like bullets at a rifle range.

"Exactly one hour?" I said to Marshall. "It wasn't even fifteen minutes!"

"Gregory!" the barista called out.

I stood. "I'll get the coffees. You may want to give Nate a heads-up."

"Nah. Let him enjoy a good night's sleep. He'll have plenty of time to be aggravated tomorrow."

Nate's aggravation, however, was the furthest thought from our minds when we got a frantic phone call from Wayne at precisely two twenty-three in the morning.

"She's dead. Under my car. Posse came to my house. Saw lights on at the ARC building and checked it out. Dead. My car. Someone's coming here from the sheriff's office. Do they think I killed her? What do I do?"

"Whoa. Slow down. Who's dead?" Every word jumbled in my ear.

Marshall sat and propped his elbows on the bed. "Is that your mother?"

I shook my head and covered the landline mouthpiece. "No. Wayne. Hold on a sec." Then back to Wayne, "Slow down and tell me what's going on."

"When the posse drove by the garage, they saw the lights on and the door wide open. They went to check and found my car on top of Betsy's body. One of them recognized her. The hydraulic lift must have failed and the car crashed down on her."

"Oh my gosh. What a horrible accident. How did they know it was your car?"

"It had a tag on it with my contact information. They immediately sent another posse member to my house to tell me a sheriff's deputy was on his or her way. What if they think I killed her?"

"Okay, stay calm, and whatever you do, don't call any of your buddies or the book club ladies. Text me your address and we'll head over."

Marshall pulled the covers off of him and stood. "Was Wayne in an accident?"

Again, I held my hand over the receiver. "Nope. Worse. Much worse. Hang on."

"Listen, Wayne," I said. "When the deputy gets there, tell him or her that you're really shaken up and will answer questions once we arrive. Okay?"

"I *am* shaken up."

"Just breathe. See you in a bit."

Marshall reached for his pants and motioned for me to speak.

"Betsy's lifeless body was found under Wayne's car. I'll tell you what I know once we get in the car. We need to go to his house. A deputy is on the way."

"I surmised that much when I heard you say the words *much worse*. I'll shoot out a text to Nate in case we're late getting into the office."

"Look on the bright side—we got four and a half hours of sleep. Some people live on that."

"Yeah, too bad we're not them."

CHAPTER 5

Two posse cars and one MCSO car with its lights on were stationed in front of Wayne's house on Beechwood Drive when we arrived. Unfortunately, so were a few of his neighbors.

"Did he have a heart attack?" an elderly gentleman asked as Marshall and I walked to the front door. "I don't see the ambulance or the fire department."

"Maybe he called 911 and then dropped dead," the lady standing next to him said. "How awful. How tragic. Such a nice man."

I turned to both of them and replied. "No, he's fine." *If you consider hearing about a dead body under your car.* "They're investigating an incident, that's all."

"On this block?" the woman asked.

"No. Near the rec center."

Then the man took the woman by the arm. "It's always something with the rec center. Come on, Bernice, I want to get back to sleep. Darn siren woke me up."

As they walked away, I nudged Marshall. "They used a siren? That can only mean one thing."

"Yeah. I know. Must be Bowman or Ranston. Or both."

I cringed, knocked on the door and let myself in. Sure enough, Deputy Ranston was standing against the kitchen counter eye to eye with Wayne. In the dim light, his jowls looked more pronounced, making his toad-like appearance stand out.

His counterpart was a few feet away tapping his iPad. A lone posse member was on his cell phone and motioned to us as soon as he ended the call. "And here I thought I'd be driving around checking on open garages. Never expected this kind of thing. We've got another posse member in the car out front. In case a crowd shows up. So far, only a few neighbors. Are you relatives of the gentleman who lives here?"

"No," Marshall said. He handed the posse his card and introduced us.

"Private eyes, huh? Guess this is some humdinger of a case."

I held out my palms and took a step back. "I'm not a detective"—*unless you ask my mother*—"but I do work at Williams Investigations."

Just then, Bowman stopped writing and approached us. "That was quick. How'd you get on the radar so fast?"

"Wayne is my mother's friend," I said.

"Don't tell me she and that entourage are on their way over with that ankle-biting dog of hers."

"No. Everyone is spared for the time being. And we drove over because Wayne phoned us."

"As you can surmise, Ranston and I are on night shift, otherwise I'd be getting some shut-eye. We need to get a statement and then take it from there. Come on, you can sit in. Looks like Ranston's in the process."

Bowman thundered ahead and I whispered to Marshall, "I don't think he's gotten too far."

Wayne pulled over an extra chair and the five of us sat at the round kitchen table. A holiday centerpiece that now held car magazines instead of goodies and a pile of napkins from Starbucks took up most of the space.

Bowman wasted no time grilling Wayne. "Were you at the automobile restoration garage earlier this evening?"

Wayne turned to Marshall and me before speaking. "Yeah. And so were Phee and Marshall. Along with my pinochle buddies and some of Harriet's lady friends from the book club. Harriet is—"

"I know." Bowman rolled his eyes. "Phee's mother. Go on."

"Your partner told me about what happened. Got to agree, it does seem suspicious. My car wasn't on the hydraulic lift when we were there. It was in one of the bays. I wanted to show it to everyone before the restoration started."

Bowman shifted in his chair. "Who else was there?"

"Yes. Who else?" Ranston narrowed his eyes and took a small pad and pen from his coat pocket.

"Well, like I said, the pinochle guys and the book club ladies."

"I'll need names." He handed Wayne a piece of paper and I tried to stifle a laugh.

"Who else?"

"The Turk sisters. Darleen and Aimee. They're in the auto club. And Holt Kavanaugh. He's the treasurer. He was there as well and he had a heated conversation with the, uh, victim. Betsy Sprig."

"Verbal or physical?"

"Verbal."

"Do you know their relationship?"

Wayne shrugged. "She was the club secretary and he's the treasurer."

Bowman turned to Ranston. "Better get that down. Could be they were more than secretary and treasurer."

"Doubt it," Wayne said. "Seriously doubt it. You're barking up the wrong tree with that one."

Bowman furrowed his brow. "What makes you say that?"

Before Wayne could respond, I broke in. "Because Betsy was sort of persona non grata. Not exactly the most well-liked person in the club. At least that's the common sentiment I heard."

"We'll need more than hearsay, but thank you, Mrs. Kimball. Kimball Gregory. Whatever."

I nodded. Bowman rubbed his chin and leaned toward Wayne. "From start to finish, tell me everything that went on in the auto garage from the time you got there until the time you left."

"I don't understand. I thought it had to be an accident. A bizarre accident."

Bowman shook his head. "Nope. Go on."

"So it was foul play and I'm a suspect?"

"No one said foul play and everyone's a suspect at this juncture in time."

I did a mental eye roll as the deputy propped a closed fist against his chin and stared at Wayne. "Now, what time did you arrive?"

Wayne took a deep breath and gave the detectives a clear and succinct version of the events leading up to Betsy's demise. I was glad it wasn't my mother they asked or they would have listened to who wore what, whose makeup was overdone or not done, and every other nonessential tidbit of gossip.

When they finished questioning Wayne, he asked the most pressing question of them all—"Is my Mustang going to be seized for evidence?"

"I can tell you this much," Bowman said, "a forensics crew will be scrutinizing everything. From fingerprints to under-the-carriage anomalies. This was no freak accident."

"You mean like something deliberate and not a mechanical failure of some sort?" I asked Bowman.

He held up his palms as if to say "Who knows?"

"That wouldn't explain what the victim was doing under the car in the first place. She wasn't working on it."

Bowman looked at Ranston. "Write that down." Then he turned back to me. "According to the coroner, there were no tools near her. It was classified as a 'suspicious death.' Won't know more until after the preliminary postmortem and a tox screening."

Wayne all but leapt from his chair. "What about my car? Was there any damage to the undercarriage? I mean, from having it land on Betsy's body."

"You'll be given a report once the investigation is completed. May want to alert your insurance company, though."

"This is a nightmare." Wayne ran his fingers across his semi-balding head. "And don't get me wrong. I feel very badly for Betsy, but I counted on that car restoration for some additional income."

"You might have to put that on hold," Bowman said.

"What about the garage? Will it be available for club members?"

"It's a crime scene." Then louder, "A crime scene! It will be cordoned off until further notice."

Then both deputies stood and walked to the door. Ranston looked at Wayne and with one hand on his hip, said, "Don't share any information to anyone. Direct them to our office. And that means the TV stations as well. They'll be crawling all over that auto garage like earthworms after a rain."

"Marshall," Bowman added, "our office will call you at a decent hour. We may be needing your assistance on this one as well. Looks like that doll will be on the back burner for a while. Good thing we've got that contractual deal with your agency. Give Nate the heads-up, will you? We're looking at club interviews for starters."

With that, both deputies exited the front door, followed by the posse volunteer, who took a step toward Wayne and shrugged. "Guess my presence isn't needed any longer. Call us if it is."

"Will do. Thanks." Wayne followed them and locked the door before looking at us. "Thanks for driving over here. Those two are about as intimidating as anything. Hey, you don't think I have anything to worry about, do you?"

Only a possible murder charge . . .

Marshall pushed his chair back. "Doesn't hurt to inform your insurance company. But don't jump the gun yet unless there's a reason to do so. You'll have plenty of time to get legal counsel if you need it."

"Legal counsel? They think I murdered her, don't they?"

"Try not to say anything to anyone. I'll give you a call as soon as I know anything. Hey, with any luck at all, maybe we'll be able to sneak a few hours of sleep before any of this gets out."

Lamentably, none of us were that lucky.

CHAPTER 6

If an hour and a half was considered to be a night's sleep, then Marshall and I were fine that morning. Somehow, we managed to get showered, dressed, and pumped full of coffee before heading to work in our usual separate cars.

"So far so good," he said when we locked the utility door behind us. "We haven't heard from your mother."

"Bite your tongue. Augusta is probably fielding that call right now. You know how she gets in at the crack of dawn."

"Relax. Wayne won't call her. He knows better."

Fat chance.

Augusta had already gotten the rundown from Nate, so if she were to get a call from my mother, she'd be "at the ready" to deal with it. Thankfully, she was fast at work at her desk with no mention of any phone calls. Then, at eight fifteen, the dam broke. Marshall and Nate had already left for a meeting with the museum curator so they were spared.

"Phee! Your mother is on the line. I'm transferring it to your office."

Please let this be anything but the news about Betsy. It hasn't even made the TV morning segment yet.

"Hi, Mom, how's it—"

"Gloria Wong just called me. She was on her way to the dog park and passed the automotive restoration club's garage. It's been cordoned off and there are at least three posse cars there and a sheriff's vehicle. If Thor wasn't in such a hurry to do his business, she would have gotten out to see what was going on. Can you find out? We were just there last night. It couldn't have been a theft. They don't cordon off buildings for that sort of thing or all the supermarkets would be shut down. Find out, will you? And call me back. By the time Thor gets done in the park and Gloria drives over there, everyone will know except me."

Heaven forbid.

"I'll see what I can do. Keep in mind that—"

"Now someone's calling my cell phone. Talk to you later."

"I was spared," I called out to Augusta.

"Not for long," she replied.

I stepped out of my office and walked to the Keurig. "I suppose I should let her know but it's only going to make things worse."

"You can't avoid the inevitable."

Sure enough, no truer words were spoken. Less than five seconds later, I got another call. This time from Lyndy.

"Hey, girlfriend, I wouldn't ordinarily phone you at work but my crazy aunt in Sun City West called. Apparently, they found a dead body in the automotive restoration club garage. Weren't you supposed to go over there yesterday? Something about seat cushions?"

"Shh! I know about the body. I'll tell you in a minute, but how did your aunt find out?"

"That's easy. She was on her usual morning stroll writing down HOA violations in her neighborhood, which is just down the block from there. She saw a bunch of news station cars pulling in and she *just had to find out* what happened."

"Oh, brother. In ten seconds, it'll be a news ribbon on all the channels, and by noon everyone in Maricopa County will know."

"So there really is a dead body?"

"Uh-huh. The club secretary. And that's not the worst. She was found under Wayne's car."

"Was she working on it? Heart attack maybe?"

"No, and no. This is pure speculation, but the existing theory is that something went wrong with the hydraulic lift and the car came crashing down on her."

"That's a horrible accident."

"It may not have been an accident." I then proceeded to tell her about what the deputies said regarding a suspicious death.

"So they think it was done on purpose? Sabotaged?"

"I have no idea but Wayne is now on the hot seat and that's enough to make all of us uncomfortable."

"I'm surprised your mother isn't all over it."

"Oh, she will be. When she finds out."

"You mean you haven't told her?"

"I was sparing myself."

"Not for much longer. Good luck with that."

"I'll need more than luck."

Lyndy laughed. "Listen, I won't keep you. Catch up with me later, okay?"

"For sure."

I rolled my neck and proceeded to do what I should have done in the first place—my work. I let two and a half hours go by before I mustered up the courage to use my morning break and relay the unfortunate incident about Betsy's demise to my mother. The midday news hadn't aired yet but I wasn't about to take any chances.

"I don't understand why Wayne didn't call me," were the first words out of her mouth. "He should have called me. Don't tell me he left a message on my cell phone. Who looks at the bottom of their phones at all those tiny little designs?"

"Deputy Bowman told him not to call anyone."

"Since when does that make a difference? Do you know if he called Herb?"

If he called Herb, it would be on the public broadcast system by now.

"No. I don't know."

"Never mind."

"Look, I'm sure it will be on the noon news but not with anyone's name. They'll just include the facts—a body was found under suspicious circumstances, blah, blah, blah. I suppose you can call Wayne once it's public knowledge."

"Noon. That's only an hour and a half from now. I guess I can wait."

"And don't go calling the book club ladies, either."

"What about Gloria? The posse wouldn't tell her anything when she and Thor walked over there. She has a right to know."

"Huh? Just because she saw yellow tape on the building? Mom, wait until the news."

"Fine. But call me if you hear anything."

"I will."

I knew the watered-down, generic version of the unfortunate incident would air shortly but what I wasn't prepared for was the proverbial break in the dam from a gossip chain that started with Paul Schmidt, of all people.

Paul was a fishing aficionado whose passion for anything with gills matched his exuberance for bait. Long story but he shared a weekly radio show with my mother and Myrna on Sun City West's KSCW. A combination of murder mysteries and fishing tips. It's inexplicable and somewhat disturbing, but somehow the audience enjoys it.

It seemed Paul, like Gloria, was in the area of the auto restoration garage that morning as well in order to snag the "longer than a day old" bread that one of the restaurants throws out. Apparently it makes for good bait. And, since Paul was friends with one of the posse members, he got the lowdown on "the dead body no one is supposed to mention."

Well, Paul mentioned it, all right. To anyone and everyone who would listen to him at Quik Stop. Nothing like filling up on gas and gossip. It was little surprise that I received another phone call from my mother before the news came on.

It was worse than the girls' room at my old junior high. Someone named Irina heard it from another lady who ran into Paul and that lady told Myrna when they saw each other at the pharmacy. There may have been more people on the rumor train but my head spun just listening to my mother speak.

"The least you can do, Phee," she said, "is find out whose body it is. And before you say another word, I wasn't born yesterday. Trust me. It was no accident. I already called Herb. It's not one of his buddies. You don't think it was one of those nice Turk sisters, do you? I'd hate to think so, but they were the only ones getting their hands dirty in that garage."

"You and the entire world will know soon enough, Mom. First, they have to notify next of kin, then go through all sorts of things to determine cause of death. It doesn't do anyone any good to speculate."

"So there *was* a dead body after all!"

"You're the one who told me!"

"But you confirmed it."

"Honestly, don't go off the rails until all the facts are in. Okay?"

In what world? That's like telling her book club ladies not to pull over when they see a sign for an estate sale.

"I don't want to find out the next bit of news from Myrna. Call me, Phee, when you know. I expect your aunt Ina to be all over this and you know how annoying she can be."

Must be a family trait.

"Fine. *When* and *if* I know."

Last thing I needed was to lose my credibility with the sheriff's office by participating in my mother's rumormongering. Still, I had a zillion questions as well, only I learned to be patient, even if it meant biting my lips, my nails, and my tongue."

CHAPTER 7

The noon news covered the grim discovery at the Sun City West Automotive Restoration Garage. Along with the afternoon news, the evening news, and the late-night news. Nothing had changed. "Dead body found under car, said to be that of a woman in her sixties or older. Deemed suspicious death. Identification to be made pending notification of next of kin."

The only difference was that the news media narrowed it down to a woman. And it opened up the field to my mother and her friends, who dutifully checked off the rosters the following day for all the sewing clubs, the bocce club, Cecilia and Lucinda's church, the small dog and pet club, the model railroad club, the ceramic club, and the bowling alley.

"Give it a break," I said when she called me at work earlier that day. "I'm sure you'll know who it is soon enough."

"I already know. Poor Wayne. He must be beside himself. Imagine, Betsy Sprig found dead under his car."

"Wayne told you?"

"No, he told Herb. That's as good as announcing it on KSCW. Listen, no one else is supposed to know, so keep it to yourself."

"Are you kidding? Everyone west of the Rockies must know by now!"

"Fine. Then we can talk about it."

"I'm at work."

"For an investigative agency."

"Yes. One that is not investigating this." *For the time being . . .*

"Betsy wasn't exactly popular with the members of the auto club. I guarantee, one of them did the deed."

"Lack of popularity doesn't constitute a reason to commit murder. *If indeed* she was murdered."

"Ask your husband and your boss to find out. They've got an 'in' with those two deputies."

"They consult for the sheriff's office, if that's what you mean."

"Consult, talk, share notes . . . it's all the same. And besides, what else could 'suspicious death' mean?"

"It means the circumstances around the death are indicative of something other than natural causes or a clear-cut accident."

"So, murder?"

"Just don't go around spouting that off. Let the forensics crew and the coroner render a decision. And whatever you do, don't say something that will send Wayne over the edge."

"From what Herb said, Wayne left the edge and is dangling over a cliff. If Betsy was murdered, he'd be the likely suspect. It was his car. *His* car, Phee."

"Anyone could have done it. The keys are at the auto garage. Look, try not to make this any worse than it is by fueling the flames."

"I'm not your aunt Ina. Or Myrna, for that matter."

"Good to know. I've got to get back to work. Catch you later."

When I got off the phone, I knew it was only a matter of time before Betsy's untimely demise would morph into a full-blown account that would stun the best crime fiction novelists. Given my mother's penchant for drama and hyperbole, it was a no-brainer. What I didn't count on was the other pending situation involving that priceless, albeit haunted, doll. Unfortunately, that nightmare would soon rear its ugly head as well.

Apparently my aunt Ina was on the Phoenix Art Museum's board of directors and she wasted no time calling my mother when my conversation was over. That prompted yet another call.

"Phee! I hope you're not busy."

"Of course I'm busy, Mom. I'm working."

"I'll be brief. Your aunt Ina phoned and she needs a favor from you. Said the office line was busy and your voicemail box was full. Empty it. Or whatever else you do."

I ignore calls like this and rarely play them back. That's what I do. It's called preserving my sanity.

"What? What favor?"

"She wants you to sneak around the unity council's office when they close for the day. The office is in North Phoenix. She's convinced someone's got the doll hidden in there."

"Nate and Marshall are already on the case. And besides, that's breaking and entering. A misdemeanor if I'm lucky. Tell her I'll pass along the word to Marshall later." *Because he doesn't have enough on his plate.*

"Fine. But don't be surprised if she calls you."

I winced, said goodbye and got off the phone before my mother thought of something else.

Meanwhile, Bowman wasn't kidding when he told Nate they'd need him on that possible auto garage murder. In order to expedite interviews, Marshall drew the short straw and wound up with Sun City West's long laundry list of players. That meant Nate had to interview members of the unity council as well as a few stragglers from the Phoenix Art Museum who weren't at work when the original questioning took place.

Both of them were expected back in the office by late afternoon since Augusta managed to shuffle around a few morning appointments with existing clients. I kept my fingers crossed they'd make headway on both cases, but knowing how those investigations work, I wasn't optimistic.

One tidbit of good news, however, was that the doll theft hadn't yet crossed the threshold to the main media news. That meant whoever had the horrible thing in his or her possession wouldn't be on their guard. And that meant there'd be a greater chance of finding it.

"What do you want for lunch, Phee?" Augusta called out. "I'm ordering from the sub shop. They deliver."

"Ham and Swiss. Lettuce, spinach, tomato, green peppers and olives. No dressing."

"Got it. By the way, someone sent an email to our office. Not sure who it's meant for so I'm forwarding it to you. Looks like someone's going to have a fun night."

"What do you mean?"

"You'll see." Then I heard her chuckle and I knew I was in trouble.

I opened the email and saw that Wayne was the one who forwarded it to our office. His note was brief, as was the email itself.

"This is Wayne. I got this email a few minutes ago from Holt at the auto club. I think you guys should attend tonight. Thanks."

Then I read Holt's epistle.

> Attention Auto Restoration Club Members:
>
> As most of you are aware, we had an unfortunate incident yesterday and it's under investigation by the sheriff's office. One of our members was found dead under a car that was on the hydraulic lift. Until further notice, our garage will not be available to club members since it is now a crime scene. Or an accident scene. Or whatever they determine. And I cannot disclose the name of the deceased either, so please don't phone me, text me, or email me.
>
> We will be holding an emergency club meeting tonight at seven at the Women's Club Room at Kuentz Recreation Center. It was the only available space so please don't call me about that either.
>
> Please note—This is an emergency meeting. We are not serving refreshments so please don't contact me about that.
>
> I strongly urge all of you to attend. We have a number of decisions to make. Thanks.

I choked down the rest of my cold coffee and walked over to Augusta. "This is horrible. A nightmare in the making. The only thing that anyone will accomplish at that meeting is to stir the proverbial cauldron."

"That cauldron's been boiling and stewing since Del Webb laid the first cornerstone. You and Mr. Gregory really should go."

I sighed. "I suppose they'll need a voice of reason."

"Voice of reason? They'll be *way* past that. You need to scope out that audience and do a little digging. I don't have to explain it to you, but chances are whoever knocked off Miss Personality will be sitting there in plain sight."

"Not plain enough. But yeah, you're right. Just what Marshall will feel like doing after interviewing them all day."

"At least he'll have a head start."

Too bad Marshall didn't see it that way when he straggled into the office at a little before five. His five a.m. freshly shaven face now resembled a cross between Brad Pitt and a homeless man. As he reached for a K-Cup, I told him about Wayne's email.

"Tonight? Really? What do they expect to accomplish other than ruffle a few feathers?"

"According to my mother, who incidentally found out about the meeting from Herb, the auto club is committed to transparency."

"That seems to be the buzzword lately. Anyway, looks like I don't have a choice. Might as well grab a pizza and head over there once we're done here. Unless of course you'd rather go straight home and leave me to fend off the hoard."

"And miss all the fun? Nah. We can leave my car here and drive to work in yours tomorrow."

"At least it's just the auto club members. We'll be spared the book club ladies."

"But not the men. They'll be worse. Herb, Bill and Kevin are in that club."

Marshall stood and didn't say a word. When he finally spoke, it was only one syllable—"Ugh."

CHAPTER 8

I expected a decent crowd at the Women's Club Meeting Room, but I didn't expect to see news vans camped out front. That meant only one thing—those investigative reporters would be inside interviewing anyone and everyone who had the slightest idea of what took place last night.

"How did they find out there was going to be an ARC meeting?" I asked Marshall. Then I caught myself. "Forget it. Those pinochle men are worse yentas than the women. Most likely more than half the audience knows the victim was Betsy."

"And the other half will glean that information in a matter of seconds. Frankly, Bowman, Ranston or both should be here for damage control."

I glanced to my left and laughed. "You got your wish. That's Ranston over by those columns in the courtyard. He's speaking with someone but I can't see if it's anyone I recognize."

"Come on, let's go inside and mosey around."

I guessed there were at least thirty people in attendance, most of them seated on the plastic fold-up chairs facing a small wooden podium that held a microphone and water pitcher. The other attendees milled about in clusters.

All of a sudden, I felt a tap on my shoulder and turned around to face Wayne. He looked as if he hadn't slept in days.

"I got a call from that deputy over there," he said. "Too bad I was in the navy. My fingerprints are on record and they match some of the prints they found on that hydraulic lift."

"Some?" Marshall furrowed his brow.

"Yeah, there were other partial prints but mine stood out. Heck, my car was on that lift a few days ago and I remember looking underneath it. I must have leaned my hand against the hoist."

"Wayne," I said, "it's circumstantial. Besides, it was probably a mechanical failure. Did Ranston tell you anything other than the fact your prints were found?"

"Uh-huh. He said the forensics crew and a failure analyst from some engineering company were looking into the matter."

"That's good, isn't it? It means they haven't ruled out an accident."

Wayne shook his head. "The coroner thought it was suspicious because Betsy didn't have any tools with her. And Ranston told me to stay put and not leave the area. That's a polite way of saying 'Get a defense attorney.'"

Just then, Holt Kavanaugh's voice all but rattled the room. He stood at the podium and directed everyone to take a seat. Marshall and I grabbed an aisle chair and the adjacent one in the back row. I strained to see if any reporters were taking notes, and sure enough, they all were.

I recognized the anchor from KPHO channel five as well as Bonnie Williams from Fox news. With any luck, Sun City West would be making headline news before the meeting was even over.

"At least my mother's not here," I whispered to Marshall. "One less thing to worry about."

Then Holt spoke. "Good evening, everyone. Sorry we have to meet under these circumstances but I felt it best to make sure we're on the same page. Now, as all of you know, we had an unfortunate incident late last night in our automotive garage. A woman's body was found underneath a 1965 Ford Mustang."

Terrific. Might as well give them Wayne's name.

Just then, a zillion hands went up in the air.

"Wait until after this information. No questions right now," Holt said. Then he cleared his throat and shuffled through a few notes. "Deputies Bowman and Ranston from the Maricopa County Sheriff's Office are handling this case. The cause of death is under investigation. I repeat—Under Investigation. That means our facility will be cordoned off for at least a week so that the forensics teams and the mechanical failure analysts can check our equipment. Last thing we need is another unfortunate situation."

Just then someone shouted, "You mean murder. Just say it!"

Holt went on as if he hadn't heard the accusation. "The sheriff's office in conjunction with Williams Investigations out of Glendale will be interviewing club members so please be cooperative. Now then, we have some important housekeeping details to attend to. I'll be brief. Since our club president is on a cruise, I was asked to conduct tonight's meeting. Don't read anything else into it."

Again, I whispered to Marshall. "If anyone has half a brain, they'll figure out whose body it is, if they haven't already heard thanks to Herb and his crew. The secretary is supposed to take over for the club president."

Marshall nodded and Holt went on. "For the time being, all automobile restorations are suspended until we can regain use of our facility. Some of you have minor repairs and you can work that out on your own for the time being. Irvin Feldstein has offered his garage as well as Harvey Lankmeyer. Irvin's got that extra garage including a QuickJack hoist. Said the four-digit garage code is the current year. No need to bother him. Just go in and be sure to clean up.

"Once we have details as to who the victim was, we can see about a nice memorial or something. I will keep everyone informed via email. If you leave me a voice message, I may not get around to it right away. Now,

I'll try to answer as many questions as I can. I ask for discretion with this situation so we don't cause a blemish to our wonderful club."

"That ship's already sailed, Holt!" someone shouted.

Then a zillion hands went up. I recognized the flaming redhead. She was one of two women who were at the workbench when we were there to see Wayne's car. Her deep, husky voice permeated the room. "The news called our situation a 'suspicious death.' Tell us what you really know, Holt."

"Wish I could, Luella, but I don't speak for the news. Next?"

Then a harried-looking man who was working on rearranging paints that night spoke up. Thin wisps of his graying hair barely covered his scalp. "All I can say is if this wasn't an accident caused by faulty equipment, then we've got a killer in our club and everyone better watch his or her back."

Suddenly the room went wild with accusations and it took Holt a good five minutes to get everyone settled down. And that was only when he decided to introduce Deputy Ranston to the club. Unfortunately, Ranston's ramblings didn't do a heck of a lot to quell anyone in the crowd. In fact, they made it worse.

The cacophony of voices, coupled with a number of gestures I'd rather not think about, got Ranston so flustered that he let the secret of the night slip out before he knew it.

"Listen, our office wants to resolve Betsy Sprig's death as much as anyone around here, so—"

And with that, the news anchors rushed to the podium, all but colliding with anyone and everyone in sight.

"Ten o'clock news for sure," Marshall muttered as he stood and headed to the podium. "Someone has to save Ranston from getting trampled."

The room had turned from Holt's somewhat authoritative meeting to a free-for-all. All that was missing was Streetman to complete the circus. It took a good ten minutes to get everyone calmed down enough so that Holt could continue. This time with an impromptu change of plans.

"People. People. Get back in your seats and calm down. This is the auto restoration club, not the Boomers club. I imagine some of you are quite stricken knowing that it was our very own Betsy who succumbed to her death beneath the Mustang. What on earth she was doing there is anyone's guess, but we'll have to leave it to the sheriff's office for a determination."

He cleared his throat and continued. "I didn't want to get into this right away but now that the cat's out of the bag, so to speak, it brings us to another matter. Knowing that we no longer have our valued secretary, we must take action. As per the bylaws, I will appoint someone to take over for thirty days, at which time we will hold an election."

"What about Richard? Don't you think our president should know?"

Luella asked.

"I'll be sure to text him or email him. Not much he can do from Barbados." Holt rolled his eyes. "Now, if there isn't anything more to discuss at this time, I'll end our meeting. Keep an eye on your emails. That's my preferred method of communication."

With that, Holt stepped away from the podium but no one left the room. Instead, small clusters of people gathered around the chairs, in the corners, near the water fountain and by the exit doors. Their garbled voices made the entire area hum. Only this was no song.

I watched, wide-eyed, as the various reporters latched on to some of the more vocal attendees.

"Poor Ranston," I said to Marshall.

"Not really. He'll say it was a ploy to eke out more information and he'd be on target. Right now, everyone's buzzing. It's the perfect time for us to wheedle our way through the crowd and see what we can find out. Much better than orchestrated interviews. You game?"

I smiled. "Always."

As Marshall walked toward the nearest talkers, I sent my mother a text. Followed by an email in case she ignored the text. Both messages were identical—*Everyone at ARC knows it's Betsy. Ranston let it slip.*

Seconds later, she actually texted back. Unfortunately, she hadn't yet mastered using emojis so mine came back with a snail, a flag I didn't recognize and a happy face. It didn't matter. I knew what was next. The book club phone tree would be spreading its branches nonstop and I'd be dangling from one of them.

CHAPTER 9

An hour after Ranston's big slip-up, Marshall and I exited the women's club room and headed home. Both of us were excited to share what tidbits we'd snatched up during our "walk-through."

"Betsy didn't resign from working the bingo games," I said, "she was asked to step down. I heard that from a group of men who were with the guy we saw arranging the paint."

"Yeah, heard the same thing. Only it was the Turk sisters who were talking to a bearded man with overalls. Don't see many of them these days. The overalls, that is."

"Yeah. I figured as much. Also found out she liked to swim, but not sure which pool."

"Forget the swimming, I got a whiff of something really interesting. Holt and the other woman from the workbench, the one with the tricolored hair, said Betsy had been scammed by one of those romance apps."

"Don't tell me. An internet café in Nigeria?"

"I don't know. Doubt it was local. By the way, Ranston told me they're expecting the postmortem tomorrow morning but the tox screen will take another week. Face it, getting crushed under a car is not a result of drugs in her system. Frankly, the postmortem isn't going to tell us anything we don't already know. It's that report from the failure analysts that we need to scrutinize. They're the best source for determining a product failure. In this case, the hoist mechanism or something related to it."

"Can they determine if the failure was sabotage?"

"Yes. They look at root causes, not necessarily the physical signs like cracking, warping, and malfunctioning electronics."

"Yikes, that could take forever."

"That's why Bowman and Ranston want to go old school with gum-shoeing. In case the analysts determine it was foul play. The sheriff's office would be one step ahead for a change."

"I think that auto club was ten steps ahead as far as jumping to a conclusion. I don't think anyone in there thought it was a mechanical accident."

"It *is* puzzling. Why on earth would she have been under Wayne's car?"

"Looking for something?" I asked.

"Can't imagine what, but hey, nothing in this community surprises me anymore."

We both laughed.

"Don't know about you, but I'm ready to dive into a bowl of chocolate chip ice cream before I turn in."

Marshall gave me a thumbs-up. "Make that two of us!"

When we got in the door, I could see the light flashing on the landline. "It's got to be my mother. Lately she leaves messages on my cell and this phone. Probably wants to explain her earlier text."

Regrettably, she didn't. Her message was unending and annoying. "Strike while the iron is hot. Take Streetman to the dog park and find out who killed that woman. And don't go on and on about toxicology and forensics dust prints and all that. We know she was murdered. While my precious fur baby does his business, you can do yours. Think of poor Wayne. I can have Streetman ready for you at five thirty. Remember, the dog park is the epicenter for valuable information."

Valuable information, my you-know-what. It's the epicenter for rumor and inuendo.

I deleted the message and walked into the kitchen, where Marshall had already started doling out the ice cream. "Anything important?"

I shook my head. "Only my mother. She thinks I should take her little Prince Charming to the dog park so I can snoop around. I don't know if she's more concerned about Wayne or the fact it might affect that buy-sell-trade event. It's going to be on TV and Jay Leno is going to host it. And get this—the radio station is going to cover it. She won't let anything stand in her way for her five minutes of fame. You know how wacky she gets when those events crop up."

"I hate to say this, hon, but she may be right about going to the park. Maybe give it a day for the information to marinate and then pop over there. Or sooner. Some of your odd leads have turned out to be good ones."

"Streetman's a nightmare in that park. Jumping on unsuspecting dogs. Picking up who knows what and refusing to spit it out, and oh—his new thing—peeing in the water bowls."

Marshall chuckled. "You'd be doing this for a good cause. Besides, we all know our office is going to wind up carrying this case so we might as well arm ourselves."

I looked at my bowl and moved it toward him. "I want another scoop!"

• • •

In the chaos of last night's ARC meeting, Nate's investigation into that priceless doll was the last thing we thought about. Until we got into the office the next morning and were greeted by Augusta.

"Better gulp down your coffee, Mr. Gregory. That investigative reporter from channel 10 wants to speak with one of our detectives. You win."

"I'm only going to direct him to the sheriff's office. They're handling the Sprig case."

"Not that. The reporter wants information on that priceless doll. Wants to run a special report tonight on the seven o'clock news."

"Oh hell no." Marshall plopped in a K-Cup and turned to Augusta. "Which reporter?"

"Tim Justin."

"Wonderful. This is going to make Nate's day."

"It would, if he were here," Augusta said, "but he got a call from his neighbor. There's a sewage backup on his street from a burst pipe and it may seep into the houses. He rushed out before the call came in."

"I knew keeping this under wraps wouldn't last long, but now having it wide open will make it more difficult to track down viable leads. Not like a missing dog or cat. That case is bound to bring out every treasure hunter and would-be psychic in the area. Heck, hidden treasure and unearthly spirits all rolled into one wooden doll. Who could resist?"

I bit my lip. "Not the book club ladies. Of course, they'll be pulled in two directions between the doll and Wayne. And we'll be stuck in the middle, getting squeezed until we're ready to cry uncle."

"What are you going to tell that reporter, Mr. Gregory?"

"The truth. Always a good idea. That way I never have to worry about what I said. Better for them to get the facts straight than concoct something that escalates. I'll shoot a text to Nate and set up a time with Tim Justin."

"And I'll busy myself with invoices."

"Not so quick, Phee. Your mother left a message for you. She said to tell you Streetman will be ready at five thirty tomorrow. Mentioned something about wearing a reversible tartan coat. Didn't ask if she meant you or the dog. Just took notes."

"The dog. It's always about the dog. And yes, I'm about to conduct intel at the dog park."

"Good deal. Nice way to start the day." Then she laughed.

And while Marshall went off to chat with a few people at the unity council office, I buried myself in invoices and unpaid bills. A productive and peaceful morning, soon to take another turn.

At a little before noon, Nate walked in, looking as if he'd been pursued by a pack of hounds. I was at the copier and was about to retreat to my office when he said, "Good luck dealing with the water and sewage municipality. If all goes well, the problem on my street will be resolved by four. If not, I'll be sporting extra deodorant in the morning. I take it our buddy is tracking down doll leads."

"Uh-huh. He's trying to stay one step ahead of the media mob."

"I know. Got his text. Got indigestion, too. I've been going over the timeline of when that blasted thing was last seen and can't narrow down the slip-up. Everyone has a different story."

"Um, when the museum said *priceless*, did they mean monetary value or historical?"

"Both. But nothing could be validated. Not like it carried a provenance, determining its authenticity. Still, its word-of-mouth is the stuff that keeps legends going."

And just as we were about to discuss antiques, Wayne walked in, unshaven and agitated. "I'm sorry to pop in like this, but I didn't know where else to go. Someone from last night's meeting told Deputy Ranston that a few weeks ago they overhead me say, 'I'll send that witch flying out of here, one way or the other.'"

"Did you?" Nate asked.

The sheepish look on Wayne's face said it all.

"Well?"

"I might have said something like that. But I wasn't insinuating murder. Just getting her removed from office."

"I take it Deputy Ranston had a little chat with you."

Wayne handed him an appointment card. "He will. About an hour from now. I was hoping one of you could join me."

Nate shook his head. "Wish I could, but that's more of a job for legal counsel. Of course, you haven't been charged with anything, so I'd suggest you go and bring someone with you. You're allowed to have an advocate."

Just don't bring my mother.

"Bring someone stable and levelheaded," I said. Then I quickly followed up. "But not me. I can't leave work."

Wayne nodded. "I'll call Bill or Kevin."

Nate patted him on the shoulder. "Good idea. And call our office when you're done if it will make you feel any better. Remember, you haven't been arrested. Or even told you were a person of interest. And Betsy's cause of death is still under investigation."

"Haven't you guys caught the latest news? It was on one of those ribbons underneath the morning TV shows."

Nate and I looked at each other and Augusta sat bolt upright in her chair as Wayne continued.

"The ribbon said, 'Unexplained death in Sun City West deemed murder. Full news at five.'"

"Looks like those interviews are going to be a lot more fun, Mr. Williams." She lifted her glasses and rubbed the top of her nose. "Wouldn't be at all surprised if you and Mr. Gregory wind up doing double duty."

Nate stood perfectly still and glared at Augusta. "Like a summer carnival ride on a Ferris wheel in Kansas right before a tornado hits."

I chalked his comment up to hyperbole but little did I know, it was the absolute truth.

CHAPTER 10

Nate immediately had Augusta get Bowman and Ranston's office on the phone. Then he stormed into his own office, presumably to find out why the entire world was informed of the murder except for the one office that was called on to help with the investigation.

When he came out of his office, he paced back and forth in front of the coffee maker. My office door was open so I watched and wondered what had ensued. My curiosity got the better of me and I stepped out. Wayne had already left and Marshall wasn't back so it was only the three of us.

"Can you believe it?" he said. "Typical Bowman and Ranston. Bowman said Ranston was supposed to call us and Ranston said he thought Bowman was. Both of them apologized profusely. Never mind. It is what it is. Anyway, I now have a meeting with those two this afternoon to 'review our plan of action.' More like devise one, if you ask me."

Marshall's day hadn't gone any better. He texted the office that he would be there in less than a half hour in order to meet with Tim Justin on "the doll fiasco." He also added that his visit to the unity council was "a colossal waste of time."

Augusta immediately ordered deli subs since none of us had eaten, and given the state of mind we were all in, we'd make Bowman and Ranston look like Mother Theresa and Mr. Rogers rolled into one.

Shortly after one, I heard Marshall swing open the outer door and announce, "I've got twenty minutes until I spin that interview for channel 10. I've never spoken with so many irritable people in one setting. Some unity council. There were four of them and they all accused each other of losing sight of that doll. So much bickering. I'll need to approach this a different way."

"You might want to approach your lunch, Mr. Gregory. Got combo subs in the workroom," Augusta said. "Protein helps the brain. We've already eaten. Our brains are full."

"She's right," I added as I stepped out of my office and walked toward him. "But I think it's my stomach and not my brain."

Marshall walked toward Augusta and patted her shoulder. "I'm taking you up on those subs. Thanks. My brain will need all the help it can get. I've got to give that reporter enough information to keep their viewers and sponsors happy, but without compromising our investigation. Boy, is this going to be a miracle."

"Were you able to figure out a timeline for the last sighting of the doll?" I asked.

He shook his head. "None of them could give me a timeline for the last sighting of Elvis."

Wonderful. I'll need to bring that little snapping turtle to the park tomorrow for sure.

"I'll let you know when Mr. Justin gets here," Augusta said. "I'll stall him so you don't have to wolf down your food."

"Appreciate that." Marshall winked at me and walked to the workroom.

"Boy," I said, "what are the odds of two simultaneous cases that seem dead-ended from the start?"

"It's not the odds, it's how well Mr. Williams and Mr. Gregory can gamble. Besides, it wouldn't be fun if more kinks didn't appear to really louse them up."

"Shh! Bite your tongue, Augusta. What else could possibly mess things up?"

It was a rhetorical question and one I shouldn't have asked, because while Nate went off to see Bowman and Ranston, and Marshall choked down his sub, Wayne called.

"You'd better take this call, Phee," Augusta said. "It's Wayne. And not even a full hour since he left. I'm transferring the call to your office. You're the only one who's free."

"But I'm not—Oh, never mind." I scurried to my desk and picked up the phone. Before I could say anything, Wayne blurted out, "Got a threatening note in my mailbox."

"A death threat?"

"Not exactly. More like a suggestion, but with teeth."

"Just read it."

"Okay. Here goes. 'Admit to killing Betsy so we can get back to work on our cars.'"

"Was that it?"

"No, there was a photo of my car enclosed. Not a real one. A printed copy from someone's phone, I imagine."

"That's not so bad."

"They used red marker to deface the car. A big skull on the hood."

"Someone's just trying to get under your skin, that's all."

"Well, they succeeded. Just like those mites that cause scabies."

"Look, call the sheriff's office and let them know. Nate is meeting with Bowman and Ranston right now. I'm sure they'll want to see that note. I doubt whoever wrote it poses a threat to you."

"To me? No. But to my car? I can't bear to think what they could do to Sally."

"Sally? Who's Sally?"

"Sally Stang. That's what I named her."

Oh brother. Worse than my mother and the dog.

"Relax. It's, I mean *she*, is under lock and key. The sheriff's office isn't letting anyone inside the ARC garage."

"That's the problem. Okay, fine. I'm driving over to the posse office now. Note in hand. Too late for fingerprints. Mine are all over it. Watch. They'll use my own evidence against me."

"I think you're overreacting. Those car fanatics want their workspace back."

"Yeah. At my expense."

When I got off the phone, I thought about the news flash Wayne mentioned. How could those technicians and analysts be sure it was murder? Did they find clear-cut evidence of sabotage? And if so, then what?

I figured Nate would have a better idea after conversing with Bowman and Ranston, but in the meantime I had plenty of my own work to do. As I refreshed my computer, I heard Augusta greet Tim Justin and hoped Marshall could keep tap dancing long enough to get through the interview.

Curious as ever, I opened my door wide enough in case their voices carried. Unfortunately, they didn't.

Forty or so minutes later, I heard Marshall and Tim from the front office. "We usually send a camera crew to film interviews but this was so last-minute, I had to resort to my phone."

"No problem. Wish I could give you more information but I'm afraid that's all I've got for now."

"Not to worry. This is the kind of stuff that grabs viewers by the elbow and keeps them in their chairs during the entire news segment. Nothing like a priceless treasure and a hidden cipher. Not to mention that whole trapped soul thing. Between you and me, someone must have fabricated it in order to pull attention away from the real matter at hand—a lost fortune. Bet whoever carries the insurance for that art museum is really steaming. Guess that'll be another interview if your firm isn't successful."

"Let's just hope it doesn't come to that. Nice chatting with you, Tim."

"Same here. Turn on the ten o'clock news."

"I'm recording it already," Augusta called out. "Got Alexa on it!"

I heard both men chuckle and the office door close. Then I stepped out and walked toward Marshall. "Sounds like it well went after all."

"More like an open invitation for every kook and nutcase in the valley to do their own treasure hunting. And every new-age psychic to charge a small fee to contact the doll's inhabitant. All we need now is your aunt Ina to offer her services."

Augusta tapped on her desk and smiled. "Ten o'clock news, huh? I'm no psychic but I predict your aunt Ina will be on the phone with you tonight before the clock tolls eleven."

"Don't say that!" I gasped. "That's all we need. She already called my mother about having me scope out the unity council office. I can't imagine what she'll come up with if she does call."

"Can't be any worse than Streetman in the park."

I shot her a look and turned to Marshall. "I don't want to know."

"Think of it as your civic duty to keep the citizens of Sun City West safe and sound. What time are you taking the dog tomorrow?"

Augusta and I both answered at once—"Five thirty."

"Wear your rubber mocs, hon. It's supposed to rain tonight."

Wonderful. A neurotic dog, a wet, slippery park, and more tongue than tail wagging. Every woman's dream.

CHAPTER 11

It started raining a little before nine and continued all night long. Finally, at four fifteen, when our alarm went off, the rain had dissipated.

"At least I won't have to carry Streetman into the park with him growling and squirming because he hates getting wet," I said. "It's supposed to clear up."

"What about the wet grass?" Marshall asked.

"Hopefully he'll be too preoccupied scoping out the other dogs to make a fuss." *If I'm lucky.*

"What exactly does your mother think you'll be able to glean from Cindy Dolton?"

"Anything and everything related to Betsy's cold, stiff body. Cindy's ears and tentacles have a wide reach and she attracts information like a black cardigan does with lint."

"Information or rumors?"

"A little of both but we can sift through them."

"In all my years as a detective, I never expected to go the gossip chain route. But if the past is any indication, I regret not doing it back in Mankato."

"I regret every part of it."

We both laughed and hustled to get going. Me to the park and Marshall to the office for an early morning meeting with Nate.

"Hold on, Phee," my mother said when I started to walk Streetman to her front door. He was already leashed and anxious to get moving. "I have doggie boots for him. Cute little red ones. They match his tartan."

"He's not going to like them."

"Once he gets used to them, he'll be fine. He doesn't like getting his paws wet."

"I thought it was just his fur."

"It's everything. That's why I enrolled him in doggie swim classes at Kimberly's Doggie Spa in Surprise. He started a few days ago."

"You what? Why would you do a thing like that?"

"Because you never know when he's going to need that skill. What if he fell off an ocean liner?"

I was about to respond when something hit me. That dog could very well wind up on an ocean cruise if my mother takes one. Heck, she drags that little nipper everywhere.

"Um, good thinking ahead."

"I bought him a doggie life vest. A nice orange one."

"And he doesn't mind wearing it?"

"He'll get accustomed to it in time."

I watched as my mother struggled with the little chiweenie to put on those boots. It was like alligator wrestling but with a smaller, cuter animal.

Yep, he'll get accustomed to that life vest, all right! When the polar ice caps melt.

"There. All set." She handed me the leash and we started for the door. Well, *I* started for the door. The dog bent down and tried to bite one of the boots.

"I'm carrying him, Mom. Much easier."

With that, I went straight to the car, plunked him in the passenger seat and prayed for the best. At least it had stopped raining. When I got to the park, I noticed most of the people converged in one corner, along with Cindy.

Then I took a closer look and winced. A woman had one of those dog throw launchers in full force. Every time she let it go, she yelled *"Wa-hoo"* at the top of her lungs. A small tan and white dog chased after the ball while everyone else ducked for their lives.

"That's the 'Wa-hoo' lady," Cindy said. "She's a snowbird from Washington. Said she left her hearing aids back there. But she said that last year, too."

Wordless, I kept watching.

"She's a lovely lady," Cindy went on, "and so is Vincent, her dog. But oh, that noise! If I hear one more 'Wa-hoo,' I may lose it. Say, what's Streetman doing over there?"

I turned to my left and watched as he furiously tried to remove a boot from his rear leg.

"My mother insisted on putting boots on his paws. Hey, at least he's staying out of trouble for a few minutes. Listen, I hoped I could ask you what you know about that bizarre death in the auto restoration garage."

"You mean Betsy Sprigs's murder? You can say it. It's been on the news."

"What have you heard that wasn't on the news? Her body was found under the car belonging to one of my mother's friends."

"Yep. Wayne something-or-other. Heard that, too. But what you didn't hear was how those analysts figured out it was premeditated murder and not an accident. My brother-in-law is a failure analyst in Seattle and his company is the one working with our sheriff's office."

Hmm, they're using the big guns on this one.

"What? What didn't I hear?"

"The tech team studied the hoist device and concluded that its composition, wear and tear, and longevity did not contribute to the failure.

It was totally hydraulic so that meant no cables or pulleys that could have been tampered with, but all someone needed to do was puncture a hole into the hydraulic line and that's exactly what happened. No accident. It was sabotage."

"So, you're telling me the fluid leaked out and the car came down?"

"Yeah. Pretty much. And the impact of the car was what killed Betsy. I don't know all the particulars but believe me, that investigation was thorough. They brought in a seasoned crew that worked twenty-four hours straight using the most accurate computerized diagnostic system. Of course, there's more work to be done, but this preliminary finding won't change."

"Um, it sounds even more gruesome with all of those details, but were you able to home in on who might have been responsible? Surely the scuttlebutt was up and running."

"Here's where it gets interesting. Betsy had issues with everyone in the club and was going to be axed from her position, but were you aware that she was also axed from working bingo?"

"Yeah, heard that too."

"Uh-huh, but what you haven't heard is the real reason. She was accused of tampering with the bingo balls by switching them out to skew the results. Face it, thousand-dollar payoffs, even split a couple of ways, still adds up."

"Could anyone prove anything?"

Cindy shook her head. "No, but let's just say more than a few people were furious. Ever watch one of those bingo games in action? Absolutely cutthroat. My guess is that someone got even. Someone who knew their way around an auto shop as well as a bingo parlor."

"But why involve Wayne and his car?"

"Probably because it was convenient at the time."

Tell that to Wayne.

I gulped. "Listen, that's not the only inquiry I've got. Have you heard anything about a priceless doll that was stolen from the Phoenix Art Museum when it went on loan to the unity council?"

"Watched the special on TV last night. I was about to tell you that I thought your husband did a good job fielding questions from that reporter, but no. I haven't heard anything yet. *Yet.* Give it time for the gossip train to leave the station. Someone's bound to know something and no one can keep their mouths shut."

"Thanks. I'll be sure to check in again when—" And just then I heard an ear-piercing shriek. I spun my head around expecting to see Streetman engaged in one of his amorous "meet-and-greets" with another dog, but thankfully it wasn't him. It was worse.

The "Wa-hoo" lady launched her yellow ball but instead of Vincent retrieving it, another, slightly larger dog went after it and snatched it up. The lady's scream was louder than her "Wa-hoos." Followed by, "Drop it! Drop it! Drop that ball this instant." As if the dog understood.

Cindy and I watched in disbelief as the woman chased after the dog, hands flailing with Vincent scurrying behind her.

"Do you know who the dog's owner is?" I asked Cindy.

"I've only seen that sheltie once or twice. Gee, there are at least fifteen people over there but no one's making a move."

They probably don't want to get hammered by that launcher. It's Sun City West's version of a lethal weapon.

Meanwhile, the "Wa-hoo" lady tore after the dog like Alexander the Great's army. But the soldiers in Alexander's army weren't running on slippery grass. At least I didn't think so. I watched in horror as one of her feet skidded out from under her and she landed facedown in what I prayed was a pile of leaves.

To make matters worse, Vincent jumped on her back and started nuzzling her neck.

"I've got rubber mocs on," I said, turning my head to Cindy. "For walking. Not running." *Don't need to be the second person breathing in the who-knows-what on the ground.*

"Take a look! The crowd beat you to it!"

Sure enough, the fifteen or so people who hunkered down at the far end of the park were now converging on the "Wa-hoo" lady, offering all sorts of suggestions.

"Get up on your elbows!"

"Move your knees in and stand!"

"Roll on your side!"

When none of that worked, two brawny-looking men rushed over and in their attempt to grab her arms, they managed to push her further into the ground. Her arms splayed apart and next thing I knew, she was facedown in the muck and mire. Or whatever it was.

Finally, she stood. Speechless. Cindy handed her one of the dog park towels that are used to sop up water messes by the benches. The woman recoiled and didn't say a word. Then she took out Vincent's leash and secured it to his collar.

"Is there anything we can do?" I asked. Her face had brown and yellow streaks running down from the forehead to her chin.

"What? I can't hear you!"

"Do you need help?" I shouted, suddenly remembering she didn't have her hearing aids.

"What I need is a shower. And better-behaved dogs at this park.

Vincent doesn't want anyone to touch his playthings."

With that, she left the park.

"I hate to think what her car is going to smell like," Cindy said.

"I'm just elated this was one incident Streetman wasn't involved in."

"Don't say that too soon. Look!"

Sure enough, the little chiweenie had managed to extricate one of his red boots from a paw and was engaged in a tug-of-war over it with a Yorkie.

"Oh brother. Just what I need." I walked over to the dog, leash in hand, just as the Yorkie's owner approached. He put his hands on his hips and shouted, "Spartacus! Let go! Spartacus, stop!"

The Yorkie paid absolutely no attention and neither did Streetman.

"I'll leash my dog," I said. "Well, not *my* dog—*because I'd rather own a tapir than Streetman*—he's my mother's dog."

The man cocked his head and squinted. "Weren't you checking out Wayne's Mustang at the auto club garage the night before Betsy Sprig's body was found?" Before I could answer, he continued. "I volunteered to organize the paint cabinets. Should have brought my noise-canceling headphones to drown her and Holt out. Not the first time they sparred, but like I told the investigator they sent, I seriously doubt Holt's her killer." Then he glanced at Streetman and Spartacus. "Who wants to risk losing a limb getting them away from each other?"

"Hold on. I can remedy this." I reached in my bag and pulled out a string cheese. I hadn't even gotten the wrapper off when Streetman let go of his boot and lunged for the treat. The man immediately snatched Spartacus from the ground and pressed him to his chest.

"Thanks. Name's Jared. Jared Loundsby. Been a club member for over ten years and Betsy was the last person I would have expected to see underneath a car."

"Because she was murdered?"

"No, because she didn't like messing up her fingernails. They had to be absolutely perfect. I was in the garage once when one of her bright red nails split and you would have thought an axle fell off of something. Nope, Betsy was more of a give-orders gal than a worker bee, if you know what I mean."

"Hmm, guess it begs the question, 'What was she doing under there?'"

"More than begs. It *is* the question if you ask me."

CHAPTER 12

I waved goodbye to Cindy and hustled Streetman out of the park, drippy wet dog bootie in my pocket. Jared wasn't the only one who questioned why Betsy was underneath Wayne's car, but I doubted anyone else was aware of her "perfect nails" obsession. That meant only one thing in my book—Betsy didn't wind up under that car voluntarily.

The minute I returned the little scoundrel to my mother, I raced to her door so I could get to the office on time.

"Call me later, Phee," she said. "And fill me in on everything. Don't forget!"

Like that would ever happen.

"Too bad you can't stay for coffee. Look behind you. Streetman and Essie are snuggling. Now she's trying to chew on his booties. At least the one he slipped off isn't ruined. I'd better take the others off of his paws."

"Great idea! He'll thank you. Bye!" I closed the door before my mother had a chance to regale me with all things related to the dog and cat.

Much as I hated to admit it, my trek to the dog park wasn't a complete waste of time. My unexpected encounter with Jared really paid off. Betsy was a thin woman. Very thin. Making it relatively easy for someone to move her body and position it under Wayne's car.

The second I opened the door to Williams Investigations, I called out, "Are the guys still in the office?"

Augusta tilted her head and smiled. "Good morning, Augusta. And how are you today? Did you sleep well?"

"Sorry about that, but I've got a hot lead. Really hot. Tell you in a bit."

Augusta pointed to Nate's door. "Make their day. From the looks of things, they'll be happy for a break."

I rapped on the doorjamb and stepped inside. "Hate to interrupt but you'll be glad I did."

The men looked up from whatever paperwork they had at the table.

"Dog park intel pay off?" Marshall asked.

My head bobbed up and down as I spoke. "Remember the guy with the wispy gray hair who sorted the paints the night we were there?" I didn't wait for an answer. "Well, he was at the park and told me Betsy never did any work on the cars. Didn't want to chip her fancy fingernails. That can only mean one thing. She wasn't under Wayne's car out of her own volition. My money is on poisoning. Or blunt force trauma. What did you find out?"

Nate shuffled a few papers and winked. "You're in the wrong profession.

Bowman and Ranston thought perhaps she was under the car in order to sabotage it, and I'm afraid the analysts concur. Not about Betsy's role, but the fact this wasn't an accident. Just got a text from Ranston."

"Cindy Dolton beat you to it! She found out from a relative who works for that company."

Nate looked at Marshall and laughed. "Why bother with official reports when we can just set up shop at the dog park?" Then, to me, "What you're saying makes sense. About Betsy. But the deputies and analysts would disagree. Thought maybe she was finishing up when the hoist mechanism gave out. Still, they put a rush on the toxicology report. If nothing else than to prove themselves right."

"They're wrong. I think she was drugged and dragged under there."

Marshall rolled his neck and then rubbed it. "Right now, the deputies are working with the only evidence they have—the physical scene and the preliminary postmortem. It showed injuries consistent with an extremely heavy object crushing her. No sign of strangling or asphyxiation. Or blunt force trauma to the head. Given the location of her injuries and the vehicle's underside, there was no doubt her body suffered severe bruises and bone breaks as a result of Wayne's car."

I let out the breath I was holding and walked toward him. "But they didn't know she really had an aversion to working on cars. And getting her hands dirty. She *had* to have been knocked unconscious. And if there's no physical sign, then for sure, someone slipped her something."

"Bowman said they found a screwdriver in her pocket that they didn't see before."

"Can't do that much with a screwdriver and a car, can you?" I asked. "And it doesn't mean it wasn't a setup. What if someone wanted to make it seem like an accident?"

The detectives looked at each other and then at me.

"We're on the same wavelength, kiddo," Nate said. "It's possible. Anything is at this point. Again, it's Bowman and Ranston's watch. All we were asked to do is help out with some interviews and consult. They know we've got that museum case going on. Still, we're definitely being pulled in two directions."

Marshall pinched his shoulders together and sighed. "Since both of us work the bigger cases hand in hand, we're feeling the pressure on that doll theft. Thanks to someone's tipoff, I had no choice but to get interviewed for the news. Otherwise, who knows what kind of a spin they'd give it." He reached for his coffee and took a swallow. "We've got a meeting later today with the fine arts shipping company that handled the transport. Gives new meaning to the phrase 'lost in space.'"

"Do you think those board members on the council are covering up for each other?"

"Too early to tell, hon."

"Much as this gives me hives, I'll see what else my aunt Ina can drum up."

Marshall took a slug of his coffee and rolled his eyes. "Just don't get involved in anything kooky with her. You know her track record."

"We all have it emblazoned in our minds," Nate said with a laugh. "That aunt of yours should come with a warning label."

Oh heck. Why stop with my aunt? The whole family should come with one, beginning with my mother. And the dog. Definitely the dog.

I left the guys to their meeting and their schedule. It was nice to retreat to my cozy office and work on accounts. The one thing that gave me the sanity I needed to get through the day. At noon, with the men out of the office, Augusta had a meat lovers pizza delivered for us.

"I had them add chorizo to the sausage, meatballs, and pepperoni. Wanted it to be well-rounded," she said. "The extra spice is good for the capillaries. I read that somewhere."

"It's good for indigestion, but I'm not complaining."

As I wiped a few crumbs from my lips, the phone rang. "I'll get it. Keep eating."

Big mistake. It was almost as if my aunt had channeled my conversation with Nate and Marshall and reached for the phone. Even Augusta heard her voice and she was seated a good distance away.

"Phee! Forget the unity council. We need to start at the museum. Why look at the tentacles when we can go after the head?"

"Huh? Tentacles? Head? I hope you're not saying what I think you are."

"The museum shipped that doll to the unity council but what if it wasn't the doll? I mean, how does anyone really know? I got your message the other day that Marshall was over there and pulled up zilch. I think we need to backtrack."

"Um, by *backtrack*, you're not suggesting we break into the art museum and poke around, are you? I think it's a worse felony than grand theft auto, given how priceless the artwork is. And I, for one, don't want to spend the rest of my life in a four-by-six cell, or whatever size they are."

"Hold on a minute." Then her loud voice. "Louis! What size are prison cells?"

"Four by eight. Why?" My uncle's voice was even louder than my aunt's.

"Phee wanted to know."

No, I really did not.

"Your uncle says four by eight. He's a wealth of information."

"Good to know, but I'm not breaking into the museum with you. I know what you're thinking."

"Don't be ridiculous. We're not going into any of the galleries. Too many lasers, cameras, and those glass-break things. My plan is to scope out their basement. It's where they keep artwork for future exhibits and artwork on loan."

"I didn't think those places have basements."

"Actually, it's the lower level by the Modern and Contemporary Art. In the Katz wing."

"And for some reason you think we can get in there undetected?"

"With the right plan, I do."

"Well, I don't."

"Phee, if that priceless doll isn't found in one piece, the museum's reputation will go right down the tubes. Along with mine. I'm on their board, you know."

Can't possibly forget.

"And what makes you think you'll find answers in the storeroom?"

"Not just the storeroom. It's where their offices are located."

"Great. So the authorities can add computer tampering to the list of charges."

"Hold on again. I hear your uncle rustling around in the refrigerator." Then, "Louis! Stay out of the tomato herring. It's for dinner. Eat that nice fat-free cottage cheese."

I rubbed my temples. "Uh, I have to get back to work, Aunt Ina. I'll talk to you later."

"Call me. This can't wait."

"Trouble in paradise?" Augusta asked when I returned to my half-eaten pizza slice.

"You could say that. Do we still have a list of bail bondsmen?"

"Why do you ask?"

"Just planning ahead."

I told her about my aunt's outrageous suggestion but instead of her usual reaction, she furrowed her brow and sat silently for a second. "Hmm, the lady might not be so far off track. Face it, even if Nate and Marshall were to secure a search warrant with help from those deputies, it would be too late."

"It won't be easy finding a new bookkeeper/accountant."

"True, but I know someone who'll make sure that doesn't happen. We just have to keep this between us."

"Uh-oh. I know where this is going—Rolo Barnes!"

Augusta grinned from ear to ear. "It's good to have friends in all the right places."

CHAPTER 13

Rolo Barnes. I thought I'd seen the last of him when he left his IT position at the Mankato Police Department and started his own cyber-investigating business. But as it turned out, he was Williams Investigations' go-to cyber-sleuth when it came to hacking computers, deep diving in the dark web, unlocking international bank codes, and a plethora of other rare and valuable skills too numerous to mention. He made Homeland Security, the CIA, and the FBI look like juvenile players. Yeah, he was that good.

He was also as looney as a fruitcake. And didn't want to be paid in cash. Only kitchen gadgetry. *Expensive* kitchen gadgetry to concur with whatever fad diet he extoled. Paleo, keto, gluten-free, sugar-free, starch-free, taste-free, you name it. Rolo tried it.

He resembled a black Jerry Garcia with an entourage of women that rivaled the ones who followed the Grateful Dead's guitarist. But his first and only love was staying one step above the law when it came to maneuvering around anything and everything in cyberspace.

"What are you suggesting, Augusta? And you know how I hate keeping things from my husband. This is his case. And Nate's. Not one of my mother's wackadoodle things. Although that'll be next. I can assure you."

"It sounds as if your aunt knows her way around that museum."

"She knows her way around the Prado and the Louvre but that doesn't mean I'm going to Madrid or Paris any time soon."

"True, but suppose the two of you stop in for a visit, and while you're there, the computer system goes haywire."

"Rolo?"

"Uh-huh. Face it, you're not going to find anything snooping around storerooms and backrooms. Too much stuff. Not enough time. But if you were to copy their files, their account information, their purchase, sale and loan information, as well as miscellaneous correspondence, you'd have a trail that would lead you right to the point of origin. If you want my opinion, it was an inside job. And with your background, you'd be able to pinpoint who, when, where, and how."

"That's industrial theft. Or intellectual theft. Or some kind of theft. Heck, I don't know, but I do know it'll come with a hefty sentence!"

"Like I said, Rolo can finesse it so no one is the wiser. And once you have the answers, you can point Mr. Williams and Mr. Gregory in the right direction."

"Yeah. To the Fourth Avenue Jail."

"Think about it. Talk with your aunt. Face it, our detectives are going to get sucked into that murder case like an unsuspecting star in a black hole."

I glanced back at Nate's empty office before returning to mine. I had to admit, Augusta's idea was tempting, but at what price? As it turned out, the universe had other ideas, and through no fault of my own, I found myself smack dab in the middle of the murkiest idea ever.

While Nate and Marshall pursued leads on the doll case as well as more interviews regarding Betsy's tragic demise, I plodded on with my spreadsheets. Until three forty-five. That's when a call came in from my mother's cell phone.

"Mom, I'm in the middle of work. Can this wait?"

"Shh! Keep your voice low."

"No one can hear me from your end. What's going on?"

"Can that cyber lunatic you work with unlock a security door?"

"A what? Where are you?"

"Your aunt Ina and I are locked in a back office at the art museum. And don't raise your voice, whatever you do."

"I won't even ask what you're doing there, because I already know. Aunt Ina couldn't get me to break into their office so she talked you into it."

"She wanted you to break into a museum? Don't be ridiculous. So, will you call that man or not?"

"I need details. And lots of them. And quick. Nate and Marshall will be back here any minute."

"Your aunt insisted I join her for lunch at one of those fancy-schmancy places downtown—Forno 301. She wanted a specialty pizza and didn't want to go with your uncle since it would give him indigestion."

"Okay, okay. When I said *details*, I meant the pertinent ones."

"That *is* pertinent."

"Is the dog with you?"

"No. Gloria Wong is stopping by to check on him and Essie. She'll bring Thor so they can play."

Why do I ask these things?

"Tell me why you're locked in an office."

"It's not exactly an office. More like a safe repository in the museum. Although we *were* in their office to begin with."

"Get to the point already."

"Fine. After lunch, your aunt insisted on having me see a Victor Vasarely—I think that's his name—silkscreen that some acquaintance of hers donated to the museum. Lots of squiggly lines. Then she *just* had to go to their office downstairs to say hello to some of the staff."

"And then what?"

I already know what. I just need to hear it from the horse's mouth.

"Your aunt excused herself to use the restroom but made a wrong turn and we wound up in a security-protected art repository. She had on one of those special VIP badges so the guard let us in."

"And they didn't know you were still there when they closed?"

"That's because your aunt lost an earring and we were on our hands and knees trying to find it."

Lost an earring, my foot!

"Go on."

"The guard must have looked around, didn't see us, and thought we had left. We heard the announcement on the loudspeaker that the museum was closing but your aunt said they always give visitors more time. So much for what your aunt knows! Now we're locked in. And the lighting is dim. It dimmed shortly after that announcement. We can't very well call the police. It would look awful for the museum. They already have one strike against them with the missing doll. So, are you going to call that cyber guy or not? I need to get home before Gloria overfeeds Streetman. She's so used to feeding that Great Dane of hers that she feeds Streetman like she does Thor."

Of course. Streetman. I wondered when she'd mention him again.

"Give me a minute and I'll call you back. Don't touch anything. Whatever you do. Oh, and look around. Are there any computers in that room?"

"Yes. With a nice big screen. Why?"

"Rolo will need to talk to it."

I ended the call before my mother said another word. Then I stomped over to Augusta's desk. "This will make your day! My mother and my aunt are locked in the art repository at the museum. When my aunt gets an idea, she's like a bull moose in mating season and nothing will stop her."

"Sounds like something did. Sorry, didn't mean to make light of it."

"They can't call the police. Looks like it's Rolo after all. Can you get me a burner phone from the file drawer? He won't accept calls unless they're on a burner."

"Say no more. Hold on."

Seconds later, Augusta handed me the phone. "I'll send him a secure fax telling him you're about to call. Once he has that number, he'll accept all your other calls."

I tapped my foot as I watched Augusta write and send the fax.

"You should be all set, Phee. Go for it."

I dialed Rolo's number and took a few short breaths. Finally he took the call. My voice was shakier than usual and I wondered if he'd notice. "Hey, Rolo, it's Phee."

"If this is about that cipher treasure that escaped the museum, I'm already on it. Tell your boss to chill."

"Um, the doll is involved, but in a roundabout way. Look, my mother and my aunt are locked inside the art repository at the Phoenix Art Museum. Can you break into their system and get them out?" *Preferably before Nate and Marshall walk through the door.*

"Depends on their security system. Do they have access to a computer?"

"Access, yes, but without a password or code, they won't get in."

"*They* won't but I will. Tell them to turn the computer on. I'll access it, find out the IP address and network, and then go from there. They *do* know not to get their fingerprints on anything, right?"

"Uh-huh. I'll call you back in a jiff."

"By the way, I'm on an intermittent fasting diet with keto overtones. Doing lots of baking. Time for a double oven."

"I'll let Nate know."

"You can also let him know that you're not the only ones trying to track down that doll. Lots of chatter on the dark web. The doll isn't what you think."

"What do you mean?"

"The treasure hidden inside is a map."

"How do you know this?"

"Trusted contacts on the dark web."

"That's kind of an oxymoron, isn't it?"

"You trust me, don't you?"

"That's different. I know you."

"And I know that you and your agency are dealing with dangerous people and a cipher I'd love to get my hands on."

"So a map, huh? To where?"

"That's what I'd like to know."

Wonderful. I've just become Indiana Jones.

CHAPTER 14

The second I ended the call, I tapped my mother's cell number and prayed she and my aunt didn't do anything else to make things worse. "Mom! Rolo said to turn that computer on. But don't leave your fingerprints on it. Grab a tissue or something."

"Then what?"

"Not sure. I'll call you back. And tell aunt Ina not to go snooping around."

"Too late for that."

I always thought that line about a "cold chill running down my spine" was reserved for horror movies and gothic novels, but in this case, it was meant for my aunt. I got Rolo back on the line and waited for his instructions. At the same time, I mouthed to Augusta what was going on. She pointed to the clock on the wall and used her thumb to run across her neck. Not as if I needed reminding that any second Nate and Marshall would breeze through the door.

When I got Rolo back on the line, I told him I'd have Augusta speak with my mother on her phone and I would continue talking with him on the burner phone. That way we wouldn't waste time going back and forth.

"Tell Augusta to call your mother on another burner. Can't be too sure."

I did a mental eye roll and informed my mother to take the next call that came in and not fuss about an unknown number. Finally, after what seemed like an extraordinarily long lapse of time, Augusta was on the line with my mother, and I was still conversing with Rolo.

"I'm in, Phee." His voice was so matter-of-fact he might as well have told me he gassed up his car or something equally mundane.

Augusta motioned to me and waved her phone. "Your mother said the computer is doing all sorts of weird stuff."

"Tell her to describe it."

Just then, Rolo spoke. "Tell your mother to look for a sequence of numbers and letters on the bottom left of the page and click it."

"Okay."

"Now what, Phee?" my mother asked via Augusta. "I'm in another screen with lots and lots of lines and numbers."

In the three or four minutes that followed, Rolo was able to take her through a series of commands that eventually unlocked the system. "This would have been easier with a reset disc but what the heck," he said. "They're still using Windows 10 so no need for a reboot."

"Now what should she do?" I asked.

"It's an admin system so she needs to get into the security system. It will be clearly listed with all the programs on the bottom left of the screen."

Sure enough, my mother found it without any histrionics. And, she was able to disengage the alarm system and open the repository door.

"Wait!" I said. "You and aunt Ina can't go running out of there. They have security guards."

"They shouldn't be running out," Rolo said. "You should be going in."

"Huh? What?"

"You heard me, Phee. Now is your chance to download their files. You want to track down this cipher doll, don't you? You're an accountant and a bookkeeper. See what that museum has been up to. Grab a thumb drive and get yourself over there."

"And what do my mother and aunt do in the meantime?"

"I don't know. As long as they keep their hands off the computer."

I looked at the clock and bit my lower lip. "It will take me at least forty-five minutes in rush hour traffic."

"Then get moving."

"And what do I do? Just open a door and walk in?"

"The system is disabled. No one knows but us. Use a side door. Or a back door. I'm pulling up a map of the building. This shouldn't be too difficult. I also disabled the security cameras. They're on an old loop if anyone looks."

"Augusta," I choked. "Did you hear that? Rolo wants me to go over there and download their files."

Augusta gave her bouffant a quick fluff and nodded. "You won't get another chance like this."

Sure, just waiting for my turn in the Fourth Avenue Jail.

"What about Nate and Marshall?"

"I'll stick around and figure something out by the time they get here. Got lots of work to do and no canasta tonight."

"Rolo," I asked, "will you be available if I get stuck with something while I'm at the museum?"

"Just don't lock yourself in. You can never be too sure with some of these systems."

"I thought you said you disengaged it."

"I did. But some of them have covert timers."

Wonderful. Just what I need.

Leaving Augusta to come up with a plan to occupy my boss and my husband, I logged off my computer, grabbed my bag and did the fastest dash on record to my car. More than halfway down the I-17 south, Augusta called.

"We may have a problem."

"What problem?" I pictured a SWAT team at the museum.

"Mr. Williams called. The curator of the museum insisted they meet with her this evening and he and Mr. Gregory are on their way over there as we speak. He said to tell you Mr. Gregory sent you a text."

Wonderful. A text.

By now, I had turned left onto West McDowell and was only a few short blocks from the museum. "You've got to do something, Augusta! Think of something! She must have found out the security system was breached."

It was a good thing my hands were on the steering wheel or I wouldn't have had any fingernails left. I would have bitten them down to the core. As I approached the building, I expected to see red and blue flashers, but instead, it was as quiet as a cemetery.

Just then, Augusta called back. "They're just turning onto the I-17. I called Mr. Williams back to suggest they meet at a coffee shop in between to save them some time but he said the curator was adamant they meet at the museum. I figure you've got about fifteen minutes on them."

"Stay near a phone."

I parked in the rear and did as Rolo said. I spied the first back door and opened it. No alarm, no flashing lights, only a dim corridor. The one thing I hadn't thought of was the fact I had no idea where I was or where I was going. I redialed Rolo's number on the burner phone and tried to keep my composure. "Where the heck am I? Went in a back door. Now what?"

"Chill. Not as if the place is about to explode. You're in a corridor, right? Keep walking and look for a stairwell to the lower floor. Don't trust the elevators. That's a whole other issue."

I hadn't given elevators a single thought until Rolo mentioned it, and by then, it was too late. I heard footsteps headed toward me, and with no place else to turn, I saw the bank of elevators and got into the first one that opened. I didn't stop to see if it had one of those illuminating signs indicating the floor the elevator was on, so to stay on the safe side, I didn't push any buttons. Instead, I stood like a statue waiting for the breath to return to my lungs.

At least I was smart enough to keep both of my phones on mute. A second or two passed and then, the elevator started. Going up. *Drat! Must be the museum curator. On the first floor.*

My mind had suddenly become a barren wasteland. No thought whatsoever of what I would say when the door opened. Sure enough, it did, but no one was in sight. That had to mean another elevator arrived before mine. I waited a second for my hands to stop shaking and then pushed the button for the lowest floor.

I arrived at another dim corridor. This time on the bottom floor where the offices and repository were located. I tapped my mother's number and told her to open the door a crack. Then, I texted Rolo and had him send me a photo of the floor plan. All the while I prayed the curator was not on her way down here. Oh, who was I kidding? Her office was down here. Any second and I'd be outed.

A quick tap and I had Rolo on the line. "You have to do something. The curator is in the building and probably headed this way."

"On it. Try not to blink."

Next thing I knew, bright corridor lights flashed like a 1970s disco.

"That should keep her entertained for a few minutes," he said. "Hurry up."

Like I needed reminding.

It took me less than ten seconds to see the open door to the repository and I rushed in.

"Shh! No time to waste. Where's the computer?"

My mother pointed and I thrust the flash drive into it and began to copy the files. Fortunately, Rolo had isolated them for me.

"It should be done by now," my mother said. "It only takes them a second or two on *NCIS* and all those FBI shows."

"That's television," I grumbled. "They need to leave time for commercials. In real life, it takes forever."

"We don't have forever."

"Tell me, where did you park the car? I didn't see it."

"Across the street in the CVS parking lot. Your aunt insisted we park there. Now I know why."

"Good. Look, no need for you to wait. Go out the nearest door and hightail it home. I'll be in touch."

"I hate leaving you here alone."

"You're not. Rolo's at the phone and most likely my boss and husband are only yards away. I'll call you when I'm done."

"You hear that, Ina?" my mother whispered. "Stop futzing around with those cardboard boxes. We need to go. Now!"

"This is the doll collection," my aunt replied. I looked her way and recognized the expression on her face. I'd seen it before when we were at Brett's Department Store in downtown Mankato when I was growing up. My cousin Kirk and I had become antsy but my mother and my aunt were so absorbed in their shopping that it would have taken a crane to extricate them.

"Now!" I pointed to the door and they scurried out. Correction. My mother scurried. My aunt stared wistfully at the boxes before she made her move. Then I looked at the computer screen. Still downloading. Rather than watch the tedious process, I walked to the boxes and picked up where she had left off. That's when I heard voices. And not ones that I recognized.

CHAPTER 15

Oddly enough, the first thought that crossed my mind was that I'd be able to drop those five or six pounds I wanted to lose, if indeed I wound up behind bars. The conversation I heard was unintelligible from a distance. Even with the door ajar as per Rolo's instructions. Then, it became clearer. And louder.

"Gonna take my break now, Stu. Checked the lighting. Must have been a glitch. Everything looks good. Gonna hit the vending machines on second. They've got Scooter Pies."

"I'm heading to the abstract art wing. Catch you later. Oh, got a notification from the company. Boss is returning to the building. She's got her own key and passcode. Not a problem."

"Never is. See you later."

I waited for my pulse to return to normal and then sent a brief text to Augusta so she'd be up to speed. Then, I looked at those boxes again. The first column had cloth dolls. And plenty of them, but the next column housed two porcelain dolls, carefully covered with packing material. I lifted the lid to the third box but instead of finding another porcelain doll, I saw that the box was empty of its contents. Only the packing material remained.

I surmised that if that box contained the priceless treasure, it had been removed and repackaged for transport. I moved the packing material around and sure enough, I was right. Inside the box was a form indicating the date of the shipment and the recipient. The notation read, "On loan." It was initialed by someone but I couldn't make it out.

Wasting no time, I called Augusta again. "Put a bug in Nate's ear to have the curator take them to the repository where the doll was last seen before transport. Come up with something. You're good at it. I can't very well tell him I've been rooting through here. Maybe the curator will recognize the initials. But wait until I let you know I'm out of here."

Augusta chuckled. "Your secret's safe for now. And give the guy some credit. He'll eventually put two and two together. Along with your husband."

"Fine. I'll deal with *eventually* when it's eventual. Meanwhile, I've got to get moving."

"Call me back."

I crossed my fingers that the files had finished downloading but they hadn't. *How long can this last? NCIS, my you-know-what!*

Then, more voices from down the hall. And this time I recognized them. No easy way out now. I approached the computer and held my breath. The red flashing light on the thumb drive had stopped blinking. Hallelujah. I went to the "safely remove" icon, pushed it and extracted the drive. Slipping it into my bag, I tiptoed out of the room and closed the door behind me. The voices were still down the corridor.

Which way out of here, Rolo? I texted.

Corridor curves left. First door is an employees' restroom. It's unlocked if you have to hide out.

I texted back—*I want to get out!*

Take stairwell ten or eleven yards down. Go to first floor and take main entrance out. Then he added, *Run like hell, just in case.*

"Run like hell?" In wedge heels, no less! I prayed the security detail was otherwise occupied eating Scooter Pies and wandering around the galleries. As for running, my feet had turned to lead and I was lucky to walk gingerly to the door. From there, with a cool breeze in my face, I charged toward my car as if it was the last spaceship leaving Mars.

Once on the I-17 north, I used Bluetooth and called Augusta. "Was that ever a close call. Never again! Never ever ever!"

"What about your mother and your aunt?"

"They're probably sitting in an eatery somewhere, stuffing themselves with pie. Were you able to lead the horse to water?"

"To the entire river. I asked him if he was going to check the last place the item was seen because that's what they do on TV. Then he told me he knew how to do his business. That's all it took."

I laughed. "Guess it's safe for you to go home now. And thanks, Augusta. I'll let Rolo know I'm safe."

"He already knows."

"How?"

"He was able to get into your car's GPS."

"Unbelievable."

I used Bluetooth and called my mother. Sure enough, she and my aunt were safely nestled away munching on Cornish pasties, of all things. My aunt knew a restaurant nearby that specialized in these British delights and since they served apple caramel ones, she *just* had to indulge.

"Nate and Marshall are in the museum. I heard their voices. I may have lost ten years out of my life getting out of there, Mom."

"Don't be so dramatic."

From the person who tops the Richter scale when the dog eats something from the ground.

"Listen. I picked up where Aunt Ina left off with those boxes but all I found was a packing slip. I had Augusta call Nate and put a bug in his ear to check it."

"Your aunt is convinced a bogus shipping company was used."

"She's not the only one. Look, it's been a long day. And it'll probably be a longer night once Marshall gets home. I have to tell him the truth. I'll call you tomorrow."

"Call me once you unload those files."

"Download. And I'm not calling you back tonight. I'm exhausted."

"Exhausted? I know my daughter. You're going to plunk them into your computer the minute you get home."

"I'm going to scan for viruses first. And yes. But I'm still not calling you back tonight. Tell Aunt Ina, no more bright ideas. This last one of hers nearly cost all of us jail time. Or hefty lawyer fees." *Or my marriage.*

Then I heard my aunt's voice. "Harriet, shall I order us the chocolate mousse pasty as well?"

"Enjoy your desserts, Mom. And drive home safe."

When I opened the door, I kicked off my shoes, plunked the flash drive into the computer, started a virus scan, and then headed to the bedroom to get into sweatpants and a top. Then I thought better of it and even though I was ravenous, I jumped into the shower instead. I needed to rinse the miserable afternoon/evening off of me and come up with some way to let Marshall know what had happened. Besides, that virus scan wasn't going to be done any time soon.

Marshall's first text said he and Nate had an emergency meeting with the museum curator and not to wait on dinner for him. His second text, that I read after toweling off, said he was on his way home but that he and Nate were stopping at the first burger joint they saw.

That gave me more than enough time to devour a full container of Noosa strawberry yogurt and a handful of saltines. By that time, the scan ended and the file was clean.

"You'd better offer up something worth the risk I took tonight," I said out loud as I stared at the flash drive, still inserted into the computer. Exhaustion may have taken over my body but my mind spun in more directions than a whirligig.

As I located the files, I heard the garage door open, followed by Marshall's voice. "I'm home, hon. What a grueling evening!"

"In here. At the computer. I take it you've eaten."

"More like shoveled. They don't call it fast food for nothing. But I will make myself a cup of coffee. Want anything?"

"I'm good." I got up from the computer and gave him a hug. As he tussled my hair, he started to laugh.

"What? What?"

"Couldn't help but notice your mother and your aunt Ina walking into the CVS across from the museum. Had to do a double take. Good thing

Nate was at the wheel. Still, he caught sight of them, too, and remarked that you aunt was hard to miss. Surprising that your mother was there. She didn't strike me as someone interested in viewing artwork."

"Viewing, snooping, casing out the place . . ."

"Huh?"

"My aunt is on their board, remember? It's a high-stakes theft and—"

"Oh no! Oh no. Please don't tell me they were snooping in places where they shouldn't have been."

"Aargh. I was hoping to ease into this, but there's no easy way around it. They weren't the only ones."

Marshall widened his eyes. "I'm going to need that cup of coffee. After what you're about to tell me, I wouldn't be getting much sleep anyway."

I pointed to the computer. "Depends on the files we copied."

It took two cups of coffee and a slice of raisin bread before Marshall spoke. By that time, I had told him everything beginning with my mother's phone call and ending with Rolo's insistence that I copy the files on the museum's computer.

"I don't know whether to chastise you or congratulate you," he said. "Chastise, because of the incredible risk you took, and congratulate because you got us to a place we'd never be able to reach on our own."

"So I guess it's a draw." I smiled.

He pulled me close and glanced at the computer. "I'll reiterate, more or less, what you said a few minutes ago. 'It depends what's on those files.'"

CHAPTER 16

"I'm as anxious to find out as you are," I said, "but first tell me what was so pressing that the museum curator insisted on a visit. After hours, no less. Was anything else stolen?"

"Stolen or misplaced, no. Disturbing, yes. Had the curator not received a phone call from their web designer this afternoon, compelling her to look at the exhibit, it might have gone unnoticed for a long time."

"What do you mean?"

"Have you ever heard of the Thorne Rooms? North wing. Second floor."

I shook my head.

"Neither have I." Marshall rubbed his chin and continued. "They're miniature replicas of actual rooms in the United States and Europe. Down to every last detail. Period furniture and all."

"Vandalized?"

"No. Compromised. There are twenty miniatures and one of them is a mid-eighteenth-century Breton kitchen. Cornwall part of England. I had to look that up. Anyway, the curator got a phone call from their web designer. The company was updating the photos for the web page and called her attention to something odd. Apparently, they noticed an extra piece in the Breton Kitchen diorama when they reshot the photo. On the floor, next to the small kitchen chair to the left, was a figurine. She immediately saw it for herself. A wooden doll, no less. It was not part of the original piece. Since the exhibit was glassed in, she couldn't very well open it from the front of the exhibit and didn't wish to call attention to it. So, she contacted us."

Again, I asked, "And?"

"She got the key from the vault and Nate and I were able to remove the piece from the wall and open the exhibit. The doll was a miniature replica of the one that went missing. And, there was a note next to it that almost required a magnifying glass. It read, "f-1." The "minus 1" in even smaller print."

"Oh my gosh. My mother and those women must never find out. This will drive them over the edge."

"It's not from the great beyond. Someone's playing with us. Or, with the museum, to be precise. Like a cat and mouse game. The first question is—'What on earth for?' and the second is—'What on earth is f minus 1? A function key? Makes no sense."

"So, now what?"

"Nate will send the miniature piece to the private lab we use and we'll see if they can pull anything discernable. Like prints, although doubtful, but substances that may lead us in the right direction. Meanwhile, it's the regular gumshoe method of questioning and probing. Unless we get a tighter circle given what's on those files you copied." He shook his head and smiled at the same time. "Notice, I didn't use the word *stole*, although—"

"It was Rolo's idea. Oh my gosh! I sound like a first-grader!"

"Hey, this business takes us places we never thought we'd be and sometimes forces us to do things we never would ordinarily consider. I like to think we abide by a decent set of ethics but when push comes to shove, we sometimes resort to the old adage that the end justifies the means. Unless, of course, the means puts people in harm's way. Right now, we're dealing with one piece of stolen artwork. But what if someone is just getting started?"

"I don't understand why Rolo insisted I secretly copy the files. Couldn't you simply ask the curator for a copy?"

"The curator may be the one with something to hide. It won't be the first time."

"I see. I'm not sure what these files will tell us, but we might as well take a cursory look. Tomorrow, I can go into depth at the office. At least it'll be part of my real job. Besides, I'm pretty much caught up on everything else for a few days."

"Okay, Sherlock, get started."

To my surprise, not only did that little flash drive contain the entire inventory of acquisitions, loans, and sales for the past five years, but a cadre of correspondence broken down by department. Recipients included other museums, industries, libraries, and government agencies. Missing was payroll and related information but I doubted it would yield us anything.

The artwork was categorized by artist name and/or type of piece, and date acquired or relinquished. The doll was labeled "cipher doll, mid-eighteenth century, wooden," and contained the date that it was first acquired and the price the museum paid to the art museum in New York. It gave new meaning to the term *priceless.*

"I can understand why the curator is frantic," I said. "The insurance company may drop them after this."

"What I don't get is why they loaned it to the unity council knowing how valuable it was," Marshall said. He rubbed the back of his neck and peered over my shoulder. "We'll need to find out exactly who orchestrated that move. Listen, it's getting late and you can pick this up in the office on Monday. Another minute and I'm liable to conk out on the floor. Thank goodness tomorrow is Sunday!"

"I just want to glance at the correspondence. Go make yourself comfortable and I'll join you in a bit."

"That curiosity gene of yours works overtime, you know."

"Good. Tell Williams Investigations to note that," I said and laughed. "Hey, do you have the employee list for the museum? I want to compare it with the incoming and outgoing mail."

"Sure thing. It's in a PDF at the office. I'll forward it to your email on Monday and you can peruse it at your leisure."

"Great! In spite of the bizarre night, I'll be overjoyed to work on something normal."

Bite my tongue! And bite it twice because, in spite of having a wonderful Sunday to ourselves, the following morning moved me away from normal and straight into bird-poop-crazy.

It began the instant I got into the office. Augusta waved a note in the air and proceeded to read it. "Tell Phee she's at least five minutes late. I waited to call her at work since she was so insistent last night that I don't bother her. Tell her Wayne called Herb and he called me. They reopened the auto restoration garage but only for painting and under-the-hood work. The lifts are still off limits. But Wayne and Herb are going to set a trap. They need someone with expertise. Like Phee. Have her call me."

I stood there, absolutely dumbfounded. So dumbfounded, in fact, that Augusta asked if I was okay.

"Oh sure. I'm perfectly fine. It's not enough my mother and my wacky aunt nearly got us all arrested the other night at the museum, but now she wants to embroil me in another one of her forays? This borders on insanity."

"Honey, it *is* insanity, but it's your family."

I rolled my eyes and walked straight toward the Keurig. "Was there anything else?"

"Nope. But it's only nine fifteen."

I pulled the flash drive from my bag and dangled it in front of Augusta. "This may be the key to figuring out what really happened to that doll." Then, in less than a minute, I told her everything that took place that night.

"You need to find a good bail bondsman and put him or her on speed dial. By the way, Mr. Williams took off for Axis Forensics Labs and Mr. Gregory is meeting again with a few key players from the unity council. Hey, you don't intend to go over to that auto garage, do you?"

"Only if they're giving away a Lexus or something similar. I'll call my mother during my break. Right now, I want to dive into that flash drive."

"Just remember to come up for air."

I grabbed my coffee and headed to the solitude of my office. But before I could feast my eyes on that file, I had to finalize a few quick invoices.

Then, I scrutinized the employee lists. Present workers, retirees, and "moved on to greener pastures" for lack of a better term. Also, those out on leave, medical and otherwise. It was almost ten and that's when I noticed a name that resonated. Resonated, and compelled me to phone Wayne.

Lucky for me, he answered on the third ring. "Wayne here."

"Hi. It's Phee and I—"

"That was quick. Considering. Your mother said you probably wouldn't get in touch until after work."

"I'm not taking part in whatever wackadoodle plan you and Herb concocted."

"I just need some technical advice."

"I'm the last person you should ask. And, in fact, you shouldn't ask anyone! Or do anything. Let the deputies deal with this."

"Is that what you called to tell me?"

"Not exactly. I need to know something. Did Holt Kavanaugh ever work for the Phoenix Art Museum?"

"I'm not sure but I can find out. Why?"

"It's for another case of ours. There's an H. Kavanaugh listed. Could be a coincidence but it said 'retired' and he'd be about the right age."

"Tell you what. I'll poke around but only if you listen to Herb and my plan to trap Betsy's killer."

"Listen? Or act on it?"

"Just listen. The deputies haven't made any headway as far as I know and they'll likely point a finger at me. So, what do you say? Can you pop over here on your lunch hour? I'll pick up McDonald's if that helps."

I looked at the clock. "I can spare a half hour. That's it. It takes at least twenty minutes to get there."

"Thanks. Do you want anything in particular?"

Yeah. A way out of this mess.

"Any hamburger will do. See you then. Oh, don't let my mother know. Last thing any of us needs is Streetman lifting his leg in the garage."

"Don't have to tell me twice."

CHAPTER 17

When I pulled into the parking lot at the auto restoration garage, I was hard-pressed to find a spot. It was like Black Friday but without the shopping. After circling the area twice, I gave up and parked near the tennis courts adjacent to the dog park.

"Is this place always so busy?" I asked Wayne the minute I stepped inside. "Or is it because it was locked down for a while?"

"It's because everyone wants to gossip and the bagel shops are full during lunchtime. Look around. Do you see anyone working?"

I glanced at the bays, the paint area, the tool benches and the corner area where a coffee maker and vending machine were. "Uh, guess you're right. Unless brewing coffee and eating junk food constitutes work."

"Yeah, about that. McDonald's was packed so Herb and I got us tacos. Hope that's okay."

"I'm fine with anything."

"Good. Herb's over by the worktable on the left. We can eat there and I'll tell you about our plan. It's ingenious."

The last time I heard the word *ingenious* when it came to describing a plan was when my mother insisted I follow a cleaning crew around in order to pry into the homeowner's dresser drawers. Now, I shudder at the term.

Other than Herb, no one was in the vicinity so we spoke freely but kept our voices low.

Wayne bit into his taco and wiped his chin with one of those brown napkins that don't do much. "Okay, here's the deal. The people who were in the garage the night of Betsy's murder were the ones who had a beef with her. The Turk sisters. Holt. And well, everyone else. I've got the names on a list."

"Go on." I bit into a carne asado taco and made a note to find out where they got it. Not because it was good, but because I needed to avoid that place.

"So, we send each of them a text telling them we know that they were responsible for the murder and that if they want us to keep mum, they'll show up at the auto garage at a certain time and place and pay us hush money. Of course, we're not really going to collect the money, we just want to find out who shows up. Brilliant! Isn't it?"

"No! Absolutely the worst plan ever. It's not even a plan. It's blackmail!"

"Only if there's a monetary exchange. I went over this with Myrna and your mother and they thought it was 'diabolical and clever.'"

"Yep. Diabolical, clever, and illegal. Good grief! Myrna and my mother? Those are the last two I'd approach for things like this."

Well, maybe not the last two. My aunt Ina is running a close second.

As Wayne started to extol the virtues of the plan, Herb cut him short. "Look over there! By the paint booth. The Turk sisters are really getting into it. We should move closer and listen. From now on, every word that anyone says in here could be a clue."

Subtlety was not a trait the Turk sisters had been blessed with. As a result, there was no need to move closer. We heard every word loud and clear, beginning with Darleen, whose voice could have been mistaken for a medieval fishwife if we weren't living in the twenty-first century.

"You could have at least told me you had my extra set of keys. I looked all over for them."

"I forgot. Shoot me! I picked them up accidently when I was at your place. They were right next to where I set mine down. I grabbed both of them and shoved them in my pocket. Pulled out the right one when I got in my car but forgot about the other. Geez, it's not as if you didn't have another set!"

"That's not the point."

"What was the other thing you beefed about?" Aimee stamped her foot but it only seemed to aggravate her sister.

"I can't believe you want to repaint the Corvette dark blue and white. You insisted on riverside red and that's what's we did. I don't know about you, but my pockets aren't that deep. Besides, we've got to swap out the engine on the VW bug."

"The dark blue and white have the nostalgia thing going for them."

"You should have thought of that when you insisted on riverside red and cream. You said they had the 'wow factor' going for them."

"Well, I was wrong," Aimee shouted back. "Deal with it."

"We need to start work on the Beetle. The Vette can wait."

"No. It can't. It has to be done now."

"I don't understand the urgency. You're being obtuse."

Then, just when I thought no one could out-shout the Turk sisters, Luella, who had been keeping a low profile, stormed over to the Turks, put her hands on her hips and gave them what my mother would have called "the Evil Eye."

"Aimee! Darleen! I heard you. A one-eared man in Saskatoon probably did as well. Don't you even dare consider commandeering the paint booth. I'm supposed to be next. My Dodge has been waiting long enough. I can't keep putting touch-up on it. The greens don't match. Besides, Betsy had me next on the list."

"Then take it up with her. Maybe a nice séance," Darleen said.

"That's not funny. And we'll see what Holt has to say about this. Once he's done talking with Jared over there."

I looked across the room and it appeared as if the men were engaged in an equally unpleasant exchange. "Are they always like this?" I whispered to Wayne.

"Nah. Sometimes they're worse."

Then, when I figured the conversation between Luella and the Turks was over, one of them said, "I know you knocked her off."

The trouble was, I didn't know if one of the Turk sisters accused Luella or vice-versa. Drat!

"Did either of you hear that?" I asked the men.

Wayne shook his head. "Herb was making too much noise unwrapping his bag of chips."

"Hey, it's not my fault the bag makes so much noise." And with that, Herb stuffed a handful of chips into his mouth.

"They're pointing fingers at each other for Betsy's murder," I said. "And by the way, what's Luella's last name?"

"Denzel. Luella Denzel."

"Like in Denzel Washington?"

Wayne shrugged. "Who?"

"Never mind. Listen, if you and Herb want to do something useful, find out more about the people in this club. Who had it in for whom, who owed who money, who cheated on who . . ."

Good grief. This sounds like "Who's on first?"

"Don't resort to cockamamie ideas that could land you in jail," I continued. "No matter how convincing my mother and Myrna are. Stick to information gathering. Then, you could share that with Nate and Marshall and they can convince the deputies to take a closer look."

"I still think our plan is faster," Herb said.

"And riskier."

The men looked at each other for a nanosecond before Wayne spoke. "Fine. We'll give it a try, but if the noose tightens around my neck, all bets are off."

I tossed the remainder of my taco in the trash when no one was looking and watched as Luella made a beeline for Holt. The Turk sisters continued arguing with each other, paying no attention to Herb, who was fixated on their performance. Yep, all was right with the world.

"This could get dicey," he said.

"Um, what does anyone know about Holt? Or Jared, for that matter?" I figured if the men wanted to do something useful, they could start right there.

"Do you think Williams Investigations would loan us a covert recording device? Like the ones on TV when they say the person is wired?" Herb asked.

"No, I don't. Just ask around. Or use your cell phone on video."

What am I thinking?

"Listen, guys, I have to get back to the office. And Wayne, don't forget to find out if Holt worked for the Phoenix Art Museum. You've got to keep your end of the deal. Ease into a conversation or something. And don't do anything irrational." *Or idiotic.*

A few grumbles from the guys and I was out the door and on my way to the car. The parking lot had cleared out a bit but it was still pretty well-packed. Off to my right, I could see the dog park and thanked my lucky stars I didn't have to venture inside.

Once I was back in the office, Augusta couldn't wait to find out what the big deal was at the auto garage. I don't know what made her laugh more, the request for a recording "wire" or the nonstop Turk sisters' bickering.

"Save me a donut for my break later," I said. "And remind me to never order from Tasty Tacos. Bland doesn't even come close."

"I'll save you two donuts." Augusta winked.

I sauntered into my office, rebooted the computer and entered my "Zen zone," the one place where numbers gave me solace and a sense of normalcy with the world. A good forty or fifty minutes later, my cell phone vibrated and I saw it was Lyndy.

"Hey, Phee, sorry to call you at work but this is my break time and I won't get a chance later. I have a date with Lyman. I just found out something and I thought you should know. My busybody aunt has been blabbering about that murder ever since it happened and found out someone was seen at one in the morning leaving the area."

"Who? What someone? Did the witness call the sheriff's office?"

"The witness is my aunt's next-door neighbor who took her dog on an emergency run to the dog park because the dog refused to go in its own yard. She saw a woman getting into her car. It was parked behind the garage but in full view of the dog park."

"Any description? Car or woman?"

"It was dark but she was positive it was a silver SUV."

"And the woman?"

"Tall and hefty. Said she carried something against her chest but she couldn't see what. She told my aunt she didn't call the posse because they only want to know if a crime was committed and there's no crime in walking or parking next to a building."

"What about reporting something suspicious?" Then I stopped myself and laughed. "Yeesh. The posse must get a zillion calls about 'suspicious' activities. I know my mother's book club keeps them busy. Anyway, I'll pass that along to Nate and Marshall. Too bad there's no surveillance behind the auto garage. Or the dog park, for that matter. Plus, she was seen getting into her car. Who knows if she left the garage or walked across the other part of the rec complex."

"True. If I hear any other tidbits that sound promising, I'll let you know. By the way, I am *so* glad you introduced me to Lyman. Dating him has been one of the best things that happened to me since I moved out here."

"It wasn't exactly an introduction. More like a—"

"Match made in Heaven?"

"I was going to say 'odd turn of events,' but yeah, 'match made in Heaven' works. I'll call you this week and we'll catch up. Thanks, Lyndy!"

"Any time!"

Lyman Neal was the manager of Herb's softball team, and through a bizarre series of events wound up dating my best friend. Who says romance is only for twenty-year-olds?"

I closed my eyes to think about that for a split second when Augusta buzzed my office. "There's someone here to see you, Phee."

"Don't tell me it's my mother. Or my aunt."

"Worse. Much worse."

CHAPTER 18

I opened the door to my office and stepped out. The odor of fish and bait hit my nostrils before my eyes took in Paul Schmidt. He stood adjacent to Augusta's desk and fiddled with some sort of lure.

He wore a large green vest with netted pockets on it and I prayed there was nothing alive inside. His red and brown plaid shirt had seen better days, as evidenced by a few holes and more than one set-in stain.

As for shoes, he wore black rubber boots and they still appeared to be wet. It didn't take a Sherlock Holmes to deduct he'd spent the morning fishing.

"Hi, Paul," I said. "What brings you here?"

"I heard about Herb and Wayne's killer trap. I told them it was a bad idea, especially since I cooked up a better one. And I think I know who murdered Betsy. That's why I'm here. You work for a detective agency. You tell me if I hit the nail on the head with this one."

Augusta flashed me a look that said, "I'm going to lose my breakfast if he stays here any longer," and I gave her a nod.

"Hey, Paul, let's talk in my office. Much more private. Want any coffee?"

He shook his head. "Nah. Don't need to take a whiz when I'm back on the road."

I did a mental eye roll and motioned him to my office. As I turned to close the door, Augusta mouthed, "Thanks."

"Grab a chair and tell me what this is all about."

Paul plunked himself in front of my desk and leaned an elbow on it. "I used to date someone in that auto club. Luella Denzel. Know her?"

"Not personally. No."

"Just as well. Got a temper as fiery as her hair. And jealous as all get-up-and-go."

"Um, what does this have to do with your plan?"

"You mean my *trap*. Everything. I'm not particularly proud of this, but I sort of cheated on Luella with Betsy back in the day."

"How far back?'

"About a year or so. And take it from me. There was no love lost between those two. Luella always said she'd knock Betsy into the middle of next week."

"Lots of people use that expression. It's just an exaggeration."

"Not when she actually attempted to do it."

"Did Betsy ever file a report with the posse?"

"No. It happened in Surprise. Luella claimed she didn't see her when she rammed her shopping cart into her at Costco."

"Okay. Fine. Now what's this about some plan of yours?" *And ten to one there'll be fish involved.*

"I'll invite Luella to join me on my boat at Lake Pleasant. It's mid-sixties but with the sun out and a jacket on, it'll be comfortable. I'll tell her I miss her company. Heck, I'll even spring for soda and chips. Then, when she's nice and comfortable, I'll do something with the engine so that it'll appear as if the boat is going to go down. I'll be sure to bounce it on the water, too."

I widened my eyes and waited for him to continue.

"Then, I tell her I know she murdered Betsy and that I'd help her with an alibi if she'd tell me the truth. I'll tell her I have a friend who works for the sheriff's office and there's ironclad evidence against her. Then, more bouncing the boat on water. And wobbling. I get her to confess. All I need is one of your recorder things."

"You can do that with your cell phone. What am I saying? That's a rotten idea. Rotten and dangerous. Worse than Wayne's and Herb's. At least no one will drown with their shenanigans."

"I thought my idea was ingenious."

Terrific. Another "ingenious."

"Ingenious, yes. Also frightening as hell. Listen, Paul, I'll tell you what I told them. Let the sheriff's office and the investigators deal with it. If you want to do something, do what you always do. Snoop around and listen. People can't keep their mouths closed around here. You're bound to hear something. Then, notify one of us. Okay? And whatever you do, don't talk about it over the air on your radio show. Or that combination fish and mystery hour with my mother and Myrna."

Paul's lips began to quiver and I almost felt bad. Almost. I thanked him for stopping by and for taking such an interest in helping a friend. "Wayne will be okay. None of us believe he's culpable. We just need to keep rational heads. Fair enough?"

Paul shrugged and started for the door. Then he stopped. "You know, I was really interested in dating that friend of yours but Lyman beat me to it. If she changes her mind, let her know I'm still available. I'll take her fishing any time."

I gritted my teeth and forced a smile. "I'll be sure to let Lyndy know. Have a good day, Paul."

When he left the office, I charged over to Augusta's desk. She took out a can of Lysol from the file drawer and sprayed it all over the place.

"Can you believe it? He thinks the garage murderer is a woman he used to date. Came up with a plan that would most likely result in another death.

This time a drowning. I think I convinced him otherwise."

Unfortunately, I didn't. Not until Saturday morning when I went in to the office for my usual every other half day Saturday. Since the lab was slow in getting results back to Nate on the miniature evidence he and the curator discovered, he focused on Maricopa County's other case—Betsy's murder. He had follow-up visits scheduled with a few of the auto club's members who had dealings with Betsy.

Meanwhile, Marshall was doing the same, only this time with some of the unity council members, including Cecilia and Louise. If nothing else, he'd get an earful about everything else. I was fastidiously poring over the information I'd gleaned on those spreadsheets from the museum, this time focusing on the chain of acquisitions. That's when a frantic call came in from my mother.

"Phee! Good. It's Saturday. You don't work in the afternoon."

I'll find work if I have to put down railroad ties.

"Why? What's going on?"

"Herb called a few minutes ago. Paul was ecstatic about some ludicrous plan he came up with to ensnarl Betsy's killer. He's convinced it's that Luella woman. You know, the redhead from the auto garage."

"I, uh—"

"Just listen. He told Herb he was going to take her fishing. Seems Luella likes to fish. Even won a lake trout contest back in Minnesota. Had to be up north. I kept up with all the Mankato news. Anyway, Paul intends to scare her into a confession while they're on Lake Pleasant. Herb and I are going over to the marina to talk some sense into him. Last thing Myrna and I need is for Paul to mess things up and ruin our chance to impress Jay Leno at the buy-sell-trade event. Did I mention it was going to be televised?"

At least a hundred times.

"Seriously? Reason with Paul? You guys talk over each other on your radio show. What makes you think he'll listen to you?"

"Herb and I will figure something out. I wanted you to know in case you wanted to join us."

"I do not. And don't do anything ridiculous."

"Relax. It's not like I'm with your aunt Ina. According to Herb, they'll be at the marina by two thirty. Plenty of time for you to change your mind."

"I won't."

"I'll fill you in later."

I was about to hang up but an unsettling thought crossed my mind. "Those motorboats come equipped with life jackets and vests, don't they?"

"I suppose. Goodness. It's not like they're going to go overboard. It's not the *Titanic*."

"No, more like the *S.S. Minnow*."

Then, she said the one word that changed everything.

"I think I may bring Streetman."

I pictured the disaster of all times. The dog in his vest, my mother anxious to see how he handles water, and a fanatical fisherman intent on catching a would-be killer. Everything perfectly lined up for a calamity. Action scenes included.

"What time did you say you were going?" I asked.

"Herb will be out front at quarter to one. We're stopping at Starbucks first."

"Okay. Just curious. Talk to you later." *Or stop this fiasco.*

In that instant I knew I had no choice if a full-blown catastrophe was going to be averted.

"Augusta!" I shouted as I exited my office and flew to her desk. "Paul is going through with his idiotic plan, and to make matters worse, my mother and Herb are on their way to convince him otherwise."

She looked up from her computer screen. "That doesn't sound so bad."

"She's bringing the dog."

Dead silence. We looked at each other like *Star Trek* mind readers before Augusta finally spoke.

"The dog's been taking swim classes, hasn't he?"

I nodded.

"Hate to say it, but you may want to drive over there before Rin Tin Tin topples the boat."

"It's not until after two. Plenty of time for me to finish up here, fortify myself with sugary donuts, and atone for my sins. Just in case."

Augusta laughed. "What should I tell the men when they get back?"

"Tell them I had a wonderful half day and was now taking care of some odds and ends."

"Odds and ends, huh?" She laughed. "That's a new expression for what you're about to do. Your mother and Herb aren't planning on renting a motorboat, are they?"

"Of course not." Then I stood still and let her words sink in. "Geez, Augusta, I hope not. My mother has no idea how to operate a motorboat."

"What about Herb?"

"Unfortunately, he does. Bragged about some excursion he took on the Intercoastal in Florida once."

"I'd say Streetman shouldn't be the only one with a life vest. I've got an old L.L. Bean one you can use."

"Thanks, but no thanks. My sleuthing stops at the water's edge."

Augusta laughed. "We'll see about that."

CHAPTER 19

Our house was on the way to Lake Pleasant so I made a quick stop, changed into jeans, a sweatshirt, a windbreaker, and my rubber all-weather moccasins. Then, I googled the water temperature in Lake Pleasant—forty-eight degrees. The coldest temp for this time of year. *Wonderful.* A horrible thought crossed my mind. Paul wouldn't be *that* idiotic to let Luella fall out of the boat, would he? I tried not to answer it. On a cheerful note, it was the sunniest month according to the website. But not if you're under water. No matter. I had no choice. I started up the car and drove the scenic route on Lake Pleasant Road to the regional park.

Known for boating, camping, and hiking, the park afforded its visitors a gorgeous getaway from the congestion of downtown Phoenix. An extra bonus were the wild donkeys found on the footpaths. And while Marshall and I enjoyed watching them, I was positive Streetman's reaction would border on over-the-top enthusiasm. I prayed those donkeys would steer clear of the marina, but what the heck? It was going to be a nightmare no matter what.

When I pulled into the marina parking lot at Scorpion Bay, I saw Herb's car parked a few yards from the building. It was hard to miss. It was the only late-twentieth-century Chevy with a Sun City West Men's Softball logo plastered across the rear window.

Please tell me they haven't rented a boat.

I charged into the office and all but toppled over a display of postcards and small Arizona souvenirs until I reached the counter. A well-built man who appeared to be in his thirties looked up from his computer screen and asked if he could help me.

"Yes. Can you tell me if you rented a boat to a man by the name of Herb Garrett? He would have arrived a few minutes ago. He's with my mother and I've got to stop them before they go out on the lake."

The man reached for his cell phone. "Is she in any danger? It didn't appear as if he coerced her into going out on the lake to fish. Looked like a nice family excursion. Dog and all."

I looked past him and could see the lake from the expansive wall-to-wall window. "I can see their motorboat. You've got to call the sheriff's office and have them send a water patrol to stop them."

"From what?" He opened a drawer, took out a pair of binoculars and focused on the lake. "Everything appears to be fine. I can't summon the sheriff's patrol for no reason."

"Oh, there's a reason, all right. They're trying to catch up with another boat to stop the man in that boat from causing an accidental, but not so accidental, water incident."

"I don't understand. Here, see for yourself." He handed me the binoculars and I could see Paul's fishing boat not too far away. Too bad I couldn't hazard a guess in nautical miles, or actual miles, for that matter.

The exasperation in the man's voice was unmistakable. "I still don't understand."

"The guy in the fishing boat may try to rock the boat and cause his passenger to land in the water. The people in the other boat with the dog want to stop him. Think hypothermia and call the sheriff's patrol."

"I can't report a non-incident or speculation."

"Keep your eyes on those boats and be prepared to make that call."

The man took the binoculars back and focused on the lake. "So far so good. The boat with the dog is approaching. Nothing unusual."

"Keep watching."

I guarantee, in an instant, the entire scenario will rival a Marx Brothers movie.

It was impossible not to watch, even though I squinted to get a better look at the distant boats.

"Hmm, the rental is pulling up to the fishing boat. Still, nothing that would raise a red fla—Oh my gosh! The dog jumped ship. Landed in the fishing boat. I don't believe what I'm seeing."

"Oh no! Has he bitten anyone? Snapped?"

"No. He's got his head in a bucket and is tossing fish around. Wait! Now he's pouncing after one of them. It's flapping around. He's got it! Latched on to it. Bit the head off. Never seen anything like it. He's going back for more. Oh no! The woman in the rental boat is leaning over the edge. Appears as if she may be screaming at the dog."

Yeah, that's always a help.

"Now will you call the sheriff's patrol?"

"A dog eating fish on a boat is not deemed an emergency."

Give it time.

I don't know what came over me, but I grabbed the binoculars. "I need to see this for myself."

"Have at it. Must say, this is a first for the marina."

I watched the scene in front of me like a bad movie that I was too lazy to turn off. Paul tried shooing Streetman away from his bucket of fish but that only made things worse. The dog stood his ground, adamant that the bucket with its glorious prizes was now his. Then, to my horror, I watched my mother put one foot over the edge of Paul's boat and hoist herself into it.

"Someone's going to get hurt. Or drown. My mother can't control that dog on a good day. Heck, she can't even remove dead things from his mouth that he picks up on his walks, let alone wiggling fish."

Then, the worst. Herb took a long rope that was in the bottom of the boat and tossed it over to Paul's boat. I handed back the binoculars. "I think they're going to tie the boats together but it's anyone's guess if they know how."

"As long as the lines go bow to stern and they take up the slack, it should be fine."

"I don't even think they know the bow from the stern. What's happening now?"

"Your mother is trying to grab the dog."

"What's the dog doing?"

"Wiggling away. Wait! He just dumped over another bucket. I think it's bait. Yep, bait. Dog's got his head in it and is chomping on worms. Oh no!"

"What? What?"

The man thrust the binoculars back at me. "This isn't pretty."

Pretty? It was horrifying. Although, I must admit, it would have won hands down for *America's Funniest Home Video*. My mother slipped on the sea of worms that was now all over the bottom of the boat and latched on to Herb, who had climbed into Paul's boat as well. That would have been bad enough, but then Herb crashed into Luella, who nearly fell overboard.

In all the chaos, no one noticed Herb's rental boat had never been tied to Paul's fishing boat. I widened my eyes as the rental boat drifted away. Suddenly, the man nudged me and grabbed the binoculars. "The marina boat's drifting. I can see it without the binoculars. I've got to radio this in."

"Now you're making the call?" I could feel the heat rising in my cheeks.

He reached for the radio and, as I gave him the binoculars, he selected the distress signal. Then, he grabbed the microphone and said, "Unmanned boat less than one nautical mile from marina, headed east, adjacent to small fishing boat. Fishing boat has four passengers and a dog. Questionable boat conduct. Failure to follow safety rules."

Then he looked at me. "At least they're all wearing life jackets. Even the dog."

Especially the dog. Wouldn't want little Lord Fauntleroy to be without one.

"I need to see this for myself."

"Here you are."

Once again, I focused the binoculars on the "catastrophe at sea." With the exception of Streetman, who appeared to be rolling in bait, everyone stood and pointed fingers at each other. Just then, two men rushed into the marina and one of them yelled, "There's a whole lot of crazy going on about a mile or so out. We can see it from the shore. Looks like a bunch of people are horsing around in a small boat. There's another boat nearby but we can't make out anyone on board without better binoculars."

Then the other guy spoke. "Better call the lake patrol. Oh, and maybe the Scorpion Bay TowBoatUS number, too, just in case."

"The sheriff's patrol was called," I said to them. "The gentleman who runs the marina made the call. The nearest patrol vessel is on the other side of the lake."

"Better hope no one goes overboard," the first man said. "Water temperature is less than sixty. That means hypothermia for sure."

Terrific. Like I don't have enough to worry about.

Suddenly, the marina operator shouted, "Another boat's approaching. Nice-sized one, too. They must have heard the distress signal." Then he looked at me. "Can you make out the name on that larger vessel?"

"Yep, it says *NoMorNY.* Wonder what that means?"

The man chuckled. "No More New York."

"Got to hand it to those snowbirds, once they get a taste of Arizona, they never want to go back," the first man said.

"That boat belongs to Arthur Sellinger. He's got a slip in the marina. Been here for years."

In a perfect world, Arthur Sellinger's boat would have approached Paul's boat and Arthur would have been able to tie the boats together and remove at least two of the unruly passengers. But forget a perfect world. This was as imperfect as things could get. Heck, it was a disaster with a capital D!

CHAPTER 20

I was glued to the ongoing fiasco in front of my eyes and gripped the binoculars so tight I thought I'd lose circulation in my fingers. It appeared as if the man on *NoMorNY*, most likely Arthur, approached the boat but suddenly veered to the right, before approaching again.

"Maybe he needs to line up his boat differently," one of the men said.

Or maybe something else is going on.

Sure enough, whatever sixth sense I had was on target. My jaw nearly dropped to the floor when I watched my mother hand Streetman to the captain of that cruiser. Well, *attempt* to hand him to the man.

"The dog's going berserk!" the second man said. "He's fighting off the captain of that boat and causing a ruckus. Oh no! The lady with the dog is now trying to get him back in her arms. This isn't looking good. Someone's going to wind up in the water!"

I closed my eyes for a split second and tried to remain calm. Nothing much had changed when I reopened them. Streetman was tugging, kicking and most likely snarling. Then, of all things, Paul got the bright idea to throw a towel over the dog. He leaned over the edge of his boat, nearly knocking my mother over, and with perfect aim landed the towel on top of the dog, who jumped out of the man's arms and into his boat, but not before causing the poor guy to fall over backward, landing on his rear.

"At least the woman and the guy didn't wind up in the water," the first man said. "Or the dog, for that matter."

"Yeah," I replied. "Until the dog realizes my mother isn't with him."

"Um, I think that's about to change. That woman is trying to maneuver herself onto the cruiser but the cruiser isn't tied to the fishing boat."

Next thing I knew, Herb tried to hold my mother back so she wouldn't land in the water while Paul got the brilliant idea to toss fish onto the cruiser. I imagined he wanted to keep Streetman occupied but it only made things worse.

The dog went after the fish while the poor captain tried to stand, losing his balance twice. Meanwhile, my mother waved her arms frantically, gesturing for the cruiser to move closer. Unfortunately, that didn't happen. The captain took control of the steering wheel and shot off like a canon.

"Is he heading to the marina?" I asked. "It looks like he's going in the opposite direction." Then, I realized why. I could see Streetman jumping up and down, tearing at the man's clothes.

"How soon will the sheriff's patrol arrive?" I asked. "This is out of hand."

Just then, I watched as Paul started up his engine and took off behind them. Unfortunately, his fishing boat lacked the speed and maneuverability of the cruiser. The only saving grace was that the passengers were no longer standing up.

Then, by the grace of God, because there couldn't possibly be any other explanation, two sheriff's patrol boats headed toward Paul. Each came from a different direction and wasted no time approaching the motley crew.

"They better find my missing motorboat before it meets with a mishap," the marina operator said. "What are they doing now? I can't see that far out."

I handed him the binoculars again and took a breath. Thankfully, my mother was still on the boat and not in the water. As for her state of mind without that neurotic chiweenie, it was anyone's guess.

"I think they've got the situation under control," one of the men said. "Both women are now boarding one of the sheriff's vessels. Hold on. Now it's taking off. It's headed toward the cruiser."

Of course it is. My mother probably hasn't stopped screaming about the dog.

"What's the other sheriff's boat doing? It's hard to tell."

The man looked at me and shrugged. "Hmm. The deputy's got his hands on his hips, and judging from the body language, he's reading those guys the riot act."

"I hope he tickets them," I mumbled to myself.

Suddenly, a different boat appeared with a sign on its side that was large enough to read from a neighboring planet. It said *TowBoatUS.* The marina operator put down the binoculars and shouted, "Hallelujah, my boat is in the vicinity." Then he walked closer to the window and announced, "Bring it home, boys! Bring it home!"

Too bad the only thing that got "brought home" right away was the dog. The cruiser showed up at the marina and docked in the captain's slip. I walked to the marina operator, thrust the binoculars back in his hand and said, "I'm going to the dock." Then I raced out of the building before anyone could say a word.

Praying that my water moccasins wouldn't lose their grip, causing me to slip, I charged as fast as I could across the deck and over to *NoMorNY.* I was about to announce myself when the captain waved and shouted, "There's a bit of a situation out there and I wound up with someone's dog. Can you notify the marina operator? Don't want to leave that little bugger alone. Seems unpredictable."

Understatement of the decade.

I looked at the man's pants and instantly calculated the damages. "I don't blame you. The dog belongs to my mother. She was on one of the other boats. Two stocky men and a redhead as well."

"I know. Looked like quite a fracas."

"I'll take the dog off your hands and pay for any damages to your clothing."

The man shook his head. "Nah, these are just my knock-around pants. Older than the hills. Besides, I've had rowdy dogs before. Although this one seems a bit anxious."

"That's very diplomatic of you. He's as neurotic as they get but my mother adores him." With that, the man handed me Streetman and I gingerly walked back to the marina.

"Do you need any help?" he called out.

Only if you're a bail bondsman.

"I'll be fine. Thanks so much!"

By the time I walked into the marina, the first sheriff's patrol vessel had returned and was docked on the other side of the building. My mother and Luella were in the midst of an animated conversation with the deputy when Streetman leapt from my arms and raced toward my mother.

"My precious little gladiator!" she exclaimed. "Momma's brave sea captain!"

I wanted to upchuck right on the spot but, instead, counted to ten before I spoke. "Do you have any idea what all of you put the sheriff's office through? Why on earth would you ever go out in a boat with Herb? You would have been better off walking on the moon with Myrna!"

"Calm down, Phee," my mother said, still stroking the dog and showering him with accolades. "Herb knows how to operate a speedboat. Besides, we didn't need another murder on our hands."

Just then Luella spoke. "What other murder? What are you saying?"

Before my mother had the opportunity to stick her foot in her mouth, Herb and Paul marched in with the second deputy.

"I was only trying to get a confession out of someone," Paul said. "For a murder."

In a flash, Luella's face turned as red as her hair and she stormed over to Paul, but not before flashing my mother a look.

"I know what this is all about," Luella said as she crossed her arms and glared at Paul. "You think I murdered Betsy Sprig so you tried to kill me! What were you going to do? Toss me overboard? Getting reconnected, my hot patootie. I can't believe I fell for it!"

"Wait, I can explain." Paul grabbed a bandana from his pocket and wiped off some bait that had dried on his vest. "I wasn't trying to kill you. Only shake you up a bit by rocking the boat so you'd confess."

The deputy who escorted Herb and Paul into the marina took out his iPad and began taking notes. Copious notes. The kind that most likely result in arrests. I rolled my eyes and watched the train wreck.

"Why on earth would I kill Betsy?" Luella shouted. Then, she paused for a moment and put her palm to her lips. "Oh my gosh. You think I was jealous of her. Jealous that you dumped me to date her. You conceited schmo! Of all things!" Then Luella turned to the nearest deputy and said, "I want this man arrested for an attempt on my life."

And, if that wasn't all, Streetman lifted his leg and peed on a display of fishing lures. I couldn't imagine anything getting worse from there, but I should have known better.

CHAPTER 21

"I wasn't trying to murder you," Paul said as he approached Luella. "But face it, there was some animosity between the two of you."

"There was animosity between Betsy and everyone who came within a three-mile radius of her! The woman was certifiable! Why don't you ruffle up Aimee and Darleen's feathers? Those two have been awfully cagey lately. And make no bones about it, there was bad blood among the three of them."

"What bad blood?" I asked. I stepped between Luella and Paul and fixed my eyes on her.

"You must be new around here. The Turk sisters registered numerous complaints that Betsy played favorites when it came to scheduling people for the bays. But that's not the real reason. About a year ago, Aimee bought one of those rhinestone clutch bags and brought it to the garage to show everyone. Somehow, it disappeared. Aimee was convinced Betsy absconded with it but couldn't prove anything."

"Why Betsy?" I asked. "Weren't other people there?"

"Yeah, the men. And they couldn't have cared less."

"Did Aimee report it to the rec center and the posse?"

"Uh-huh. Filled out all the forms but that's as far as it went. Bad blood ever since."

Then Luella turned to Paul. "And don't forget Holt Kavanaugh. Betsy was certain he embezzled money from the club, but again, couldn't prove a thing. I always assumed he failed to report cash contributions and played around with the figures, but nothing I could prove."

Behind me, my mother frantically wiped the lure display with her supply of baby wipes while continuing to coo at the dog. The deputy, who had exhausted his note-taking, motioned to my mother, Luella, and the men.

"I'll need detailed statements from all of you. Might as well take a seat over there by the poster of the rules for boating. Might be a good time to study it. I'll start with Mr. Schmidt. That's the name you gave me when I approached your vessel."

"Yep. That's me." Paul dusted off his pants and followed the deputy to a spot away from everyone else.

Then Luella walked over to my mother. "I want to thank you. You don't even know me and yet you risked your life because you thought I was in danger."

My eyeballs spun in the back of my head. I was dying to tell her that the only reason she went with Herb was because she didn't want Paul to muck up anything before their big engagement at the buy-sell-trade event.

Forty-five minutes later, Paul showed us his desk-appearance ticket for the town of Peoria and the rest of us were told to abide by boating rules. Herb had to pay the towing fee for the rental, which he insisted be split between him and Paul because he was "on a rescue mission to save Paul's butt."

With my afternoon already wasted, I tried to get out of there as soon as I could. I told my mother I'd call her later and started for the exit when Luella ran toward me and whispered, "There's more to those Turk sisters. They're always sneaking around and I wouldn't be surprised if they had something to hide and Betsy found out. Still can't believe that idiot Paul thought I would kill someone out of jealousy. Boy, talk about an inflated ego. From now on, the only fish I want to see are the ones on my plate when I order out for dinner. By the way, I'm riding home with your mother and Herb. Don't want to be anywhere near Paul."

"He really has good intentions," I said, "unfortunately, his approach is somewhat primitive."

"Somewhat Neanderthal, if you ask me."

I laughed and got out of there before any other catastrophes took place.

If there was a silver lining to the afternoon, it was the fact that Aimee, Darleen, and Holt vied for top position on my suspect chart. But unless I was willing to go into Bowman and Ranston territory, there wasn't much more I could do.

Nate and Marshall were involved as well, even if it was on the periphery. Still, I knew that Herb would moan and groan to my mother about "poor Wayne" and that she would feel compelled to get those book club ladies embroiled in escapades that would make my blood run cold.

Aaragh! Like it or not, I had to crank my sleuthing up to the next level and I figured I might as well start with the Turk sisters and a friendly little chat. That meant asking Wayne when he thought they'd be at the garage. I made a mental note to phone him when I got home, but things took another turn, nearly blindsiding me.

Marshall had gotten my text about the marina debacle and burst out laughing the minute I got in the door.

"It's not funny," I said. Then I laughed too. "Oh, what the heck. It was a regular sideshow. Streetman eating freshly caught fish and rolling in bait, Paul rocking the boat, Herb losing his rental boat . . . what can I say? I went there knowing full well it was going to be a mess but I honestly didn't expect it to be that much of one!"

"Think of the good news. We're not dealing with a snappy chiweenie who now reeks of dead fish and bait."

"Not yet, anyway. Listen, I did manage to get Luella's take on the suspects. The Turk sisters are in the running with Holt."

"I'm afraid Bowman and Ranston will have to sort it out because our own investigation at the unity council and museum just took a hundred-and-eighty-degree turn."

"When? When did that happen?"

"About twenty minutes ago. Good thing I thought ahead and picked up subs at Mr. Pickles on my way home. They're in the fridge. I'm going to eat and run because Nate and I will need to return to the museum and meet with the curator again."

"On a Saturday evening? It can't wait?"

"I'm afraid not. It's waited too long already. One of the unity council members was rearranging their storeroom this afternoon and found the missing package from the transport company. She notified their board as well as the museum and our office."

"That's great! End of story, right?"

Marshall ran his fingers through his hair and shook his head. "Nope. More like the beginning."

"I don't understand."

"When the woman opened the box to remove the doll, she realized the doll wasn't the one depicted in the photos. Someone packed a different doll and shipped it. That means the theft originated at the museum, not the unity council."

"How do you know the woman told the truth?"

"The unity council recently installed a surveillance system since they received threats from some outside sources. Not knowing if it was a hoax or not, they decided not to take any chances. She contacted the IT company that monitors the surveillance and they forwarded us a copy of the video. It was pretty clear she cut the cardboard box to retrieve the contents. Then she stopped dead in her tracks and reached for her cell phone."

"Oh my gosh. I really need to concentrate on that chain of acquisitions as well as the pieces that were loaned to other museums. I barely got started."

"Please don't tell me you intend to drive back to the office?"

I chuckled. "You should know me by now. I made another copy of those files and the flash drive is here, in my desk."

"Good, because I don't want to worry about you while Nate and I are downtown."

"Relax, I'll be in my Zen zone, looking over those spreadsheets."

An hour and a half later, I was still in my comfort zone, sweatpants and all. Unfortunately, I wasn't turning up any viable information. Most of the acquisitions were for Asian art and they were all carefully documented.

Loans were another story, and I barely got started when my mother called.

"You didn't have to drive all the way over to the marina, Phee. Herb and I would have been fine."

"Fine? You nearly fell out of a boat and drowned. Or died from hypothermia."

"I had everything under control."

Except the dog.

"You can't keep taking chances like that. Like it or not, there's a murderer out there and who knows who that is."

"I couldn't very well leave Herb to deal with Paul on his own."

"Never mind. At least it's over with for now."

"Yes. For now. But not Monday night."

"What's Monday night?"

"The book club ladies are meeting at Louise's house to come up with a plan to ensnarl the killer."

"Did you say *ensnarl*? And why Louise's house? Why not Bagels 'n More where you always go?"

"We don't want to be overheard. Voices carry."

"Since when has that ever bothered you? Those book club voices were probably heard in our nation's capital. I'm surprised the FBI hasn't come looking."

"Honestly, Phee. Besides, Louise doesn't want to leave her parrot alone at night. He's having issues."

"Well, don't make his issues worse by bringing the dog. Now tell me, what exactly were you thinking and who exactly were you thinking about?"

"We can go over that on Monday night."

"What? I'm not going."

"Phee, we need you. Those women get so off track that any little thing sends them off on a tangent. One minute we're talking about some politician and the next it's someone's recipe for chopped liver. You have a good way of keeping everyone focused."

"I'll spare an hour and that's it. But only if you agree not to do anything rash or chancy or—"

"I can only speak for myself and I'm the epitome of clear and level thinking."

Tell that to the sheriff's lake patrol.

"One hour!"

"Oh, and before I forget, don't wear anything floral. The bird goes bonkers."

"It's nearly winter. And he better like my Coyotes sweatshirt!"

CHAPTER 22

It seemed Nate, Marshall and Augusta thought it was a good idea to "stop it in its tracks" when I told them about my mother's book club and their next move to round up Betsy's killer. It was Monday morning and little headway had been made by the men when they met with the curator on Saturday night and looked over the museum's storage areas yesterday. I wasn't faring any better either, unless blurry eyes counted for something. I had pored over those spreadsheets for the remainder of the weekend and came up as dry as the Sahara.

"This is so exasperating," I said as I poured extra cream into my coffee. "I know I'm missing something but I can't put my finger on it. The loans to other museums and such run the gamut from two-dimensional art to small figurines and keepsakes. Every one of them is clearly documented and accounted for. And, the shipping company has been the same for the past five years."

"Aha!" Augusta announced. "The shipping company. Wouldn't be the first time someone was on the take and repackaged something."

Nate, Marshall and I looked at each other and then at Augusta.

"Go on," Nate said. "This should be interesting."

Augusta fluffed her bouffant and stretched her arms out in front. "Suppose someone from the shipping company knew someone from the museum, and they hatched a little plan. The museum person couldn't very well steal the item or switch it, but the carrier sure could. He or she had access to the packing materials, the labeling, you name it."

Nate scratched his head. "Hate to say it, but you may be on to something. It's worth looking into."

"I'll remind you of that, Mr. Williams," Augusta said, "when it's time for a raise."

He winked at her and headed into his office. Marshall gave my shoulder a squeeze and muttered something about having salads ready for us when I got home from Louise's tonight.

"He probably should have a smorgasbord of pain relief pills when I step over the threshold. That bird of Louise's is an advertisement for migraine medicine."

"Uh-huh. That would explain why Mr. Williams is sometimes cranky in the mornings. If he forgets to put a cover over Mr. Fluffypants' cage, the thing squawks like crazy when the sun comes up."

"I know. Too bad he got stuck with his aunt's pet. For Louise, it was a deliberate choice. Like Streetman. Go figure."

The rest of the day ambled on with the usual clients and both detectives in and out of the office. Augusta and I ordered giant subs for lunch since I knew I'd be chewing my arm off by the time I got to enjoy Marshall's salad.

I remained in the office until six fifteen, catching up on invoices and studying those museum spreadsheets. As much as I wanted to discover even the teeniest anomaly, I didn't. Everything appeared the way it should. Like it or not, I came to the conclusion that the files didn't hold the clues we had hoped for. And as far as the murder investigation went, I crossed my fingers Nate and Marshall would have better luck today.

When I pulled up to Louise's new house on North Vista Drive, I edged my car between Shirley's oversized Buick and a late-model Toyota. Louise had sold her larger house about a year ago and moved into an HOA area where the outdoor maintenance would be taken care of and the size meant less cleaning. It also meant a front bedroom for her bird, since he commanded an entire room of his own. I try not to think about it.

All of the book club ladies were seated in the spacious living room/dining room area, including my aunt Ina, who wanted to escape Uncle Louis's saxophone practice for a while. Too bad she wasn't familiar with the parrot or she would have thought twice.

Thankfully, the bird was in his own room with the door closed and the only thing I heard was some faint chatter.

"Glad you could join us, Phee," Louise said. "Make yourself comfortable anywhere. Since I bought that large sectional, I've got so much more seating room." She motioned to the coffee table and a console table a few feet behind the sofa. "I've got crackers, pretzels, gluten-free cookies, and assorted candies. Help yourself. There's also coffee in the kitchen on your right. I made a fresh batch this morning and reheated it."

Great. A woman after my mother's own heart.

"Uh, thanks, I'm fine. I had a huge lunch, and I can only stay an hour." Then I turned to my mother and gave her the look that said "I meant it. One hour."

My mother cleared her throat, looked at everyone, and spoke. "Poor Wayne continues to get the stink-eye from everyone in that auto garage and he's twitchy about that note he got telling him to confess. If you want my opinion, it might be the real killer since they always pass the dirty deed off to someone else."

"Yes," Myrna exclaimed, "just like in the book *Gone Girl.* What do they call that?"

"Suspense," Cecilia answered.

"No," Lucinda said. "It's called deflection. Has its own name. Like—"

An hour, my you-know-what. We'll never get past this conversation until eight thirty.

"It doesn't matter," I announced. "Just get on with it, Mom."

My mother motioned for Myrna, Cecilia, and Lucinda to stop talking. "It's no surprise those deputies are moving at a glacial speed. And we can't risk living and working in an environment that's harboring a dangerous killer."

"I don't think Sun City West is harboring him or her, Harriet." Shirley bit into a pretzel and gracefully spat it into a napkin. "The killer has to be a resident. And an auto restoration club member."

"Exactly," my mother said. "That's why we must begin Project Gear Shift. It's our code for the plan we've loosely outlined."

At the word *loosely*, I knew the plan hadn't gotten much further than its name. Still, I persisted.

"Tell me more. Like details."

"That's where you come in, Phee. You're the one who's good at this."

What? Since when?

"Keep talking, Harriet," Shirley said. "Tell her what we've got so far."

My mother took a breath and for the next full minute described how the ladies would "tail" the Turk sisters as well as Holt and Jared. They would split up into teams and covertly find out what those folks were up to.

"Where are they spending their off time? Who are they mingling with? What purchases are they making?" She went on and on until I'd had enough.

I held my palms up and she stopped talking. "I seriously don't think that's going to get you anywhere. Except maybe getting arrested for stalking. You need to be more specific. Like trying to figure out a specific, as opposed to generalized, motive that any one of them would have to knock off Betsy. And in order to do that, you have to ingratiate yourselves with them. Although I don't know how that's possible. It's not as if any of you are conversant with automobiles. It may be a better thing for Herb, Bill, and Kevin to do that since they worked on Wayne's car."

"They'll mess it up," Cecilia said. Then she turned to Lucinda. "Remember how Herb tried to help when Roxanne Maines was framed for murder?"

"I sure do. It was impossible not to."

"Okay, ladies, how about this? Since Herb, Bill, and Kevin are really the only ones who can work in that garage with Wayne, what if one or two of you offered to work alongside them. That way you'd be privy to all the chatter that goes on. And chatter leads to clues."

"That's a splendid idea," my aunt said. "But unfortunately, my schedule is totally booked. Between the opera committee and the fact that I'm on the board at the art museum, it wouldn't be feasible. Especially the art museum. I haven't had a decent night's sleep since that precious artifact was stolen."

"As long as I don't work with Bill, I'll be fine," Myrna said. "It's bad enough I have to deal with him on my bocce team."

"Put me down for working with Herb." My mother handed me a notepad and a pen.

"Um, I thought that was something you'd do. I need to get home. It'll be an hour in less than ten minutes."

And then, just as I thought I could make a graceful exit, I got a text message from Marshall. "Excuse me, everyone. I need to read this." I looked at my phone screen and couldn't believe what I read—*"On my way to auto garage. Woman found passed out in paint booth. B & R on scene. Possible sabotage."*

"Yep, better get home before dinner spoils. Let me know what you decide. Have a nice night."

"Are you all right, Phee?" my mother asked.

"Fine. Absolutely fine. Just don't want a mushy salad for dinner."

I charged to the door and thanked Louise for her hospitality. Then I started up the car like a NASCAR driver and hightailed it to RH Johnson Boulevard. From there to Meeker Boulevard, where I saw a swarm of posse cars, a fire truck and an ambulance.

No coroner's van. Things are looking up.

Without wasting a second, I parked adjacent to the walking track and headed to the building, nearly colliding with Tim Justin from channel 10 news. The same reporter who interviewed Marshall about the doll.

Up close and personal, he looked even younger than he appeared on television.

"Excuse me," I said, "but how did you get wind of this so fast?"

"My uncle plays on a bowling league here. I caught a little of his game when I heard sirens out front and thought I'd see what was going on. Not usual to have so many posse cars plus emergency responders and—oh, look—is that a HAZMAT truck pulling in? Must be something worth reporting."

I stared at the truck and didn't say a word.

Tim looked past me as if I was invisible. "The EMTs are bringing someone out on a gurney. I'll see what I can find out. There are at least four posse members by the front entrance."

"It could be nothing with nothing. People faint all the time. Or fall. Lots of falls in senior communities."

"Not with this kind of response." Next, he picked up his cell and spoke. "Get a camera guy over to the auto restoration garage on Meeker in Sun City West. Something's going down."

Then, to me, "You don't think this place is about to blow up, do you? All those chemicals and whatnot?"

And just as I was about to answer, two more fire trucks pulled up and I was suddenly on overdrive.

Chapter 23

I recognized one of the posse volunteers as a woman I'd seen before and thankfully she, too, seemed to recognize me. She motioned me over and kept her voice low. "You're Sophie Kimball- Gregory, right?"

I nodded.

"Your husband and your boss are inside. You can't go in but I'll let them know you're here."

"Thanks."

Meanwhile, Tim Justin introduced himself to the other posse member and showed him his press identification. Like me, he wasn't allowed inside, but a sheriff's deputy came out to speak with him. I imagined the carefully constructed narrative would be the one that would air on TV later tonight.

"Phee," Marshall said as he stepped outside. "I didn't expect you to drive over here. Just wanted to give you a heads-up."

I gave him a hug and stepped back. "You should know me better by now. Tell me what's going on. And relax, none of the rumormongers at Louise's house know what's happening. Not yet anyway. And certainly not from me."

"Okay, let's talk way off to the side where no one can hear us."

We skirted around to the back of the building and made sure no one could catch our conversation. Then Marshall spoke. "Aimee was found passed out, barely breathing, inside the auto paint booth. This never should have happened. It's a twenty-thousand-dollar structure with a cross flow to prevent that sort of thing. And, according to Jared, who was also there along with Darleen and Luella, it was fully functional earlier in the day when someone else used it."

"Who? What someone else?"

"Nate's getting all of that information."

"What about Aimee? Is she going to be all right?"

"She's breathing. The EMTs treated her and rushed her to the hospital."

"Holy cow! You said possible sabotage. What are the deputies saying?"

"It's Bowman and Ranston. That should answer your question."

"Tim Justin is here, by the way."

Marshall rubbed the back of his neck. "No surprise. He's quite the go-getter when it comes to breaking news stories. Nate and the deputies are speaking with everyone who's in the garage—the people I already mentioned plus Wayne, Kevin, and Bill." Then he looked around to make sure we were still alone. "The deputies may be tight-lipped, but Nate and I strongly suspect tampering with the mechanism. We'll know more when the forensics crew arrives. They should be here any minute. No sense having you wait. It's going to be a long night."

"Want me to bring you guys back some coffee or anything?"

"One of the posse volunteers called his wife and she's making a late run to Dunkin' in Surprise."

"Good. Keep me posted. Say, what makes you and Nate believe it wasn't an accident?"

"Someone stuffed the exhaust ventilation fan with wads of accumulated lint. Possibly from their own dryer. They also punctured small holes in the hose that pressurizes the paint, so toxic fumes could leak out. This was no accident. It was planned."

"Wouldn't the system have shut off automatically?"

"Not right away, even though they've got the most efficient option. Apparently, there are a few kinds. This one's a downdraft system, according to Wayne, where the draft runs right down from the ceiling to the floor. It's the cleanest option for painting. It wouldn't matter, really. Once something is clogged, it's clogged."

"I suppose the forensics crew will be studying the fibers from that lint."

"They'll be analyzing it, all right, but who knows how long that's going to take. Right now, it's fingerprints and the usual protocol. Bowman plans on heading over to the hospital to get a statement from Aimee once she regains consciousness. Meanwhile, it's back to getting statements from everyone. Too bad the only surveillance is the front of the building and it's been acting up lately."

"Tampered with?"

Marshall shrugged. "Hard to tell. The IT team from the sheriff's office will have a better idea. Meanwhile, I'd better get back inside. Don't wait up. I'll call if anything new emerges."

We gave each other short pecks on the cheeks before I walked back to my car and Marshall to the scene of the latest possible crime. Going to sleep at my normal hour was never going to happen. More thoughts crossed my mind than ants on a watermelon.

Once home, I made myself comfortable and nuked a pot pie. Marshall would have to make his salad another time. Then, I plopped myself on the couch with my half-used marble composition book and did something I should have started days ago—a murder map.

I drew a stick figure of Betsy in the middle of the page, and with spikes and cartoon-like bubbles attached, I filled in the suspects—Aimee, Darleen, Luella, Jared, and Holt. I was hesitant to add Wayne, or any of Herb's crew, for that matter, but I did add a side note indicating he, along with Kevin, Bill, and Herb, were part of the auto restoration club.

Then I filled in the pertinent data:

Holt—treasurer, verbal altercation with Betsy, accused of cooking the books

Aimee—club member, ongoing scuffles regarding facility use

Darleen—ditto to Aimee

Luella—rivals for Paul's affections. Ew!!!

Jared—No real info. Club member for years.

Mystery person who used paint booth during the day.

Other woman at workbench the first day.

That was seven suspects and four of them had motives for murder. They also had means and opportunity. I made a mental note to ask Marshall what he knew about that other woman. Especially since he or Nate must have interviewed her. I did remember that the folks they interviewed from that morning all indicated they had been in the facility most of the day and said no one else had come in.

The good news—it narrowed down the suspects. The bad news—it narrowed down the suspects. Nate had always said we were better off with a long list of suspects rather than a handful, but if we wound up with a short hand, it would make it easier to look for connections. I hoped he was right.

Then there was Aimee. Was her accident, or possible attempted homicide, in any way related to Betsy's demise? And if so, what was the common thread? And who held the needle?

I studied the list of suspects two more times. The last thing I wanted to do was to elbow my way into the investigation when Nate and Marshall were asked to assist. Then again, they were also knee-deep in mire with that missing doll. I figured if I could keep things low-key and under wraps, I might be able to find some information that I could unceremoniously pass along to them.

I knew detectives used sites like TLOxp and IRBsearch as well as a number of government sites, but armchair sleuths were relegated to Facebook and other similar social media options. I'd been down that road before and I figured with a little help from Lyndy, we might be able to help move the investigation along.

"You want me to what?" she asked when I called. "Stalk people on Facebook and Instagram?"

"Not stalk, study. Dig deep on their profiles. Hobbies. Friends. Friends of friends. Think of it this way, we'll be leading the horse to water but when he finds it, he'll think he was the one who discovered it."

"Oh, brother. Why the sudden push?"

"Pinky swear you won't breathe a word of this."

"I'm not back in junior high."

"Fine. Just don't tell Lyman. Or anyone."

"I won't. Now tell me what's going on."

I broke the promise I made to Marshall less than two hours before, but I knew Lyndy would keep her word. At least better than I did. When I finished, she was stunned.

"That auto restoration garage is becoming a house of horrors," she said. "Are they sure it's not an accident?"

"They're sure. Just waiting on the official word. So, will you do it? Dive into social media on my suspect list? We'll divvy it up. It'll save time."

"Beats the crossword puzzles. At least this time I don't have to impersonate anyone. Or worse. I don't, do I?"

"It'll be like that old ad for the Yellow Pages—'Let your fingers do the walking'—only they'll be clicking a mouse instead."

"Text me the names and I'll get started."

"We can compare results over paninis at Twisted Italian on Thursday. Since tonight is Monday, that'll give us three days to do this. It shouldn't take that long."

"What about dinner and Marshall?"

"He's got a full week of late nights. Besides, I'll bring home some of that special bread and the homemade gelato."

"Boy, it sure didn't take you long to become a devious wife."

"I'm not devious, I'm exercising my role as his helpmate."

"Remind me to call emergency services if I ever need help."

"Very funny."

We agreed on later in the week and split up the names. I got the Turk sisters and Jared. Lyndy picked up Luella, Holt, and the mystery person pending Marshall's ability to find out who that was. The other woman was still up for grabs.

"What about the doll case?" she asked. "What's happening with that?"

"It's a Ping-Pong ball. Now back in the art museum's court. I'll tell you more later."

"Gee, and the only interesting thing in my office is that we're getting a software upgrade. That'll mean more work, not less. My gosh, I'm sounding like my cranky aunt. Hope it doesn't run in the family."

"Got news for you. It runs in all our families."

Chapter 24

A few minutes after my conversation with Lyndy, Marshall phoned. Short and to the point. "Hey, hon, just wanted to let you know I'm heading over to the hospital with Bowman. Can you believe it? He actually insisted I join him. Said Ranston told him that he tended to intimidate people. Wanted me along for the ride."

I laughed. "What are Nate and Ranston doing?"

"Checking out the scene and talking with witnesses. I'll be home as soon as I can. Get some rest. Or at least make a stab at it."

"Not the best choice of words."

"She was asphyxiated. No blood involved."

"For now. All of this is so bizarre."

"Take a breath. It won't be for long."

I hoped he was right but I didn't give it too much credence. Marshall and Nate were the proverbial optimists while I went to the dark side first and worked my way backward from there.

It was almost midnight when Marshall crept into bed. Half awake, I asked him how it went and he told me they were keeping Aimee overnight for observation. She was able to breathe on her own but still somewhat disoriented and dizzy. The oxygen was helping. No permanent damage.

"That's a relief. Does she remember anything of significance?"

"Not really. Said the paint booth was empty when she arrived, so she hooked up her paint supply, drove the car in, made sure everything was closed and began the process. That was the last thing she recalled before being shaken by someone."

"What someone?"

"She doesn't remember, but according to the deputies, it was the monitor on duty—Mike Odell."

"Does she have any idea who could have sabotaged the booth?"

"Nope. Maybe later when her head clears. Ranston said the monitor was absolutely shocked. Still, perpetrators can be pretty good actors."

"I know."

I closed my eyes and before I knew it, it was morning. Marshall was already in the shower so I made us coffee and toast, which we chomped down before he rushed off to see Aimee.

As I let the warm water wash over me, I couldn't help but wonder why on earth someone would want to harm her. Unless they thought she was the one responsible for killing Betsy. Then again, it didn't appear as if anyone was that attached to Betsy in order to seek revenge.

When I arrived at the office, I shared my thoughts with Augusta, who had already gotten the news from Nate.

"Sounds like that auto restoration garage needs an *Enter at your own risk* sign," she said. "Anyway, Mr. Williams got a fax from the forensics lab about that miniature doll with the creepy note. It sent him racing out the door."

"They found fingerprints? A match?"

Augusta shook her head. "I read the fax and they found smears of paint on the doll. They analyzed it and it was some sort of metallic paint. Mr. Williams thought maybe the burnished coloring was blood or nail polish but he couldn't tell. Anyway, it was good old-fashioned metal paint."

"Like Rust-Oleum?"

"I suppose. Not house paint or that sort of thing."

"Another needle in a haystack. Anyone could have been painting anything. This is so frustrating."

Just then, Marshall walked into the office, having just come back from the hospital. He rubbed his temples and sighed. "Two nurses had to ask Darleen to lower her voice. I can still hear it reverberating in my ear. She was at the hospital for Aimee's discharge. Screamed at her, 'If you hadn't barged into the paint booth, Luella would have been the one in the hospital and not you.'"

"Oh, brother," I said. "Were you able to find out more about the incident?"

"Uh-huh. Seems Luella was next on the paint booth list. I phoned her but she wasn't the person who used it before Aimee got there."

"Don't they have to sign in or something?" I asked.

"They do, but whoever it was scribbled their name. Impossible to decipher."

"What about the monitor on duty?"

"Mike was on duty but he got called away, and by the time he got back, the person who used the paint booth before Aimee did was long gone."

"Couldn't anyone tell who it was? I mean, given the cars in the garage?"

Marshall rolled his neck. "No one bothered to look. Lots of cars in there. Not to mention the parking lot behind the place. Anyway, Nate's got a full day. He has to confer with the curator again on the off chance that the red paint on the miniature was being used for a museum art project. Oh, and get this—the curator didn't authorize the loan to the unity council. Her assistant did. Unfortunately, every time Nate has spoken with her, she's bawled her eyes out."

"I would, too, if it resulted in such a loss for the museum," I said.

"Looks like your little mystery is growing, Mr. Gregory. That's two unknown people you need to identify." Augusta reached across her desk for a half-eaten donut and took a bite. "At least from what Phee said. The workbench woman with the tricolored hair and the secret car painter. I think you'd have better luck with the car painter. The workbench woman may be tougher. It's wintertime. Lots of women go for tricolored hair this time of year. Blends the fall colors with the winter ones. Much better than all those shades of gray."

Marshall widened his eyes. "Thank you for that choice bit of information. I'll be sure to note it. That woman at the workbench the first day never signed in, and according to the Turk sisters, they didn't know her."

I crinkled my nose. "You mean no one bothered to ask while they were all working?"

Marshall shrugged. "Apparently not. And she left without anyone noticing. So, yep. Two unknowns. Could be worse. Meanwhile, I've got some paperwork to do and then I'll be at the posse office before I head over to chat with the folks at the shipping company."

"There's no doubt in my mind," Augusta declared. "It was attempted murder in that paint booth. Don't get me wrong, I like DIY projects myself, but not when it means working in an enclosed space. Been around cow fumes long enough to know what toxic odors are like."

"Good to know." Marshall started for his office. "And yeah. All of us agree with you. The evidence points to attempted murder. Except for one nagging thought."

"What's that?" Augusta shoved the rest of the donut in her mouth and waited for a response.

"Aimee may not have been the intended victim. She barged in and commandeered the paint booth, but Luella was next in line. Now, to figure out what she and Betsy might have had in common."

"Not Paul?" I all but gasped.

"Good grief, no. I'm thinking money. Or information that someone didn't want leaked out. Heck, anything at this point, but not Paul. Definitely not Paul."

Augusta and I looked at each other and tried not to laugh but it was impossible.

"I'll leave you two hyenas to yourselves," Marshall said with a smile. "But holler if you need me."

With that, he retreated to his office while Augusta and I tried fruitlessly to stop laughing.

"I'd better get back to my desk, Augusta. Plus, I now have another person to scope out. Mike Odell, the other monitor."

"You should make a full-time job out of your armchair sleuthing."

"Unfortunately, it doesn't pay."

The next hour and a half were blissful. Spreadsheets and tallies with numbers that made sense. Then, the obnoxious ring from my cell phone.

Clearly, it was an omen for what awaited me at the other end.

"Phee! Why do I have to hear these things from everyone except the one person who should be telling me what's going on? I had to listen to Herb first thing this morning. He got off the phone with Wayne and couldn't wait to knock on my door. I swear, that man can smell toasted bagels from the other end of the county."

"If it's about the incident at the auto garage yesterday, I planned on calling you." *Maybe not until the next century, but still . . .*

"That's one murder and one attempted murder. Herb said it was Aimee Turk. Was she the sister with the blue streak in her hair or the one with the brownish hair who looked like Shirley Temple?"

"I'm not sure. It doesn't matter. Listen, the deputies as well as our office are looking into the matter. Best thing you and the ladies can do is what we already decided. Stick with your Project Gear Shift plan or whatever you're calling it, and work covertly with the men in the garage. That way you'll pick up information and pass it along without causing a ruckus." *Fingers crossed.*

"None of us want to get our nails greasy."

"Fine. Do paperwork. Organize shelves. Anything but stalking. Okay?"

"Fair enough. But keep me posted this time. I don't want to get the news from Herb. I want it straight from the horse's mouth."

"Uh, thanks, Mom. Good choice of words. Catch you later."

I went back to my work and prayed she wouldn't mess things up. Nate left word with Augusta that the lab was able to identify the wood on the miniature doll as pine but that didn't help much. Along with balsawood, it was a standard hobby wood for miniatures, railroad scenes, and all sorts of crafts. However, they were able to discern one more thing. And that came from the note, not the doll. The paper showed signs of demodex. Otherwise known as eye mites. Irritating parasites that can cause itchiness, scaly skin, and red eyes.

"Mr. Williams figured whoever wrote that note must have rubbed their eyes while cutting it to size before adding it to the diorama at the museum," Augusta said when I walked into the outer office.

"Anyone can show signs of mites. Heck, it's always allergy season here in the Phoenix area. How would anyone know the difference?"

"The lab did." Augusta opened her desk drawer, took out a compact mirror, removed her tortoiseshell eyeglasses and stared at her reflection. "Long as I don't see anything, I'll be fine. Meanwhile, Mr. Williams and Mr. Gregory will have to be on the lookout for museum staff with running, red eyes."

"Maybe they won't have to do that if another, better clue comes along."

Augusta chucked. "Must be nice to be a dreamer."

Chapter 25

When Marshall returned from the posse office and the shipping company, it was almost time to close the office.

"Hope Nate's afternoon went better," he mumbled as he marched straight to the Keurig. "Can you believe it? The posse office got hit with a number of phone calls regarding the paint booth. Glad the forensics crew finished up in there and it will be ready for use tomorrow."

"Why the posse office and not the rec center?" I asked.

"I was about to ask the same thing, Mr. Gregory," Augusta chimed in. "But Phee beat me to it."

"No surprise on the happy rumor train. Seems someone in that illustrious community thought a dangerous toxin was in the air at the auto garage, and get this—according to Ranston, who took the call, the woman at the other end wanted to know 'how much time do we have left?' Unbelievable."

"You should be used to that sort of thing by now. Spend ten minutes in the dog park and it will be a great refresher."

He gave my shoulder a squeeze and retrieved his coffee. "At least your mother and her book club can feel free to do their on-site snooping or whatever they've named it. The garage will be up and running. Since the paint booth was sabotaged by stuffing the ventilation with dryer lint and puncturing a hose, there was no real damage once they replaced the hose, so the sheriff's office deemed it safe to reopen. The hoist situation is another story entirely. The entire hose system has to be replaced and that will take time."

"Poor Wayne. They'll never get to his car before that big event."

"They've got other hoists. Not state-of-the-art like the one in question, but workable for sure. By the way, what was the name of your mother's latest plan?"

"Project Gear Shift." I rolled my eyes. "At least it should keep them out of trouble and somewhat focused."

Marshall all but spat out his coffee. "That'll be the day."

• • •

It took less than a day for Marshall's comment to be fully realized, but when it did come to fruition, even he was as stunned as ever. My mother had divvied up the "investigative assignments" so that no one would be left out. Except my aunt Ina, who wished to remain as far away from oil, gasoline, and grease as possible.

Lucinda and Cecilia would work alongside Bill, while Myrna and Louise would annoy the heck out of Kevin. Wayne got the best end of the deal with Shirley riding shotgun, so to speak, and it came as no surprise that my mother chose to do her sleuthing alongside Herb. I figured if they could survive the boat ride from Hades, teaming up in the auto garage would be child's play. At least on paper.

The following morning, after Marshall had already left for the office, my mother called to let me know she and Herb would be joining Wayne and Shirley at the garage.

"Herb doesn't know a thing about cars," I said. "Except maybe reverse-neutral-drive."

"Aimee's out of the hospital and she's going to be there to help Wayne. His car is on another hoist and they're going to start work on the undercarriage. I think that's the word Herb used."

"And what will you and Shirley be doing?"

"Tidying up and eavesdropping."

"Sounds like a wonderful plan." *I will never retire.*

I did the breakfast dishes and hurried off to the office as well.

"You just missed Rolo's call," Augusta said before I even had a chance to take three steps in the door. "It was a humdinger. Sent your husband scurrying out of here."

"What about Nate?"

"Finishing up a minor case in Surprise, then over to the posse office. MCSO got the official lab report on that lint and those deputies want to go over it with him."

"Must mean they don't know where to start."

"You said it, not me."

"What about Rolo's call? What did he have to say?" I ambled over to the coffee maker, plopped in a K-Cup and waited for Augusta to respond.

"He thinks he may know more about that map. Seems he's been immersed in that dark web tracking it down."

"What did he say? What does he know? Gosh, I hope that map isn't one of those symbolic things like hieroglyphics."

"He's not sure. *Yet.* But according to his contacts, he *is* sure of one thing—the map leads to an actual treasure. He believes it's the loot that thief stole in the late seventeen hundreds."

"It wouldn't surprise me if one of those 'dark web dwellers' knew about it and somehow orchestrated that theft. Too bad we'll never figure out their identities."

"We won't, but Rolo might. The guy is a veritable genius when it comes to that stuff. Then again, it's what makes him as neurotic as your mother's dog."

"No kidding. So where did Marshall go?"

"To track down those staff members at the museum and at the shipping company who have computer skills beyond the norm. Then back to Rolo for their profiles."

"Boy, those cases get more and more tangled. Glad all I have to do is my regular work today. It will be blissful."

Worst words ever spoken. An hour later, *blissful* was the last sentiment I'd use to describe the rest of the day.

"Phee!" Augusta shouted. "Your mother's on the line. Said your phone went to voicemail but she doesn't trust it. Said there was 'a situation' at the auto garage."

"Situation as in another body or just a general situation?"

"Lots of yelling in the background, but it sounded as if people were chasing something."

"Oh, brother. I'd better call. Thanks."

Wonderful. This is all I need.

"Got your message, Mom. What's up?"

"Louise stopped by the garage after getting Leviticus's nails trimmed at the vet and—"

"Her parrot's name is Leviticus?"

"Yes. Now listen. He was in one of those bird carriers but it didn't latch properly so now he's flying all over the place. Pooping on cars."

I tried not to laugh. "Can't Louise rein him in with a treat or something?"

"It's not like a dog or cat. We need you to drive over here and help. Everyone else is too hysterical."

"Even Herb?"

"He's no help. He's doubled over laughing and so is Wayne."

"I'm not a bird catcher. Call Paul and see if he can bring over some fishing nets. That's the best I can think of."

"We still need you."

"I cannot, for the life of me, imagine why, but I'll drive over on my break and skip lunch. But don't expect a miracle."

When I told Augusta, she nearly spat out her coffee. "I'll order us something from the deli so you won't starve. Have fun."

I could still hear her chuckling as I exited the office and made a beeline for my car.

There were a half dozen or so vehicles in the parking lot at the garage but plenty of parking. I hesitated at the door, not wanting to open it, but it didn't matter. Someone had the foresight to lock it. A quick rap and Aimee opened it slightly. I noticed the blue streak in her dark auburn hair was now red, along with the rest of her hair.

"Hurry up," she said and motioned. "That thing is going wild."

"How are you doing?"

"Fine, now. That was scary for sure. Can you believe this mess? A screeching, pooping parrot. All we need. Jared can't help because he has vertigo. Just watching that bird is making him dizzy."

I did a mental eye roll. Of course, I could believe it. It fit in perfectly with all the other nonsense that seemed to surround my mother and the book club ladies.

Paul had beaten me to the garage and was fast at work spreading out netting, as if he planned a week on the bayou catching shrimp.

"Can you get him to fly lower, Louise?" my mother asked. She waved at me and rushed over.

"Lordy, Louise, do something!" Shirley watched as the bird swooped, dove, and pooped.

"Paul thinks he can toss the netting over Leviticus. See if you can help him, Phee. You're younger and more agile."

"Whatever."

And while Paul was ready to launch into action, Leviticus was not. He had positioned himself on the top shelf of a supply closet and wasn't going anywhere. The only saving grace was that my mother hadn't brought the dog or the cat.

"This should be a piece of cake," Paul said to me. "I'll drag that ladder over there and toss the net on the bird. The net and bird should drop down and you can grab him. Keep the net on him."

"I'm not about to let him loose. What if he bites?"

Louise walked toward us and looked up at the parrot. "He's only done that once in a while when he's nervous."

"Pray he's not nervous," Shirley said.

"Here!" Aimee handed me a pair of work gloves and I couldn't get them on fast enough.

I glared at my mother and mouthed, "You owe me. *Big* time."

Paul lumbered up the ladder with the net hanging over his shoulder. Leviticus, meanwhile, began to preen his feathers, oblivious to Paul and his net. At least that's what Paul thought.

With a less-than-graceful toss, the net opened wide in the air, but not before Leviticus flew to another shelf, where he knocked down small cardboard boxes that bounced against the car hoods below.

"Try again," Louise begged. "He'll tire out."

I had a horrible feeling that Paul would reach the point of exhaustion hours before Leviticus, but I kept it to myself.

"Now he's perched on the edge of the shelves where the work overalls and rags are," Wayne said. "If he topples those boxes, it'll be a pain folding up everything. Better hope he doesn't—Oh heck no!—Look out everyone. Boxes are falling all over!"

And with that, Project Gear Shift was heralded in a new direction.

CHAPTER 26

Thirty seconds later, a barrage of boxes hit the ground and scattered towels, rags, old jeans, old overalls, and unrecognizable fabrics all over the place.

"This is going to take forever to sort out and repack," Aimee said. "By the way, where's that bird?"

We looked around and none of us could spot Leviticus.

"He couldn't have gotten out," I said. "All of the doors are shut."

Louise went from agitated to outright panic. "We have to find him. He could be trapped anywhere. My poor Leviticus. Start looking! Please!"

We stepped over the miscellaneous materials on the floor and tried to hunt down the bird. I noticed Paul off to the side of the room and tried not to chuckle. He stood like a sentry, fishing net gripped to his hands. "I'm on it."

Meanwhile, the rest of us moved about gingerly so as not to get the clothing, towels, or rags dirty. Heaven forbid they'd need washing. Then, my mother yelled, "Those overalls! They're moving!"

Louise and Paul raced over with Paul tossing the net over the coveralls and over Louise. She lost her balance and landed on her rear next to a bench grinder. Meanwhile, the blue denim fabric rose up and down and I was positive Leviticus was the one beneath it.

"Paul, don't remove the net until I say so, but someone get that bird's cage. I think I can grab him. Overalls and all."

I bent down and slid my hand under the net, careful not to lose sight of the moving lump. Then, I placed my hand over it and told Paul to yank away the net. I don't remember breathing at the point when I felt the bird's body. With part of the overalls on top of Leviticus, I shoved him into his cage and closed the door. I was faster than a Las Vegas blackjack dealer. And my stakes were higher.

Louise rushed over and showered the bird with so much cooing and swooning that it made my mother's overtures to Streetman and Essie seem mild.

"I might as well start the cleanup by folding these coveralls," I said. As I stood with one hand holding on to a pant leg, a paper dropped out of a pocket. I reached down and picked it up, figuring I'd toss it in the trash. That's when I realized what it was and that everything was about to change.

"It's an old newspaper clipping from the *Arizona Republic*. It's about the Phoenix Art Museum lending the 'priceless' doll to the unity council for their celebration."

"Just throw it away, Phee. One less piece of litter. We already know they lent it and lost it." The annoyance in my mother's voice was obvious.

I scanned the article and turned it over. An advertisement for window shutters. In the spaces between the large ad print, I noted what looked like scribble and I read it out loud. "Call Kev re: shipping date. Move time up."

As I studied the note, my mother proceeded to fold the overalls. And then, a gasp that sounded like a car misfiring. "These belonged to Betsy. She sewed in a name tag. I haven't done that since you went to camp, Phee."

"Let me see." Sure enough, the overalls belonged to the late Betsy Sprig.

"I didn't think she worked on cars," Wayne said.

"She still had to look the part," Aimee replied. "Credibility and all of that. What a poser."

"Did Betsy have any dealings with Kevin?" I asked Wayne. "I mean, how many Kevins are out there?"

He shook his head. "I don't think so. He would have told me."

"It's odd that she would have clipped an article about that museum doll."

"Oh goodness, Phee," my mother said. "People clip all sorts of things from the paper."

The words *shipping date* were like an itch that wouldn't stop. True, it might have referred to anything, but still, it seemed more than a coincidence.

"Maybe you're right."

Then, without any rhyme or reason, my mother furrowed her brow and held out her hand for the note. "Hmm, maybe *you're* right, after all. Oh my gosh! That note is about the death doll. The death doll! Betsy knew the museum was delivering it to the unity council and found a way to prevent it from getting there. Then, someone who also wanted that thing found out and murdered her."

"Thank you, Nora Roberts, but I think a little more evidence is called for. And right now, my office is calling me to get back to work. Lucifer, I mean Leviticus, is back in his cage and all's right with the world. I'm taking off."

And just as I headed to the door, I heard a loud knock and an unmistakable voice—"Unlock this door. This is Deputy Bowman from the Maricopa County Sheriff's Office."

Oh heck no. Could my day get any worse?

Since I stood adjacent to the door, I opened it and looked straight at him. "Good afternoon, Deputy Bowman. I was just leaving. Needed to put a parrot in a cage."

"Is that supposed to be a code for something or some text message thing?"

"Uh, no. It's Louise's parrot. The one squawking in the background."

He raised his head and shuddered. "Never mind. I have an arrest warrant for Holt Kavanaugh and my office was informed I could find him here."

"He's not here," Aimee called out, "but check the—"

"Holt?" my mother yelled. "An arrest warrant for Holt? *That's* who killed Betsy?"

"Lordy, and I thought he was such a nice man." Shirley put her palm to her cheek and shook her head.

Then everyone rushed toward the deputy and shot off more questions than bullets on a firing range. An exasperated Bowman waved his hands in the air and told everyone to pipe down.

"He's not being arrested for murder. Understood? It's another issue entirely." Then he looked at Aimee. "Where did you say he might be?"

"Next door at the Men's Club. They play euchre this time of day."

"Must be nice," Bowman muttered under his breath before stomping to the door. "Again, not murder. Don't fuel up those rumors." The door slammed behind him, and for a moment we stood in silence.

"You think one of us should check out the Men's Club?" my mother asked. "I'm not sure if women are allowed, and Louise certainly can't go with that bird, but maybe Wayne or Herb might want to mosey over there."

"Whatever it is, you'll only make things worse, Mom. Leave it alone. I'm sure everyone will be privy to that information before nightfall. And no, I don't think it has anything to do with murder or stolen 'death dolls.' Talk to you later."

I left the place in record speed and couldn't wait to get back to my desk and my peaceful world of spreadsheets, invoices, and glorious paperwork. But so much for wishful thinking. Even Augusta warned me when I described the fiasco at the garage. "Once things get started over there, the dust storm becomes a tornado."

Was she ever right! Midway through my pastrami on rye sandwich, my phone vibrated.

Not now. This is a nightmare.

"Phee! It's your mother."

"Uh-huh." *Like I wouldn't recognize the voice.* "Whatever it is, I'm not driving back over there."

"I called to tell you that Herb and Wayne walked over to WSCW's radio station in the Men's Club and were able to go down the corridor and overhear that deputy arresting Holt. I thought you'd want to know."

"Does it have anything to do with our cases?"

"You never know."

"Fine. What did they charge him with?"

"Stealing club assets from the auto restoration club. I'm not sure how he did it, but he did. Or at least they think he did or they wouldn't have charged him, right?"

"I suppose. And no, I'm not going to look into it. I have enough on my plate."

"I wasn't about to ask you. But I did need to tell you what the men heard."

Before I could eke out a syllable, she spewed out the words that Herb and Wayne overheard—"That harridan! That miserable crone! I should have strangled her when I had the chance."

"I would take that with the proverbial grain of salt. You know how people get when they're under stress."

"I sure do. Tell your boss and your husband to bump Holt up on the suspect list."

"Fine. Just stay out of it. Okay?"

"There's more."

"What? What more?"

"Another deputy escorted Holt out of there and Deputy Bowman made a phone call."

I rubbed my neck and prayed the call would end soon. "And?"

"It was to his office. They're searching Betsy's house again. You know what that means. I don't have to spell it out for you. 'Stealing club assets,' my you-know-what. They're going to charge him with murder."

"And someone will charge you for slander if you spread that tidbit around. Mum's the word. I repeat—Keep this under wraps."

"You don't have a single reason to concern yourself."

"No, I have a trillion."

CHAPTER 27

Next thing I knew, Nate phoned the office and Augusta was only too happy to share the news.

"Mr. Williams is now on his way to Betsy Sprig's place. Boy, that was fast for a search warrant from the sheriff's office. Then again, they may be working off the original one."

"What do you suppose they'll find there that they didn't the last time?" I asked.

"They were probably looking for evidence of some sort of altercation if she was killed elsewhere and moved to the garage. This time, I'll bet they're looking for any communication between her and Holt that would be considered a motive for murder. I've read enough crime novels. They arrest you for something else while they look for evidence of the real thing they want to charge you with."

"Isn't that illegal?"

Augusta shook her head. "Not if the first thing has credibility. And face it, they wouldn't have taken Holt into custody if they didn't have proof to back up the claim that he stole club assets."

"Theft is one thing. Murder is another."

"Sounds like cause and effect to me," Augusta said and grinned.

At that moment, the phone rang and she answered immediately. "I figured as much, Mr. Williams. Phee's mother told us about the arrest. What? Here, Phee can fill you in. It's her mother."

She handed me the receiver as I pinched my shoulder blades back and proceeded to describe everything from Leviticus's escape to Holt's arrest. He kept muttering, "No surprise. No surprise."

Then he explained he was on his way to assist Deputy Bowman and hoped to be back before too long and that Marshall had some moderate success with the shipping company and that our office would need to cross-reference names and profiles with museum employees for possible relationships.

"Our office? As in Rolo?"

"Our office as in supplying Rolo with the information. He'll take it from there. He developed a program that sifts through data to find even the most miniscule links."

"The stockholders in IKEA will be pleased."

"Don't remind me."

"Rolo's got my vote," Augusta said when the call ended. "I hate cross-referencing. And to think we did it without the use of technology. Who went to school where, who lived near each other, who had the same beautician. Dredging up all those pesky details on people's lives."

"My mother and her book club would be in seventh heaven doing that. Go figure. Anyway, I'm going back to my office. Don't want the keyboard to get cold."

About an hour later, a second call came in from Nate. Augusta had just finished getting some preliminary information from a new client who wanted our office to locate a twin sister who had been raised by an adoptive family. Something that had become more and more familiar to us, especially with DNA testing so readily available.

"Phee," she called out. "You're not going to believe this. Betsy's house was ransacked. Ransacked! Everything looked fine from the front, but when the MCSO deputies and Mr. Williams got inside, it was totally trashed. Had to have happened after the original search. Going to be a long afternoon for sure. They've got to speak with the neighbors and all that hoo-ha."

"Is Marshall headed that way?"

"He will be. Mr. Williams said he texted him."

"Betsy's house isn't far from the auto restoration garage. If any of those folks pass by, the news will be all over the community. I'm sure the deputies are cordoning off her place as we speak."

"Are you thinking the same thing I am? That maybe she had info on Holt and Holt tore the place upside down to find it?"

I shrugged. "Could be. Lately, nothing surprises me anymore."

Just then, a text appeared from Marshall—*Break-in at Betsy's. On my way. Don't wait on dinner. Will call later. Xo*

"Well, that makes it official. Nate and Marshall are knee-deep in this case whether or not they want to be. And as for my mother and her friends, I'm keeping my fingers crossed they stay out of trouble while they snoop around the garage. It was the only way to prevent them from executing one of their notorious plans."

"What about you? You're not going to sit on the sidelines."

"Lyndy and I are doing armchair snooping. I've got the Turk sisters and Jared. And so far, social media hasn't exactly panned out. Jared isn't on it and only Darleen is on Facebook. And not with much info, either. In fact, her profile picture is a wing of an airplane."

"Didn't you say they were retired airplane mechanics?"

"Uh-huh. And the only photos she has are of airplanes, including cockpits, turbine engines, fuselage, and slats. Who on earth would care?"

"Other airplane mechanics. Was the same way with my late uncle Horace, but that was before computers. He always carried photos of his dairy cows in his wallet and showed them off."

Suddenly, I had a thought. Not my greatest, but still, better than nothing.

Against my better judgment, I phoned my mother as soon as I got back to my desk.

"Are you still at the garage?" I asked.

"No. Why? Did something happen that I missed?"

"Not at the garage. And don't go yammering about what I'm going to tell you. Betsy's house was ransacked. MCSO and our guys are over there."

"I bet Holt did it."

"Don't say anything. And whatever you do, don't go snooping around over there."

"Honestly, Phee."

"Are you going back to the garage later?"

"Not today. Tomorrow morning. After breakfast at Bagels 'n More. Shirley and I need to compare notes."

"About that, did you or any of the ladies happen to find out anything about Betsy's ex-husbands? Nate said two of them passed away decades ago and the other one lives in Florida. They seriously doubt he had anything to do with her death. And he wasn't in her will."

"He might not be in her will, but the house belongs to him."

"What?"

"I found that out from Cecilia, who has the same house cleaner. I thought I told you."

"No, you didn't."

"Fine. According to the house cleaner, the divorce agreement specified that Betsy could live rent-free in the house until she died but she had to pay the taxes and homeowner fees."

"Is that common? I mean, with older people and second marriages?"

"More common than you'd imagine. Why? You don't think the guy wanted her out of there and had her killed?"

"No, that would be a long shot. Timing, situation, all of that stuff. I wondered if maybe Betsy had something of value in the house and when he was notified of her death, he flew out here to find it."

"He didn't have to ransack the place and destroy stuff."

"Not destroyed. Messed up. Augusta told me that nothing was broken. Just drawers pulled out and emptied, furniture cushions removed, files dumped, paintings off the walls, but nothing seriously broken. And whoever it was didn't have a key. Nate said they jimmied the patio door lock. Betsy didn't have one of those dowels on the bottom to keep it from opening."

"Glad I have a dowel. And Streetman. He's better than a Roman sentry!"

Too bad he wasn't around in Caesar's day.

"Anyway, if you hear anything more from Cecilia, or anyone, for that matter, let me know. And remember, steer clear of Betsy's place. It will be crawling with investigators and they don't need your help. Or Streetman's."

"I can't help it if the dog needs refreshing walks."

"Not on the other side of town. Talk to you later."

When I ended the call, I was certain my mother and her crew of yentas would be camped out across the street from Betsy's house. Nothing ensures that someone will do something like telling them not to. It's like a law of physics, only with human nature.

I figured her presence wouldn't cause that much harm, but past experience should have taught me otherwise.

It was nearing closing time when Augusta took a phone call from Gloria Wong, my mom's former neighbor and unofficial member of the book club. Augusta called me over to her desk and propped her head on her elbows. "I hate to tell you this, Phee, but that was Gloria Wong. She said you'd know who she is."

"Uh-oh. I can only imagine what's coming."

"Gloria could only speak for a few minutes because of the barking."

"Please don't tell me she's anywhere near my mother. She's got a wonderful, well-behaved Great Dane, Thor, who plays with Streetman. I hope they haven't gotten into any mischief."

"Uh, about that . . ."

"Cut to the chase. I'm bracing myself." *Along with every part of my tense body.*

"Okay. Gloria was on her way to the dog park when she passed Betsy's house and pulled over. Your mother and a bunch of ladies were across the street watching."

"Of course they were. Now give me the bad news."

"Naturally, your mother brought the dog, but he was in his stroller. That was before Thor rushed over and knocked the stroller to the ground, where it came undone and Streetman escaped."

"He's loose in the neighborhood?"

"That would have been the better alternative. No, he and Thor raced across the street to the side of Betsy's house, sniffed under one of the bougainvillea bushes and began digging. When anyone approached, both of them barked, and according to a witness, 'the little one bared his teeth.' Oh, they're still barking."

"Were Gloria and my mother able to leash them?"

"Yes."

The tension in my neck subsided and I took a breath. "Good. Whew!"

"Uh, not exactly. Those dogs dug up some sort of remains and now an entire forensics crew showed up. Gloria thinks there was something else in there but the deputies won't let the crowd get any closer. Then, to make it worse, one of the ladies shouted, 'Is it one of her ex-husbands?'"

CHAPTER 28

"Nate and Marshall must be pitching a fit, and I don't even want to think about Bowman and Ranston. And as for a dead body under one of her bushes, it's not *Rear Window*. When Marshall gets home tonight, I'll text you the full story."

"You don't have to. Mr. Williams always calls to keep me informed so we don't get blindsided."

That was one of the things I really liked about Nate. All of us knew what was going on at all times. Our agency was family with a trust factor that couldn't be found at other places of business.

"I'm not going over there. Dog crisis is over. Unexplained remains dug up. And now time for me to grab a bite and make something Marshall can eat later. Besides, I have my own snooping around to do. On paper. On the computer. But nowhere near my mother or her crew."

"Smart thinking."

When I got home, I tossed granola into yogurt and called it supper. Then, I made tuna salad for later and pulled out my murder notebook. The one pressing question I had was simple: Why couldn't anyone identify that woman with the tricolored hair who was at the garage the first day we showed up? With time on my hands, I called Wayne.

"Doesn't anyone have an idea who that could have been?" I asked. "Her hair was a few different shades of red."

"That describes all the women in the club whose hair isn't gray. I asked the Turk sisters when we first found out about Betsy and they weren't looking. That lady was at a workbench on the other side of the room. No one saw her leave. And I was told she didn't sign in."

"What about the person who used the paint booth before Aimee? Have you heard anything?"

"Sorry, no."

"Well, keep your eyes and ears open. Are you at the garage right now?"

"I'm home. I left a little while ago. Aimee's helping me make up for lost time on the Mustang. She's anxious to paint that VW of hers. Since Luella was next on the list, and not her, she's not worried that she was the intended victim."

"What about Luella? She must be scared stiff."

"Didn't you hear? MCSO has a deputy posted in front of her house. They think whoever sabotaged the paint booth will make another attempt. This time on Luella."

"Hmm, that begs the question—What did Betsy and Luella have in common?"

"Not much from what I know. But then again, it's not as if I pay attention to anything anyone says."

"Well, start paying attention now. This is getting really tangled up. By the way, any word on that note you got? The one that accused you of knocking off Betsy?"

"It's been shoved under the rug. Even the deputies think it was a disgruntled club member. But now that the garage is open, I don't expect any more threats. But I'm still a suspect, or person of interest, or whatever you call it since it *was* my car."

"It'll get sorted out. Meanwhile, stay vigilant. And thanks, Wayne."

I busied myself for the next two hours and also touched base with Lyndy. We were both desperate for a good swim but it was way too cold, even if the water was heated.

The good news was that her amateur sleuthing paid off. She found out that Holt was let go from his former job as an auditor, amid rumors of tampering with the books. Unable to make anything stick, his company gave him a nice severance pay plus his retirement. As Lyndy put it, "Who said crime doesn't pay?"

As far as I was concerned, it was one more reason to believe he might be the killer. *That*, plus his physique. He was strong, no doubt. Unfortunately, her search on Luella wasn't as fruitful, but she wasn't about to give up.

"Still on for dinner this week?" she asked.

"Absolutely. Marshall's going to be tied up so any day works."

"Tomorrow? Twisted Italian?"

"Fine. I'll get takeout to bring home for him."

I went back to my own internet snooping and before I knew it, Marshall was home. He kicked off his shoes, plopped on the couch and groaned. "I feel like I'm ninety years old. What a night. Were you aware that your mother and her entourage were at the scene of the crime?"

"Aware, annoyed, aggravated, you name it. Gloria called our office and Augusta got stuck getting the details. Seems that little nipper-snapper and Thor dug up something."

"I was about to get to that. More than 'something.' As much as the dog is a nuisance, he may have uncovered a decent clue."

"Really?" I thought my eyes would bulge out of my head.

"The 'burial spot' was recent and it had the remains of a cat with its collar and ID. All in a little box."

"Did anyone know Betsy had a cat?"

"That's just it. She didn't! Hated dogs and cats, from what the neighbors said. The cat actually belonged to her next-door neighbor, who buried it in her own backyard not too long ago. How it got moved to

Betsy's property is anyone's guess. When Ranston notified the neighbor, because the tag was still on the collar, the woman got hysterical. Like I said, what a night!"

"I can imagine."

"That's not all. The deputies thought the only thing under that bush was the cat, but then, Thor continued digging and unearthed another box. One that never would have been noticed if it wasn't for those huge paws of his."

"Don't tell me it was another cat! Was Betsy off her rocker?"

"Not another cat. Or dead thing. This time the box was a metal one. Not cardboard. And it contained a Ziploc freezer bag with an unsealed envelope in it. Naturally we donned gloves and took a look. It was a yellowed paper with handwritten instructions for assembling and disassembling something. Bowman and Ranston think maybe the hydraulic lift, but the sabotage was in the hoses, not the mechanism. All of this begs the question—What was Betsy up to?"

"Other than reburying the neighbor's cat?"

"Lately, nothing surprises me. Now it's up to the scrutiny of the Maricopa County Forensics Lab. It could take weeks. Meanwhile, Ranston returned the deceased feline to the neighbor."

I covered my eyes and shook my head. "What else is new?"

"I'm starving, that's what."

"Come on, I made tuna salad and bought fresh bread."

"Hallelujah!"

To make the evening complete, my mother called with her version of "Streetman's heroic behavior" at the scene of a crime. I didn't think they gave as much credit to the recipients of the Congressional Gold Medal. I told her not to get too carried away at breakfast tomorrow with Shirley, but I knew it was a lost cause.

• • •

Marshall left early the next morning for a meeting with Nate and the deputies. This time at the Starbucks on Del Webb Boulevard since Ranston insisted the posse coffee was destroying his stomach lining.

By the time I got into the office, Augusta was only too eager to share what she'd learned about the meeting.

"Mr. Williams called. They'll be in soon. Said to move any early appointments around because they needed a few quiet minutes to speak with us."

"Wow. They've never done that before. Must be something really secretive. Or worse. I'd better fortify myself with more coffee right now."

"Same here. Only with a French cruller."

I forced myself to concentrate on the file of invoices that sat on my desk but my mind drifted. Marshall hadn't said a word to me this morning about any such meeting, so I figured whatever it was, it had to have originated after he conferred with Nate and the deputies.

Sure enough, I was right. As soon as the men walked into the office, Augusta rapped on my doorjamb. "We're going in the workroom. Good thing I brought morning munchies. We may need them."

That or Pepto-Bismol.

"Sorry for the cloak-and-dagger, ladies," Nate said. "Both of you look as if a bomb's about to drop. It's nothing that staggering, but it is urgent if we're going to succeed with our investigations."

"Did you want any coffee?" Augusta asked the men.

"We're fine." Marshall chuckled. "Ranston had a good idea for once—meeting at Starbucks." Then he turned to Nate.

"Might as well get on with it. Both of our cases are moving way too slow for our comfort zone. And since Betsy's murder presents a generalized threat for the community, we need to focus our concentration there. However, that priceless bit of history needs to be solved ASAP. So, we all agreed to 'push the envelope.'"

"Huh?" I looked at everyone.

Marshall leaned forward and kept his voice low, even though we were the only ones in the office. "We're making headway with our investigation but gumshoeing is a long, time-consuming process and time is something we don't have. So, we're going to set a trap to catch the culprit."

Augusta jumped to attention. "Like a sting? Like in the movie with Paul Newman and Robert Redford? I loved that movie. What role do I get to play?"

"Uh, no roles. We're not making a Hollywood production. What we're going to do is lure that thief out in the open. And we do it by dangling another priceless piece of art. We already spoke with the museum curator."

"She's going to loan out another piece?" I widened my eyes.

"Only on paper. And in the papers. Hear me out." Nate pinched his shoulder blades and took a deep breath. "We create a fake story for the newspapers telling them that the Phoenix Art Museum decided to loan the unity council another priceless artifact for their unity week. Which, incidentally, is fast approaching. Therefore, the rush."

"Then what?" I asked.

"We describe in detail what the object is and when it will be shipped. We even take a bogus photo of it. Whatever it may be. Most likely another hideous doll. Only this time, we explain that the new object's value is in the rare stones that were embroidered onto its clothing and in its eyes. The curator will get her art and design department to fabricate it."

"It's brilliant, really," Marshall added. "The thief or thieves won't be able to resist. With proper surveillance in place at the shipping office, we'll be able to catch whoever is behind it and hold him or her dead to rights. The deputies have already spoken with the company management and they're on board. They don't want to blemish their reputation, and agreed that if the switch was made by one of their employees, they want to find out right away and deal with it."

"You mean *fire* them," Augusta said.

"Turn them over to the sheriff's office, but yes, most likely fire them, too." Nate laughed. "Now, what this means for both of you is that our office will be articulating the plan while Bowman and Ranston work with their forensics lab on the new evidence. Rolo will be designing the surveillance so it will be virtually undetectable."

"Won't that take a long time?" I glanced at Augusta, who crinkled her nose.

Nate shook his head. "The guy's got it down pat. One of his buddies will be responsible for installing it."

"I didn't know he *had* any buddies in the Phoenix area."

"You'd be surprised, Phee, at the myriad of Rolo's contacts. Sometimes I don't want to know."

I nodded. "So what do we do?"

"Begin by writing a description and fake provenance for the piece of art. I'll find out more details once I chat with the curator. She's expecting my call at ten. Then, contact the local newspapers and media with the story. The museum will call the unity council and work it from their end."

"And if the thief takes the bait?"

"Not *if*, when. Those facilities function twenty-four hours a day to get their shipments out. And we need to be ready to jump in as soon as Rolo gives us the word. He's got an artificial intelligence program that was designed to process every frame in the video feed, analyze them and report anomalies right back to him."

"I'm not sure I'm getting all of this, Mr. Williams. You're telling me a robot's going to find out if someone switches the contents of a shipment box?" Augusta fluffed her hair before resting both hands on the table.

"Pretty much. And it's AI now. Artificial Intelligence. Welcome to the twenty-first century."

"I preferred the twentieth when those things were in science fiction movies."

I looked at Augusta and then at Nate and Marshall. "It's better than plodding along."

"As long as the new piece of art isn't cursed, I'm fine with it, Mr. Williams."

"Good to know."

When we left the workroom, I was relieved that the new direction would provide the momentum we needed. What I didn't count on was that it would also provide a workout that I never would have imagined.

CHAPTER 29

That night, Lyndy and I met for dinner at Twisted Italian, a stone's throw from our neighborhood. Marshall had tons of paperwork to tackle in the office so he was relieved I'd be bringing his pasta primavera home along with garlic bread.

"Okay," Lyndy said. She sipped her club soda with lemon and tore off a piece of Italian bread. "Did you know that Luella is going to be running the auto club meetings until Holt gets his 'Get Out of Jail Free' card?"

"How'd you find that out? And so soon? Yesterday you said you hit a block wall."

"That was yesterday. My aunt told me this morning. She found out at her condo association meeting last night. It wasn't a secret. Nothing is in that community. And that's not the only thing I learned. Luella owed Betsy money from a gambling trip she took to Laughlin a few months back."

"Your aunt again?"

Lyndy grinned. "Who else? It might have been chump change, but still, it might be a motive for murder."

"But Luella was a target, too. She was supposed to be the one in that paint booth but Aimee showed up first. That's why the sheriff's office posted a deputy by her house at night."

"If it's the same killer. There never seems to be a shortage of unbalanced people."

"That's an unsettling thought if I've ever heard one."

Lyndy took another sip of her soda. "That's why dating's been scary. Until I met Lyman. Even if we did start out on shaky ground."

"That was my fault. And Marshall's."

"And Paul's."

"At least it worked out."

"For sure."

Then I told her about the plot to trap the art thief in the act and Lyndy was mesmerized. "Too bad that couldn't be done with Betsy's murder," she said. "Then again, it might result in a second murder."

"Heaven forbid."

We decided to keep on digging and sharing notes. Both of us agreed that once the creepy priceless doll thief was located, the MCSO deputies and our office would be able to devote themselves entirely to the murder. *If* the thief was caught.

"You're not going to tell your mother, are you?" The expression on Lyndy's face was a mix of fear and concern.

"Are you kidding? Only if she pesters me. So I suppose, yeah, I am going to wind up telling her. If only to get her off my back. I mean, it's not as if she was going to do anything about it."

Stupidest words ever spoken! No sooner did I walk into our house when Marshall told me my mother called there twice. Once to let me know my voicemail was full and once to inquire about the ongoing investigations.

"I'll call her after you eat," I said. "The pasta's still warm so enjoy it."

"I'll be fine. Give her a buzz and get it over with. Then we can relax tonight."

"Shall do. I'll be in the bedroom. Putting on comfy clothes and bracing for her gab-a-thon."

"Better you than me. I pulled an Aunt Ina when she called and rang our own doorbell. Got to admit, it worked."

"You learn fast." I gave him a kiss on the forehead and trotted off to change clothes and make the call.

My mother answered on the first ring. "Wayne told Herb you called him today."

"Uh, hi, Mom. And yes, I did."

"Tell me what's going on. The women are getting antsy. Well, Louise, Shirley, and Lucinda are antsy. Cecilia's practically a basket case and Myrna's becoming a regular storm trooper. Everywhere we go, people ask how close your office is to finding out who killed Betsy."

"They're working on it."

"It took less time to build the Transcontinental Railroad."

"Fine. Here's the deal. Bowman and Ranston need to concentrate on Betsy, but they still have that doll artifact to find. So Nate and Marshall came up with a plan to expedite the process."

"Go on."

I explained about Rolo and the artificial intelligence, hoping it would waft over her head, but it didn't. In fact, her aversion to anything that wasn't human was mind-boggling.

"You're telling me they're letting a machine figure this out? Spy on people and catch the culprit? That's the most ridiculous thing I've ever heard. I have a much better idea. We'll do it! There are enough book club ladies. Plus Herb and his cronies. They've got nothing better to do. Except for Wayne and his Mustang."

"Oh no. Definitely no. I can see where this is going and my answer is no. Plain and simple—*no*!"

"You don't have to be a part of it. We're perfectly capable of rooting around on our own. We are mature adults, you know."

In what alternate universe?

"All you need to tell me is where that mailing company is located and we can take it from there."

"I don't know. Seriously. I never bothered to ask Nate or Marshall."

"Fine, if you want to play that game, Phee. But Gloria Wong's older daughter, the one who doesn't live with her, works for FedEx and she'll be able to tell her mother the names of those companies and we'll narrow it down."

"And then what? You're all going to get inside like a hoard of Vandals?"

"Job applicants."

"Oh, give me a break."

"Do you have a better idea?"

"Yes, stay out of it. No more scenes like the one on the lake. Rolo's got it under control. Besides, you're already keeping an eye on things at the auto garage. That's enough for now."

I figured my mother would leave well enough alone, but oh no! She just *had* to interfere. Unfortunately, I didn't find out about it until it was too late.

• • •

It was a few days later and Williams Investigations had already put "the plan" in motion at the shipping company. In fact, the feature article in the *Arizona Republic*, along with smaller articles in the local *Independent*, described in detail the value and beauty of the "Nantucket Doll," said to have rare stones set into its eyes and sewn into its clothing. Augusta and I marveled at the imaginative prose we used to create what sounded like a genuine artifact. That is, if you didn't read it too closely, or bother to research it.

To cover ourselves, the curator embellished the article with similar doll histories in the hope that our reference would get glossed over in the minds of readers. Except, of course, for our thief.

The fake doll was securely packed and picked up by the company the following Monday morning for delivery to the unity council. As far as they were concerned, it was an added, albeit fake, bonus exhibit.

"I had to use the leftover wrapping from our roast beef subs the other day," Augusta said. "We ran out of newspaper and I didn't have time to buy wrapping paper. No worries though. The paper from our subs was dry. Shouldn't be a problem."

"I don't think anyone will notice or care."

"Good. Paper is paper."

In the interim, not much progress had been made on Betsy's murder or the mechanical instructions found in the box beneath the dead cat. In fact, those were photocopied and sent to Rolo by MCSO as per the advice of our agency.

"Everything's in place for 'the sting,'" Augusta told me when I got into the office that morning. "According to Mr. Williams, the driver is supposed to pick up the package tomorrow and get it to the shipping office by the close of the day. That means he or she will do the dirty deed sometime tomorrow night."

"The driver may not be the one who's going to repack it." I watched as the coffee dripped into my cup from the machine and looked around.

"Doesn't matter. Once the surveillance catches the action, the deputies will swoop in. According to Mr. Williams, MCSO will have an unmarked vehicle in place."

"What about Nate and Marshall? Are they expected to swoop in as well? Marshall rushed out to work while I was half asleep. Something about a text."

"Search warrant for Holt's house. A tip-off from someone. Most likely bogus. Sour grapes. That sort of thing, but still, Bowman and Ranston are checking it out and wanted our crew to join the fun."

"Oh, brother. Guess that means Holt is still in lockup."

"Uh-huh, but he's expected to be out on bail this morning. Presumably after they search his house. Of course, that's only for our ears."

"That should be interesting. I wonder if he'll be conducting the next auto restoration club meeting or if it will wind up in Luella's lap."

Augusta tucked a small curl behind an ear and shrugged. "There are days when I'm so glad I live on county land."

I retreated to my office and buried myself in the joyful bliss of numbers and spreadsheets until midday rolled around and Augusta took out her secret stash of Entenmann's donuts. I was about to bite into one when my cell phone vibrated and the caller ID was my mother's.

"It's like she has a secret sense that compels her to call me whenever I'm inches away from a donut or candy bar."

"You could let your voicemail get the call," Augusta said.

"Nah, I'll only wind up getting a longer one later." I chewed quickly and answered.

"What's up, Mom?"

"Just wanted you to know that all of us are now celebrating Wayne's progress on the car. We're going to the Homey Hut for dinner and pie à la mode tonight. In case you want to join us."

"What progress? And no, I'll pass but thanks anyway. And Marshall's really tied up."

"Aimee has gone out of her way to help Wayne. She's practically been living underneath that Mustang. Turns out the transmission was in tiptop shape so only a tight end had to be replaced."

"A tight end? I think that's football."

"Hold on a minute—Shirley! It was a tight end, wasn't it? On Wayne's car?"

Then I heard Shirley's voice. "No, a tie-end. And control arm bushings. Whatever they are. And the stabilizer. Whatever that does."

By now, my eyeballs rolled in their sockets and I was anxious to end the call.

"Okay, sounds good. Glad Aimee's helping. I've got to get back to work. Thanks for the invite."

"Wait! One more thing. Wayne found out from Dave, the monitor, that Luella's going to be conducting the next auto restoration club meeting since Holt is out of commission. Nice way of saying 'locked up until further notice.' You don't think he did it, do you? Because if he did, they'd make a big deal of it. If you want my opinion, those deputies are keeping him under lock and key until they find the real killer. Naturally, your aunt Ina has a different take altogether, and I—"

"Mom! I don't have time to get into it. I've got scads of work to do. We'll chat later."

Much, much later.

"Fine, but don't say I don't keep you informed. Which is more than I can say for the information you dole out."

"That's because it's information. Not rumors or innuendo."

"It's close enough."

Or light-years away.

CHAPTER 30

Nothing new at Williams Investigations as the day drew to a close. Well, almost nothing. I got an exasperated-sounding text from Marshall. He drove back to the museum to review days of surveillance footage of the Thorne Room in a Hail Mary attempt to see if the perpetrator was visible from angles that might have been overlooked prior. At a little before five, he texted again: *Sorry, hon. Still working on the cryptic message some lunatic left us. Home by seven the latest. I'll eat anything.*

I took some frozen chicken from the fridge, along with a package of Korean BBQ rice, and made a quick salad to top it off. And while cooking had never been my strong point, *preparing* was a skill set I had mastered completely.

With plenty of time on my hands, I revisited my murder map and jotted down a few "musts." Like tracking down the elusive tricolored hair woman and finding out who used the paint booth before Aimee showed up. Short of hiring a medium, I was about to give up on both counts when I realized something about one of the mystery people—We knew the time Aimee got into the booth, and according to both monitors, only one other person used it that day. As for the prior day, both said there were no problems whatsoever.

That meant I had a general timeline, even though I didn't have a video feed of the area surrounding the garage. Then, I realized something and could have kicked myself for not thinking of it before. Without wasting a second, I called Louise in the hopes she hadn't left yet for the Homey Hut.

"Phee! Is everything all right? I was just on my way out the door. Too bad you can't join us tonight."

"Yes, very disappointing." *Like a root canal getting canceled.* "Marshall's working late and he'll be exhausted when he gets home. I won't keep you, but I need to ask you something. Remember when you mentioned an eagles' nest in one of those tall palm trees adjacent to the dog park? My mother mentioned that the book club even celebrated it. Is anyone from your bird club videoing it?"

"Why, yes, Imitra Patel. Lovely woman. Owns a few cockatiels and a budgie. Why? Are you interested in watching the eagles' progress?"

"Actually, I wondered if she could share the video from the night Aimee was nearly asphyxiated. We might find the culprit."

"Hang on, I'll get you Imitra's number. It's in my list of club contacts."

"Oh, and one more thing, please don't mention this to my mother. She'll call me at all hours demanding to know what I found out."

"I won't say a word."

Five minutes later, I had reached Imitra and she invited me to stop by and watch the video as well as visit with her birds for a few hours. I asked if I could get a copy instead and she was more than willing, but needed one of her friends from the computer/technology club to do it. That meant waiting another day.

"No problem," I said. "I can pick up the video anytime and I'll be more than glad to pay for expenses."

"Don't be ridiculous. We all live in this community and if my video helps to catch a killer, or whoever tampered with that paint booth, I'd be doing my good deed for the day."

We agreed I'd give her a call the following afternoon and for the first time in a while, I was upbeat about my own sleuthing. I glanced at the time when I ended the call since Marshall would be home any minute. I set out plates, napkins, and utensils, figuring I'd plop the chicken and rice into the microwave as soon as he got inside. Too bad his grand entrance coincided with a frantic phone call from my mother. In that split second, I knew dinner would have to take a backseat to the latest catastrophe from Sun City West.

"Wayne's going out of his mind, Phee. He's at the garage. Wanted to check on his car before driving over to join us. It's gone. *Gone!* That's grand theft auto! He called the posse and the sheriff's office. Good thing we're still in the parking lot. Looks like we're going to wind up having a late-night dinner at the Texas Roadhouse instead. Right now, we're all going over to the garage."

I swear she got that all out in one breath while I tried to process how someone could drive off with Wayne's car right in front of everyone at the auto restoration garage.

"I don't understand how that could have happened."

"What's to understand? The keys are right there, and according to Wayne, that Mustang is quite coveted."

"And quite in need of repair. And a paint job."

Just then, Marshall came inside and announced, "You won't believe this. Bowman texted me and Nate. Someone stole Wayne's car. They're on their way to the auto garage."

"They'll need backup. And it looks like it's going to be you and Nate."

"Huh?"

"My mother and her entourage are on their way over as well. Wayne and the guys were supposed to join them for a Homey Hut dinner but now everyone is headed over to the latest crime scene. At least it's a missing car and not, well, you know . . . another body."

"I'll swing by McDonald's and we can eat on the way over there. If nothing else, Nate and I will be needed to help manage the scene."

"At least the dog won't be there. The women were already at the Homey Hut but hadn't gone inside yet."

I grabbed a warm jacket and followed Marshall to his car. "I may have some good news. There's an eagles' nest across from the auto garage and it's being filmed by Louise's bird club. Full view of the auto garage. We may be in luck finding out who was there before Aimee succumbed to the fumes."

"You astonish me, hon. Never would have imagined that."

"To be honest, it didn't cross my mind until tonight. Then I phoned Louise and got in touch with Imitra. She's the woman with the video feed. Anyway, I'll be getting a copy tomorrow afternoon."

By now, we were buckled up and on our way to Sun City West with a quick stop on Bell Road for burgers and fries.

By the time Marshall pulled into the parking lot adjacent to the auto restoration garage, I had wiped the grease from my French fries and swallowed the last bit of Coke. "Yep, the crowd's all here. Look at the lineup of Buicks."

Unlike the time before, we were able to walk right in and join the yammering group of book club ladies and pinochle players. Bowman's voice rattled the walls as he fired off questions, observations, and general grumbling to no one in particular.

"What do you mean no one saw the car leaving the garage?"

"How does a classic car leave the garage without anyone being aware of it? Or the driver, for that matter?"

"The opening and closing of the garage door should have caught someone's attention!"

"Did everyone here leave their hearing aids at home?"

Meanwhile, Wayne paced around the garage, pausing every few minutes to sigh and mutter, "Poor Sally Stang," when he wasn't pitching a fit about calling his insurance agent.

Other than the crew that accompanied my mother, only the monitor was there along with Jared and Darleen. I watched wide-eyed as he was grilled by Deputy Ranston, whose raspy voice sounded more like a croak. "You mean to tell me you didn't see anyone drive off?"

The monitor shook his head. "No one drove off while I was here. I don't monitor very often and when I came in, that Mustang wasn't here. I checked the attendance list like your partner asked me and the only names are Jared Loundsby and Darleen Turk. And they got in after I did."

"Who was the monitor before you?"

"Dave. I have his phone number on the directory list."

Ranston muttered something and tapped the number into his phone.

Just then, Nate appeared from the back of one of the bays and approached Marshall and me. "According to Jared and Darleen, who are over there with Darleen's VW, Aimee was supposed to do some undercarriage work on the Mustang. They have no idea if she was the one who drove it out of here or if someone else did. Darleen called her cell but it went to voicemail."

"You don't suppose something happened to her, do you?" I asked.

The look that Nate and Marshall gave each other was one I recognized. They had another thought entirely. Still, it gave me chills when Marshall said it. "She may have stolen the vehicle herself. Bowman told me that MCSO and the Surprise Police Department have a BOLO on it."

"At least the news stations didn't show up. That's all we need." I looked around, and as far as I could tell, nothing had changed. Wayne still muttered and the mixed group of yentas still yammered. Then, out of nowhere, we heard more than one siren and raced outside to see what was going on.

With red and blue flashers behind her, Sally Stang made a grand entrance to the front of the building, brakes squealing and a crowd rushing over as if it was the Indy 500.

"What the hell?" Aimee slammed the car door behind her just as Bowman shouted, "Hands over your head! Hands over your head."

CHAPTER 31

"Are you serious?" Aimee kept her hands in the air and looked at Bowman. The red and blue flashers from the sheriff's car behind him accentuated Aimee's red hair, making her appear more like a troll than a petite senior citizen.

By now, everyone in the garage and its vicinity had charged to the parking lot to get a better view of the scene. As Bowman walked toward Aimee, she shouted, "What is the matter with you people? I didn't know it was a crime to blow out the carburetor on an open road. All that gunk clogs it up and I wanted to make sure I didn't have to replace it like I thought."

"Carburetor? We're talking grand theft auto!"

"What? You thought I stole Wayne's car! I'm working on the darn thing, for goodness' sake! And I told the monitor I was going to give it a run for its money on Route 60—Grand from Meeker to 163rd and back. Didn't he say anything? And by the way, can I put my hands down now?"

Bowman nodded and turned to Ranston, who stood two or three feet to his left. "Where's this monitor? Don't tell me he suffered a memory loss and forgot she told him she was taking Wayne's car out."

"Dave's shift ended a while ago," Jared shouted from behind a crowd of onlookers. "Mike took over as the monitor. Guess Dave forgot to tell him."

Again, Bowman turned to Ranston. "Who's this Mike?"

At that moment, Wayne elbowed his way through the growing crowd and apologized profusely to Aimee. She shrugged and said, "Forget about it," before asking Bowman "when the stupid flasher lights would shut off."

"Obviously, it's not grand theft auto," I said to Marshall, "but I have a feeling it'll be a long night, nevertheless."

"Got that right. The statements alone are going to keep our two deputy friends busy for sure."

And then, a voice from back in the crowd that was worse than chalk on a chalkboard. "Phee! What's going on? Have they put her in handcuffs yet? Shirley and I can't see a thing from here."

"We can't either, Harriet," Myrna added. "Cecilia's on tiptoes and all she can see are people's backs."

I squeezed Marshall's forearm. "Catch you in a bit. I'd better get over to the women before they make things worse."

"I think the men are doing a pretty good job already." He pointed to the far side of the garage, where Bill, Kevin, Kenny and Herb were engaged in a louder than usual conversation. To make matters worse, someone in the crowd yelled, "She better not be armed!"

That set off a series of responses that no one expected.

"She's armed!"

"Duck to the ground. We could be collateral damage."

"Who has a gun?"

"I should have brought my Daisy Air Rifle. No law against that!"

With no way to quiet the crowd, Bowman had one of the deputies blow the horn on the sheriff's car and hand him a portable megaphone.

"Attention! Attention! No one is armed. There is no danger. I repeat—No danger. I insist you leave the area at once. Everything is under control. I repeat—Everything is under control."

I glanced to my right and tugged on Marshall's sleeve. "I wouldn't be too sure about that. Look who just arrived."

Sure enough, Paul Schmidt thundered through the crowd, fishing pole in hand. "I'm here to help if you need me!" But that wasn't the worst. On his heels were at least four large dogs that were dragging their leashes.

"They must have gotten a whiff of fish," I said. "Look! They're still attached to their leashes."

And then, a flurry of dog owners charged the area and shouted for their dogs.

"Winston! Get over here!"

"Buddy! Come here. Now!"

"Miss Petunia! Come to Mommy!"

And on and on it went. More dogs joined them and more frantic owners followed.

I couldn't keep my eyes off the circus of dogs and their owners. "This gives chaos a whole new meaning. Thank heavens Streetman is home."

"That's the only shining light in this entire debacle," Marshall said. Then, he and Nate took off to corral the dogs while Bowman and Ranston did the best they could with crowd control. Lamentably, their best wasn't good enough, because more people came out of the woodwork to see what was going on.

The bowling alley emptied. The card groups at the Men's Club exited their building and the exercise fanatics on the walking track ambled over to where we stood.

It took two hours and thirty-three minutes to get everything under control according to KPHO channel 5 news, who got the word and sent a team over to cover the situation.

When everyone had left the area, except for my mother and her book club, along with Herb's buddies and the auto restoration club members, Nate rubbed his temples and sat on a stool near one of the bays. "I've never seen anything unravel so fast in my life."

Across from him, Darleen grilled Aimee as if she was hiding state secrets.

"What's the matter with you? You should have told me instead of Dave what you were doing. Half the time he doesn't remember what he ate for breakfast. And last week he had his shirt on backward but no one wanted to tell him."

"I thought he'd say something to Mike."

"Well, he didn't. And now look around."

"At least Wayne's carburetor is good."

Darleen then announced she was going home and if everyone was smart, they'd do the same.

"Do Darleen and Aimee live together?" I asked Wayne once Darleen left the garage.

"No way! There would be a double murder if they did. I think Darleen lives in one of those condos on Camino del Sol but I'm not sure about Aimee."

"It doesn't matter. I was curious, that's all."

"Well, I'm exhausted. Had enough excitement for one night." Nate started for the door and then spun around and took a step toward us. "Maybe my timing's off but it shouldn't take that long for someone to drive from Meeker to 163rd and back. Then again, I could be off. It's been a long day. See you in the morning."

I was about to say something to Marshall when Nate left, but my mother and her entourage headed our way.

"All that fuss over nothing," my mother said. "We're going to the Texas Roadhouse. You're welcome to join us. Myrna wants the Road Kill dinner. That's all she's been talking about."

"We had burgers before we got here, but thanks, Mom. Enjoy your meal."

"Paul's joining us. I better not sit upwind from him."

My mother headed out and I looked past her to see Aimee, Wayne and Jared chatting. Next thing I knew, Aimee left the garage but drove Wayne's car back inside a few seconds later.

"Guess everything is honky-dory for now," Marshall said.

"I'm not too sure. Isn't that Darleen by the door? I thought she went home."

Sure enough, Darleen returned, handed Aimee something and shouted, "You left your artificial tears at my house. Try Visine next time." Then she took off without saying anything else.

"Come on, hon, let's make a break for it while we still can."

And while the garage floor was concrete and flat as could be, the same couldn't be said for the parking lot. Small pebbles were everywhere and I stumbled over them, catching myself at the last minute and losing one of my heels. I bent down to retrieve my shoe and brush the pebble away when I realized it wasn't a pebble at all. It was a tiny wooden miniature of a man. Roughly hewn, as if the artist was still working on it.

"You okay?" Marshall offered me his hand.

"Fine, but someone lost their project. It still needs work." I handed him the miniature. "They must have a miniature club in Sun City West."

He scrutinized the tiny doll, and for a moment remained speechless.

"What are the odds? It can't be."

"It can't be what? There are a zillion clubs here. They probably even have one for cultivating mushrooms."

"Not that. This little thing looks similar to the one we found in that diorama at the museum. Only that one was completely carved with a splash of hobby paint. I know this is going to sound as far-fetched as all get-up-and-go, but—Oh, never mind. I'll turn it over to the forensics crew and see what they can tell us."

"You seriously don't think whoever stole that artifact was here at the garage tonight?"

"Common sense and reason tell me no, but hey, it's not as if I can ignore it. Meanwhile, see if you can ask Shirley if she knows who might be into working with miniatures. She's got a good handle on the crafts and sewing clubs. Who knows? It might put us on the right track."

Or derail us altogether.

"I'll call her tomorrow. Let her enjoy the Texas Roadhouse with the gang."

"And let us enjoy one night of relative peace."

CHAPTER 32

The next morning, Wayne couldn't wait to share more good news. He phoned the office to thank us for "rushing over in his time of need, even though it was a false alarm." Then he went on to tell Augusta that Aimee had completed all of the undercarriage work on his car and that now they could concentrate on "what's under the hood."

"I don't know why men are so fascinated by anything with wheels," she said as she unwrapped a package of Trader Joe's black and white cookies. "Far as I'm concerned, it's transportation. Plain and simple. Get me from one place to another on time."

I chuckled. "Or to an auto auction or event where it translates to lots of moolah."

"It must have been quite the night, huh? Mr. Gregory mentioned something about finding another miniature doll that was the same size as the one from that exhibit in the museum. He left to drop it off at the MCSO lab."

"It's probably nothing with nothing but they're desperate for clues or links, or anything. Say, has Rolo gotten back in touch?"

"Yes. I was about to get to that before Wayne called and before Mr. Williams and Mr. Gregory took off. Mr. Williams is meeting with both rec center monitors today. Guess a new guy is in the mix."

"Yeah, Mike. Getting back to Rolo, what did he tell you?"

"Those instructions that were found under the dead cat aren't mechanical instructions after all. Well, not for a car anyway."

"What?"

"According to Rolo, the instructions are for a coded locking system. Like the ones for opening a secret-compartment cabinet safe from the mid-1800s. Mr. Williams immediately called the sheriff's office but they didn't find a safe in Betsy's house. They also had their staff look into storage units in the area to see if she rented one. Hmm, must be nice to have a big staff. Anyway, she didn't. Rent one, that is."

"Maybe it wasn't her safe."

Augusta held out the black and white cookies and I took one. "Boy, does this get more and more convoluted. The deputies asked around to see if any of the neighbors or auto club members knew anything about it. So far, nothing. If Betsy *did* have a safe hidden somewhere, and there was something valuable in it, then it might have been a good motive to knock her off."

"What about the ex-husband? Did anyone ask him?" I consumed the cookie and wiped the crumbs from my lower lip.

"It was the first call Bowman made this morning. They're two hours ahead of us in Florida. And no, the guy had no idea. Said Betsy didn't have anything of real value when they were married."

"And Bowman believed him?"

Augusta nodded. "Apparently so, because the guy didn't seem that interested in finding out more about the safe's instructions. If he had the safe, he'd want to know how to open it."

"Good point."

I took a second cookie for good measure and trotted off to my office. Less than an hour later, Nate breezed in and announced, "You're not going to believe this. While I was in the auto garage, having a nice chat with Mike, Bowman sent Marshall and me a text. Seems a woman registered a facilities complaint with the rec center, alleging that the ventilation system at the auto restoration garage wasn't working properly. Said she would have taken it up with the president of the club but he's 'on a cruise somewhere' and the next in line is 'a jailbird.'"

"Good grief." I stepped away from my desk and into the outer office. "All of that in a text message?"

"Bowman doesn't write text messages. He uses the app to write long, old school letters. Anyway, it gets better. She was the person who used the paint booth prior to Aimee. Said she didn't sign in because she didn't intend to be there that long. Just needed to touch up a fender that her 'moron husband' scratched."

"That's why I'm single," Augusta said and grinned. "Don't have to worry about my car fenders. Or moron husbands."

Nate did a half eye roll and continued. "Seems the woman who submitted the complaint got lightheaded when she started spraying the car fender. Said she'd used that paint booth before for longer jobs and never experienced lightheadedness. She stopped immediately, cleaned up fast and bolted out of there for some fresh air."

"Why didn't she report it to the monitor?" I asked.

"She said she didn't see him and didn't want to stick around and breathe more toxic air."

"That was Dave on duty? Right?"

"No, Mike. Dave was on duty in the morning. Mike stepped out to grab a coffee from Memo's because 'the coffee in the auto garage was like watery tar.'"

"Oh, brother." Augusta leaned her elbows on her desk, propped her head in her hands and looked directly at Nate. "That's a little too coincidental in my book."

"Did you get her name? Is it someone from that first day?" I chomped at the bit like a horse on its way back to the barn.

"Not according to the sign-in, but as we know, it's very 'loosey-goosey' in that garage."

"Did Bowman get her name?"

"Sure enough—Kevelyn Viviani. He's looking into her right now."

"I think I can do one better. Give me fifteen minutes."

I darted into my office, picked up the phone and dialed my mother before I had second thoughts.

Her voice was the usual siren. "What did you find out? And someone needs to tell Paul to take a shower when he's done fishing. Imagine if I brought Streetman over there. You know how he is with odorous things."

I know how he is, period.

"Okay, I've got some news, Mom, but I need to ask you a question first. Do you know or know of a woman by the name of Kevelyn Viviani?"

"No, but give me fifteen minutes to launch the B4M phone tree. Which, by the way, now includes Herb's pinochle crew."

"Phone tree? That went out in the eighties. Can't you use email or text messaging?"

"I can text your aunt Ina, Shirley, Myrna, and Lucinda. Cecilia's convinced someone is watching and Louise doesn't know how to text."

"It's the twenty-first century!"

"Fine. I'll do both. Will that make you happy? And why the interest in that Viviani woman? Do the deputies think she's the murderess? What did you find out?"

"She was the person who used the paint booth before Aimee got there but she left because she thought the air in there was toxic. So, no, she is not the murderess. But, she may know something."

"Give me fifteen minutes."

Fifteen minutes. Must run in the family.

"Okay, thanks."

"What else do you know?" The impatience in her voice was evident.

"Rolo figured out the note underneath the dead cat is for operating a coded locking system to a safe."

"Aha! There's money involved. I knew it. Money and murder go hand in hand."

Now it's money and murder. Usually it's a love affair gone wrong.

"We don't know that yet. Look, I've got to get back to work. Call as soon as you find out about Kevelyn."

"Will do."

I let Nate know that my mother was "on the trail" and that if anyone could find out about the woman, she would. Then I remembered I had told Marshall I'd contact Shirley about that miniature I tripped over. I placed the call right then and there so I wouldn't forget.

Shirley's voice was its usual pleasant one. "Hmm, sorry, Phee. Sun City West doesn't have a miniature club, but wait a minute—Cecilia's church is making a big display with miniatures for Christmas. Maybe she'll know something. Oh! Another call's coming in. It's your mother."

And before I could say another word, she said goodbye and took my mother's call. At least I was assured of one thing—my mother would be a regular bloodhound tracking down Kevelyn.

Next, I phoned Cecilia, who told me she'd check the list of the women in her church and see if any of them, or their spouses, belong to the auto restoration club.

"This is the most exciting thing I've done in ages, Phee. Just like Sherlock Holmes."

"Uh, I wouldn't go quite that far, but yeah, it would narrow things down on the off chance that the miniature I found was made by the person who put the cryptic one in that museum display."

Finally, with all my calls made, I focused on the quarterly taxes. A short time later, my mother called.

"You'll be happy to know that the antiquated phone tree paid off. Good thing we put Gloria Wong on it because she's the one who knew who Kevelyn was."

"Go on."

"Kevelyn and her husband are transplants from Scottsdale. Must have gotten too expensive there. Gloria said the husband used to collect classic cars but downsized when they moved here. Thor was in the same dog training class as their dog, Beamer. Also a Great Dane. That's how she knew who Kevelyn was. Now, if Streetman was a bigger dog, I might have considered training but—"

"Okay, okay. I got it. You've been a terrific help. Thanks, Mom. Talk to you later."

"Is Nate still in his office?" I asked Augusta when I got off the phone.

"In with a new client. They should be done soon. Been there for a good half hour."

"Let me know when he steps out. My mother tracked down Kevelyn Viviani."

"Sometimes I think the two of you should start your own agency."

"Bite your tongue."

By late morning, Bowman had met with Kevelyn and came up with a winner as far as our unknown suspects were concerned. Kevelyn was clearly the mystery person from the paint booth, but she was also the tricolored hair woman from that first day. Boy, talk about dumb luck. He let Nate and Marshall know that he had no reason to suspect her of anything, other than not signing in on the day we all visited the place to see Wayne's car. And, had it not been for the fact that the hose tampering was done with small punctures to the rubber, Kevelyn might have been the one in the hospital and not Aimee.

"Do you think she was the intended victim?" I asked. "Maybe someone knew she was going in there at that time."

"Nope," they replied in unison. Then Marshall spoke. "Remember, she rushed in to use the booth. It wasn't planned. Luella was the one who had signed up. And speaking of which, she still has a deputy posted by her house at night. Ranston said they haven't been too successful figuring out who tampered with those hoses."

"Oh my gosh! The hoses! Same deal with the hoist, right?" I all but jumped up and down. That's got to be the perpetrator's MO. It's easier to puncture a hole in rubber than to do something really complicated or messy. It has to be the same person! And I'm thinking it's a woman. Someone familiar with knitting needles, or crochet needles, or the back of a decorative pin, or maybe even a tiny shish kabob skewer. A regular homemaker with a penchant for murder."

"And a burning desire to rev up an engine at the same time. If you're right, I'd be cross-referencing sewing clubs with the auto restoration club." Augusta looked directly at Nate. "I'm right, aren't I?"

"It's logical. And it shouldn't be too difficult," he said. "Not as complex as employee lists and backgrounds. Good thing we've got Rolo on it."

"We've also got Cecilia and Shirley."

Augusta and Nate crinkled their noses and Marshall laughed as I continued. "Cecilia's looking into who's in the auto club and working on miniatures for her church. It's a long shot, but I found an identical one in the parking lot by the auto garage. Just like the cryptic doll in the museum's diorama. I'll ask Shirley to compare names of auto club members with those sewing groups."

Nate rubbed his neck. "I almost feel as if we should be compensating both of them for their time."

"Trust me, they *are* being compensated. Cecilia thinks she's the next Sherlock Holmes and Shirley won't be far behind. Plus, they're really motivated to catch a killer. Lots of bragging rights."

"Only in Sun City West." Augusta popped a cookie into her mouth and smiled as she chewed it.

"If we can't catch a killer, maybe we'll have better luck with a thief." Nate took a step toward Augusta's desk and she held out the cookies for him. "Tonight's the night," he said. "The shipping company works with a strict deadline for shipments so we expect to nail our perpetrator as soon as the day shift ends."

I gave Marshall a nudge and smiled. “I’ll have leftovers from the freezer for when you get home. And don’t worry, it’s not like my mother’s freezer. I don’t have stuff from the Ice Age.”

“Uh, Nate and I will grab a burger. Don’t defrost anything.”

Augusta smirked. “You see, you *are* turning into your mother, after all.”

“Not funny! I track things down orderly and sequentially. In fact—Oh my gosh! Oh no! I completely forgot!”

“Forgot what?” everyone asked at once.

“I was supposed to call Imitra from the bird club and get that eagles’ nest video. With the theft of Wayne’s car last night and everything else, I completely forgot. I’ve got to call her right now!”

With that, I scampered back to my office and rooted around for Imitra’s number. I wound up with voicemail and left her an apologetic message asking her to please call me. Aargah! It was as if everything spiraled around me and I struggled to keep things in balance. Even the Flying Karamazov Brothers had their limits.

CHAPTER 33

I knew my mother's yenta-ing would eventually pay off, but Lyndy was also on the case regarding the mystery woman. Only now, I had a name and location. So as not to interrupt her at work—heaven forbid someone's medical billing would get fouled up—I sent her a quick text. A half hour later, she texted back: *On it. Called my aunt. Her snoop circle should be able to find out something. Later.* It was followed by a happy emoji.

Given the phone activity in the outer office and the entrance door opening and closing, I knew Augusta hadn't slowed down. To clear my head, I walked to the deli and brought us back a late lunch, since the guys had left on other business. Finally, at a little past two, Imitra returned my call.

"I'm on my way to a high tea at the Spicery in historic Glendale," she said amid a background of chips and chirps. "Last-minute invitation. Anyway, I have to pass your office and I'll be happy to drop off the video for you."

Finally! Something in my favor. I thanked her and told her how appreciative I was.

"No worries, Phee. None of us need a killer or saboteur on the loose."

Then, another stroke of luck. Lyndy called back.

"You won't believe this! Not in a million years. My aunt's neighbor knows Kevelyn. According to the neighbor, she and her husband were quite the car aficionados in Scottsdale."

"Yeah, I knew that much from Gloria Wong, whose dog was in the same basic training as Thor. Don't ask."

"Okay, but did Gloria know that they lost most of their investments in a Ponzi scheme that went wrong? It was big news a number of years ago. I'll see if I can find out more."

"See if there's any relation or mention of Betsy Sprig, will you? Maybe we'll come across a connection."

"Or a motive for murder?"

"That, too."

"You *do* realize that if we track down her killer, the ones who'll get the credit are Bowman and Ranston."

"They always do. They could be in Manitoba and still get the credit."

"Oh brother."

The looming cloud that hung over me dissipated when I got off the phone. At last our cases weren't stagnating. I figured Nate, Marshall and the deputies would catch the doll thief and I'd be able to zero in on who murdered Betsy. Too bad my bubble of optimism was about to burst without notice.

Imitra arrived at our office at a little past three and handed me the flash drive of the eagles' nest. "This goes back a few weeks," she said, "so you'll have to fast-forward to get to the date and time in question. I'm not sure how to do that. However, you may enjoy watching the daily activities of the eagles as they prepare to nest."

Worse than my mother's videos of Streetman playing with Essie.

"Thank you. I really wish I had the time, but I've got to find out who went in and out of the garage about the time Aimee Turk was asphyxiated."

"I understand. I really hope this helps you. Anyway, I've got to run. They're serving Queen Elizabeth Tea today and I don't want to miss it."

I walked her to the door and thanked her again. Augusta glanced our way, and as soon as Imitra was a few yards away, she said, "Queen Elizabeth Tea, huh? Got to add it to my bucket list."

"Really?"

She shook her head. "Nah. I'd be more likely to be adding royal stout or whiskey."

"This film is going to take me longer than I anticipated, but since Marshall will be tied up tonight, I'll have plenty of time. Meanwhile, I'll scan it for viruses just to play it safe."

By day's end, I was itching to get home and watch the video, even if it meant a snooze-fest. I didn't want to risk missing even the slightest detail since the auto garage was in full view, just past the nest.

"If you hear anything, let me know," I said to Augusta as she closed and locked the door behind us.

"You'll probably hear from your husband first, but sure, if Mr. Williams contacts me, I'll let you know."

"Same here. I'm keeping my fingers crossed they'll be able to nail that thief tonight and the museum will be able to recover its creepy doll."

"Um, not to get your hopes up, but they'll be able to prove theft of the *setup* doll. Not the original. They'll have to get the perpetrator to confess."

"I know. But Williams Investigations can be quite persistent."

"Worst-case scenario, have your mother sic that dog on them."

"More like pee on the person, but sure."

When I got home, I changed into sweats, grabbed a yogurt with granola, and with a full cup of coffee, sat at my computer to watch the eagles' nest. The video dated back to when the birds first made their nest and I thought I'd fall asleep in my chair. But then it picked up and I watched the two venues simultaneously. An eagle laying eggs and people going in and out of the auto restoration club garage. Nothing unusual. I had no idea how to check the time or date. Other than bothering Rolo, I resorted to Google, and after browsing a few websites, I found one with directions for determining date, time, and metadata. I chose to forgo the metadata. I had enough to deal with.

After the first hour, I took a short break to give my eyes a rest. No word from Marshall but it was early. Then, back to the video. By now, the female comfortably rested on her eggs, taking short food breaks while the male took over. And nothing of interest at the auto garage. As I continued watching, I realized the female did most of the sitting while the male did most of the food hunting when he wasn't protecting the nest. One thing for sure—I'd either find out who might have tampered with those hoses or become an expert on eagle nesting.

A cup and a half of coffee later, I got a brief text from Marshall: *Still a waiting game.* It was followed by a hug emoji. I returned to the screen and finally got to the date that Aimee succumbed to the toxins in the booth. Now I had to pay close attention to who would walk in and out.

At eight fifty-three a.m., Dave unlocked the door and went inside. Ten minutes later, Jared entered the building. I could have easily fast-forwarded it to the evening when Aimee was discovered passed out on the floor of the paint booth, but the culprit most likely punctured those hoses way before that time. Grabbing a pen, I jotted down every person I saw on that tape, including the time they went in and the time they exited.

Dave (monitor): 8:53–noon, 6:00–(n/a deputies arrived)
Mike (monitor): noon–6:00
Jared: 9:03–10:42
Luella: 11:15–1:00
Darleen: 12:56–2:40
Jared: 3:16–4:44
Wayne: 3:24–6:10
Bill: 3:30–5:00
Kevin: 3:30–5:00
Herb: 3:30–5:00
Unidentified male * identity later discovered, Irvin Feldstein: 5:10–5:55
Unidentified male * identity later discovered, Harvey Lankmeyer: 5:10–5:55
Kevelyn: 6:15–6:35
Aimee: 6:48–8:16 when taken out by gurney

I surmised Mike had a six-hour shift from midday to six and Dave worked both ends of it. True to her word, Kevelyn was in and out of the place. Only twenty minutes. No other club members showed up that day. That meant whoever sabotaged the paint booth had to be someone on my list. I immediately crossed off Wayne, Bill, Kevin and Herb as well as Aimee, Luella and Kevelyn. Aimee was the victim, Luella was most likely the intended victim, and Kevelyn was the person who noted something "iffy" in the paint booth and notified the rec center. That left six possible offenders, two of whom I didn't recognize. At least it was a start.

The voice in the back of my head told me I needed to share this with Bowman and Ranston, but I wanted to savor the moment a bit longer before shooting off a text to them. Besides, they were knee-deep catching a doll thief, and knowing how linear both of them worked, why add to the confusion just yet?

Instead, I used my cell phone camera and took a few screen shots of the two men I couldn't identify. Then, I texted it to the B4M book club as well as Herb's cronies. Someone was bound to know. And someone was bound to tell Louise since she didn't text.

Sure enough, five answers came within minutes.

"Harvey Something or Other"

"Irvin or Irving. Not sure of last name."

"Arvin Feldstein."

"Harvey, last name starts with an *L*."

I must have rolled my eyes at least half a dozen times. Then I remembered that Marshall had a list of the auto restoration club members and I went to get it. Easy enough. There was only one Harvey. Harvey Lankmeyer. And the other name was Irvin Feldstein. Then it dawned on me. The night that Holt conducted the meeting to inform everyone of Betsy's death, those two men volunteered their own garages for work on cars since the auto garage was cordoned off.

With two new players in the mix, I called Lyndy and we agreed to check out their social media, if any, as well as the usual rumormongering from my mother's friends and anyone her aunt came in contact with. Since time was of the essence, we didn't have a moment to spare.

At least it kept me occupied while I waited to hear from Marshall. I envisioned a quick and tidy response to their "sting," but so much for quick and tidy.

Chapter 34

It was almost eleven and my eyes were blurred over from staring at the computer screen. First to see if I could find out anything from social media on Harvey or Irvin, and then to move to local news since neither of the men had any social media whatsoever.

Lamentably, the only information I found was from the Sun City West club news in the local papers, and that was in the form of photos with both men showing off their vintage cars at a show last year. Talk about a snooze-fest. At least I had the other option working in my favor—the gossip chain. Lyndy agreed to call her aunt in the morning, and I'd do the same with my mother.

Still no further news from Marshall. Whoever was behind the package swapping took their sweet time. I put my cell phone on the nightstand by our bed and turned in. No sense falling asleep at my desk, or worse yet, trying to stay awake, only to become a zombie at work in the morning.

As I pulled the drawstring to the bedside lamp, another text from Marshall came in, preceded by an angry emoji. It read: *We've been played. No visible action but lots of treks to the women's room by quite a few workers. I'm thinking the action's going on in there but nothing we can do.*

Against my better judgment, I texted back: *Am wide awake. Can be at that facility and check out ladies' room if you can get me in. And don't say it's dangerous. It's a ladies' room. Not an arms bunker.*

Next text: *Is this Phee or Harriet?*

Then, before he could text back, I added: *Might not be a bad idea if she came. Distractions always work.*

I knew they were desperate because he responded in two words: *Do it.*

Less than an hour later, my mother and I pulled up to the shipping office in Surprise. Well, my mother, me, and Shirley because my mom didn't want to leave Streetman and Essie home alone. And even though Shirley offered to babysit at this beyond-late hour, my mother insisted they come along for a ride. Both of them in the small, shared pet tote.

"Shirley will be our backup in the car in case something goes wrong," my mother said.

"We're not making an arrest. We're not law enforcement. We're simply going to find out what may be going on in the restroom. After all, what better place to pull off a packaging switch? Especially in those large handicapped-accessible rooms."

The shipping facility resembled a mini-version of the huge Amazon warehouses that are always featured on TV. Separate counter area with a night receptionist, and behind him, a large area with conveyer belts and packages as well as a small forklift. I could see at least a dozen people working under those miserable fluorescent lights.

Marshall stepped out of a room to the left of the counter and motioned my mother and me inside. Nate, along with Bowman and Ranston, was seated in front of a large computer monitor watching different screens of the workers. With them was the company manager. After a few hellos, Nate said, “Rolo’s at the other end of this.” His comment was followed by Bowman, who looked at my mother and crinkled his nose at her bag. “Please tell me Cujo isn’t in there.”

“He’s not,” I replied, before my mother could answer. “So, what is it you want us to do?”

“It’s simple, really. Phee, you go into the stall next to the handicapped one and keep an eye out for anyone who goes in with packaging materials. Or unusual bulk, as if they stuffed something under their clothes. Then again, it was a small package. Anyway, you should be able to see enough from the side slits once you’re in place. If not, improvise. But be careful.” Nate kept his voice low.

“And my mom?”

“Harriet should hang out by the sinks. Fiddle with her hair or makeup if anyone comes in and watch what they do. If they go into a handicapped stall, knock on the one Phee is in and pretend it’s free. Then go inside and see if you can get a peek too. See if anything is getting repacked.”

“Then what? “I asked.

“Use your camera and try to get a photo so we can identify the culprit. But text us first.”

“Got it.”

“Be sure to walk in separately,” Marshall said. “And thanks, both of you. This most likely is our last chance to pull this off.”

“What about the men’s room? What if it’s a guy?”

“I’m already on it,” Nate said. “It’s anyone’s guess at this point.”

I took a breath and had the night manager direct me to the ladies’ room. He had already informed the receptionist to buzz me inside the working part of the facility. Soft music played in the background, and other than some indiscernible chatter from the workers, it was relatively quiet.

So quiet, in fact, that I heard my footsteps on the tile as I made my way to the restrooms. A few minutes later, my mother and I were both in place.

“This is just like a scene I remember from *Rizzoli and Isles*,” my mother whispered.

“Shh! Don’t talk.”

“All I said was *Rizzoli and Isles.* Besides, we’re the only ones in here.”

“Again, *shh!* Anyone could walk in.”

Refraining from speaking is not a trait my mother, or anyone in my immediate family, was familiar with. I kept having to shush my mother until, at long last, the door to the ladies' room opened and Shirley, of all people, walked in.

"Shirley! What happened? What are you doing in here? Where are my fur babies?"

I opened my stall a crack and whispered for both of them to keep their voices down.

"Lordy, Harriet, I had to use the ladies' room. Give me a second. Streetman and Essie are in their stroller and are being watched by the nice man at the counter."

With that, Shirley went into the front stall and I held my forefinger up to my mouth. My mother nodded and I closed the stall door. With any luck, Shirley would exit and whoever was behind the doll theft would make an appearance. So much for pipe dreams.

Two seconds later, we heard someone yell from the main work area, "There's a dog on the conveyer belt. I'm shutting down the operation!"

The next scream came from my mother. "My Streetman! It's got to be my Streetman!"

Yep. No doubt in my mind.

As if it was well-rehearsed, my mother, Shirley and I raced out of the ladies' room in perfect synchronization as we charged into the huge warehouse packaging room. Sure enough, the "Prince of Chaos" sat bolt upright on the conveyer belt, scanning the room as if he was getting tired of waiting for the machine to start up again.

My mother raced toward him and in that neurotic dog mind of his, he must have thought it was a game. He jumped off the conveyer belt and ran across the room in the opposite direction from my mother.

The employees, in an effort to corral him, ran as well, making it even more exciting for Streetman. He ducked under counters, toppled over boxes, and at one point, which I'd like to forget, lifted his leg and peed on a trash can.

"At least the cat didn't escape," someone announced.

It was followed by another comment, "Are we shipping animals now?"

Suddenly my phone vibrated and it was a text from Marshall: *Man at front desk said dog chewed his way out of the meshing. The cat is in another compartment and sleeping. Once we catch Streetman, it's back to the original plan. Hang tight.*

"Hang tight?" More like pray for a miracle.

As the hamster-wheel chase around the facility continued, something hit me. Now would be the perfect time for the perpetrator to repack the new priceless relic, aka the Nantucket Doll with rare gems for eyes.

I spun around and hightailed it for the ladies' room once again, certain I was right. That snippy little chiweenie provided the perfect distraction for the culprit to get on with business. Too bad he wasn't working on our side.

Back in my cramped, uncomfortable stall, I waited for someone to make an appearance. Outside the room, I could still hear voices as well as pounding footsteps on the tile floor. I surmised Streetman was still on the run.

And then, I heard a woman's voice right outside the door. "Let go of my bag, you little scoundrel! Let go!"

It could have only been one "little scoundrel." My mother's! I was tempted to race out of there and nab the dog but I held back. Augusta would later tell me it was my sixth sense working overtime, but the truth was, I had wedged myself between the toilet and the toilet tissue dispenser and it was too much of an effort to move quickly.

Instead, I kept my eyes glued to the sink, fingers crossed the woman would be my long-awaited thief. Sure enough, the door swung open and in she walked, a hair-wrap covering most of her brownish red curls. She placed her large bag on the sink with Streetman at her legs still pulling on the bag's long straps.

Good grief, that dog is such a nuisance. He's going to ruin everything.

Outside the restroom, I could still hear voices.

"Where'd that dog go?"

"He was under the forklift a minute ago!"

"Behind the water cooler."

Apparently no one knew that Streetman followed a woman into the restroom. But why follow her? The dog *was* strange, I'll admit that much, and he did have a tendency to attach himself to certain objects, but her bag? Unless . . .

A few seconds later, the woman removed a wrapped object from her bag and Streetman went wild jumping and whining. I squinted for a better look and recognized the deli wrapping Augusta used when she ran out of paper.

Roast beef! He smells the roast beef! This is it! We've got our thief! I immediately shot off a text to Nate and held my breath.

Please don't let my mother storm in here. Please don't let my mother storm in here.

He texted back: *Stay where you are.*

Too late! Everything happened at once! My mother and Shirley charged through the door in an effort to nab the dog, causing the woman to grab everything and flee from the place as if it was on fire. By that time, I'd extricated myself from the stall and watched in semi-disbelief as Streetman went berserk.

Clearly, in that canine mind of his, there was no way he'd give up what he thought was roast beef. In a nanosecond, he was at the woman's heels, barking and pawing as she made her way across the large packaging facility, my mother and Shirley in fast pursuit, only this time joined by Nate, Marshall, the deputies and an endless number of employees. It was a circus gone awry.

And then, just as the woman was inches from a side door, Streetman pulled on her pant leg and she stumbled, causing a tower of empty boxes to scatter all over the place, along with rolls of packing tape that had now become major tripping hazards.

As everyone fumbled to reach her, she disappeared through the dark parking lot, and by the time the men were out the door, it was too late. She was gone.

"What's that dog eating?" my mother asked, more concerned about Streetman's latest find than our miserable failure to catch a thief.

I looked at the parking lot, where Streetman was obviously chewing on something. "Probably the roast beef packing paper Augusta used."

My mother charged toward him. "Nope, it's a—Oh my gosh—he found a dead thing!"

I ambled over, expecting to remove the contents of his find from his mouth. "Mom! It's not a dead thing. Look! It's a wig. A brownish red wig. When that woman tripped, it must have fallen off, along with the scarf she had on because that's also in your dog's mouth."

Then, before she could say a word, I continued, "Don't touch it. It's DNA evidence. Maybe this won't be a failure after all."

"Lordy, it will if Streetman doesn't give it up," Shirley said.

Next thing I knew, Bowman's voice boomed from behind me, "Ranston—grab an evidence bag!"

CHAPTER 35

Nate and Marshall checked the outside surveillance video of the parking lot, but whoever that woman was, her car wasn't visible.

"It's not a total loss," Marshall said as my mother, Shirley and I headed to my car.

"No, Streetman had a field day." I shot my mother a look and she shrugged. Her voice was as nonchalant as ever. "This is at least the fourth time I've had to get the meshing replaced on that carrying tote."

"Maybe that should tell you something."

"Yes. They don't make things like they used to."

Marshall made sure we were all safely inside the car before leaning over to give me a kiss. "Drive safe. I'll be back soon."

"You, too."

Thankfully, he got in the door about forty-five minutes later, exhausted but not defeated. "That wig was a mix of blond, brown and red colors. You know who else has that color hair, don't you? Kevelyn. Tomorrow we're going to have a nice little chat with her. Maybe we won't need the DNA evidence after all."

"See if you spot a bruise on one of her hands. Streetman jumped up and sort of nailed her. No blood, but it might be black and blue."

"Not exactly incriminating, unless we're talking Streetman, but yeah, it's a conversation starter for sure."

Both of us dragged ourselves to bed and didn't stir until morning. Then it was the usual race to the office and waiting game to find the results from the wig DNA. In between my usual spreadsheets and tax preparation, I revisited my list of comings and goings from the day Aimee was asphyxiated. Mired in work, I hardly noticed the time.

A strange and unsettling thought entered my mind. If the sign-in sheet was accurate, then someone had to be lying and I was pretty sure who that was. Then another disturbing thought hit me when I checked the time sheet again—the saboteur would have known who would have seen them at the time in question. And that "who" was Wayne.

"Augusta," I called out, "I need to run something by you."

I pushed my chair back and walked into the main office. Augusta was fixated on something on her computer and lifted her tortoiseshell glasses when I approached her desk. "I think I may know who's responsible for puncturing the hoses in the paint booth," I told her. "And I'm afraid Wayne may know as well, but he doesn't realize it. Most likely, he crossed paths with the culprit and now I'm worried that he may be in danger."

"Whoa! Pull in those reins and get to the point. It's almost lunchtime. Don't want to die of starvation while I wait for you to spit it out."

"Fine. Here's my thought. Luella was the intended victim. Not Aimee. Aimee simply barged in and used the paint booth, but it was Luella who scheduled it. Meanwhile, Kevelyn went in because no one else was using it and she reported to the rec center that there was a suspicious odor. I think she was the one who punctured the hoses and feigned her own 'near miss' with the fumes. She could have told the monitor or left a note, but she didn't. Why? Because she had to make sure the next person in the booth would succumb to the fumes."

"Hmm, you may be on to something."

"I know I am. According to what I found out, the punctures were enough to release the toxins but not right away. They wouldn't have posed a danger to Kevelyn if she got out of there fast, but they certainly would have for the next person in. In this case, Aimee."

"So Kevelyn creates her story and no one is the wiser."

"Not unless they analyze the sign-in sheets. And she covered herself this time. Not like that first day when she didn't sign in and no one knew who she was. This time she signed in but with unrecognizable writing. But at least she could later say she had an alibi."

"Honestly, Phee, you should be putting a plaque on your door."

"No way! Besides, it's only speculation on my part. Not until I can prove something. Oh my gosh! I'm bouncing up and down to tell Nate and Marshall."

Then, as if Wayne could read my mind, he called our office and Augusta handed me the phone. "Must be your lucky day. It's Wayne."

I held my hand over the receiver. "Please don't tell me someone tried to go after him."

Augusta clenched her teeth and shrugged as I said hello to Wayne.

"It's me. Wayne." I rolled my eyes and he continued. "I wanted to let you know that I checked and Holt had nothing to do with the Phoenix Art Museum as far as anyone knew. But get this—rumor has it he was fired for, hmm . . . now, what was it? Oh yeah. Fiddling with the books from his auditor job."

"Yeah, I heard that, too. Not sure if it has anything to do with Betsy or Aimee. Anyway, there's something you ought to know. And don't tell my mother or Herb. Or anyone, for that matter. Okay?"

"Fine. What is it?"

"I have reason to believe you may be in danger. Remember the day when Aimee lost consciousness in the paint booth? Well, you were there when it all went down and I think you might have even locked eyes with the culprit only you didn't realize it."

"Who? What culprit?"

"Kevelyn Viviani."

"Kev? That doesn't make sense."

"Did you just call her Kev?"

"Yeah, why? Don't tell me it's one of those socially incorrect things to say. I never know what to call people these days."

"Uh, nothing." *Yet.*

"What about my being in danger?"

"I think Kevelyn was the one who punctured the hoses in the paint booth and pretended she was a victim, too. But you would have seen her bounce out of there as if nothing happened. It takes a while for fumes to escape from small hose punctures. If she's as diabolical as I think she is, you should be on guard."

"On guard? I should call those deputies!"

"No, not right now. It's conjecture on my part."

"What? Trying to kill Aimee?"

"Like I said, it's conjecture. But be on your toes, that's all. And don't work on your car alone."

"Don't worry. I've got help. Aimee's been a lifesaver. Doing all sorts of things to get Sally Stang a great price."

"Remember, not a word. Especially where Herb is concerned."

Augusta took the receiver back and looked up. "Sounds like he's still vertical."

"Vertical but who knows for how long? I honestly think Kevelyn is our culprit as far as Aimee and Betsy are concerned. Now, even more so. There was a note my mother found in the pocket of Betsy's overalls that read, 'Call Kev re: shipping date, move time up.' I thought it was for someone named Kevin. Now I realize it meant Kevelyn, not Kevin. And time up for what? And why would Kevelyn murder Betsy and go after Luella?"

"Money, revenge, jealousy, blackmail. Pick one."

"Marshall said he and Nate were going to speak with her this morning. Kevelyn's hair color matches the wig Streetman sunk his teeth into. The men think maybe it's a wig Kevelyn's been wearing. Plus, she said she worked part-time for a distribution company or something like it. Kind of fits the bill so they're checking."

"And what are those deputies doing in the meantime?"

"What do they always do? Delegate it to Williams Investigations."

"Could be a double whammy, Phee. Kevelyn turns out to be the doll thief and the murderess. Of course, getting that to stick is a whole different story."

"Yeah, we're probably getting way ahead of ourselves. What time did Nate say they'd be back?"

"He didn't."

"Well, I've got my own work to do so I'd better get at it while I can."

"Huh?"

"I don't know. I just have a feeling something's about to get in the way."

"Can't blame you. It always does."

Marshall got in about an hour later while Nate went back to the museum to follow up on that miniature from the diorama. In the interim, three walk-ins set up appointments for what Augusta deemed "minor investigations."

I could hear him chatting to Augusta so I stepped out of my office.

"Good news, bad news, hon," he said. "Kevelyn *does* work part-time at that facility but said she got off work two hours before we arrived. I checked and her time sheet said as much. Asked her if she knew anyone at work whose wig resembled her hair and she said no. Said most of the workers are men who wear baseball caps to cover up their bald heads."

I tried not to laugh as he continued.

"We had the manager go through the employee list and match it to the workers who were there and it seems like we were duped. Whoever it was snuck in there or worked in tandem with someone. We are now back to where we started."

"Maybe the DNA will tell a different story." I then expounded on my theory about Kevelyn feigning her toxic fume encounter so she could go after Luella.

"That's going to be tough to prove, but it does make sense. Certainly more than anything else has at this point."

I mentioned Betsy's note about Kevelyn and her reminder to move time up. "Did it sound like they were into something together?"

"Way too nebulous. It could have been a lunch date or something equally innocuous. As far as shipping goes, that could have been anything, too. Face it, we've got to go by hard evidence and right now all we've got are a wig, a scarf, and a miniature." He squeezed my shoulder and winked. "Don't worry, we've worked with less. Besides, Nate may pull up more from the museum."

And while Nate "pulled it up," it was Rolo who put the final yank in place.

CHAPTER 36

Finally! Friday came around and good news wafted our way. Well, at least it seemed as though it did when Nate breezed through the door an hour or so later. His voice was chipper and faster than usual. "May have gotten a break today," I heard him say to Augusta through my open door. I immediately stepped out.

"What kind of break?"

"When the museum gave us the employee list, it was the abbreviated copy. First name, last name. I sent it to Rolo for further scrutiny and guess what?"

"What?" Augusta and I asked at once.

"Seems they had a night security employee by the name of Darleen Turk Westly four years ago. Her name appeared as Dar Westly so it got passed over."

Augusta sat up straight and moved closer to the edge of her desk. "One of the Turk sisters, I presume? And don't those night security workers have keys to everything?"

Nate nodded. "Appears that way. Of course, that doesn't necessarily spell theft, but it sure spells coincidence. And that's not all. Bowman and Ranston got the lab report back on the miniature Phee found in the parking lot. The forensics techs compared it with the one from the diorama and they were carved from the same wood."

"Isn't wood, wood, Mr. Williams?" Augusta had moved so close to the edge of her desk, I thought she'd fall forward.

"Not the *type* of wood, the exact *piece* of wood. Both miniatures came from the same log, or slab, or whatever you call it. Easy to infer that the same person carved both of them."

"Oh my gosh!" I tapped my foot without realizing it until Augusta pointed to the floor. "That means someone who was in or around the auto restoration garage also made an appearance at the museum."

"Not an appearance. A calculated act. We've still got a long way to go on this, but—cripes—What are the odds that the museum theft is connected to the auto restoration garage? One in a zillion?"

"Can't say I'm surprised, Mr. Williams." Augusta moved back to her usual spot at the desk and glanced at her computer screen.

Nate chuckled. "Me either. Marshall called Darleen and they're meeting at the auto garage. It was either that or the posse office."

Against my better judgment, I let my mother know what was going on and she, in turn, promised to "light a fire" under Cecilia to find out if anyone who made miniatures for her church was connected to the auto garage. Good. I was off the hook for now. Or so I thought.

Two hours later, my mother called back.

"We're going to regroup at Bagels 'n More tomorrow morning. The tide is turning. The ship is coming to shore. The—"

"For goodness sakes, Mom. I don't know what book your club is reading now, but enough with the cliches. And what do you mean by 'regroup'?"

"The buy-sell-trade event is coming up soon and the auto restoration club needs to get past those disturbing events."

Or closer to Jay Leno?

"You mean *murder* and attempted *murder*?"

"I was trying to be euphemistic. Anyway, the book club ladies will be meeting to take an inventory of where we are with our unofficial investigation."

"What about the men?" *Please don't tell me they're coming, too.*

"It's only us women. We can't get anything done with them around. They have absolutely no concentration. None whatsoever. And if a good-looking waitress walks by, Herb is useless for at least a half hour."

"What do you hope to accomplish? Other than gossip and whine."

"Don't be snarky. We need to see what steps we should take next."

"You're not the detectives. And neither am I."

"No, we have a vested interest. Truly vested."

"Vested as in being seen with a celebrity?"

"That, too. Face it, no senior community wants a killer running loose. We aren't as quick or agile as we once were."

"No, but you're smart and clever. That counts for something. Have fun tomorrow with your 'regroup.'"

"Oh, I thought you'd be joining us. I was counting on it. We all were."

Just then, I heard Marshall's voice and cut to the quick with my call. "I'll talk to you later, Mom. Got to run." With that, I ended the call and walked out of my office and stood in front of Marshall, blocking his way to the coffee maker. "Hey there! Nate said you followed up on that lead with Darleen. Any luck? Augusta and I are chomping at the bit to find out."

"Phee's the one who's chomping. I always take things in stride." Augusta fluffed her hair and sat straight up.

Marshall chuckled. "Darleen was elusive, let's put it that way. But she didn't argue the fact that she did work at the museum while she was still married to some 'nitwit.'"

"What's your take on it?" I asked.

"She's holding back. That's where Rolo will come in. Whatever she's hiding, he'll dig it up."

"Better hope it's not a body." Augusta continued fluffing her hair.

"I'm hoping these mismatched puzzle pieces come together. Luella was the intended paint booth victim and Kevelyn was most likely the perpetrator, even if she wasn't the woman in the wig from the other night. But as far as anyone knows, there's no connection between those women and the museum. Unless Darleen fits into the mix, and that's something we don't know yet."

"I'm banking on Rolo and that dark web of his. Mainly because I don't want to wind up coaxing information from Cindy Dolton in the dog park again. Streetman's done enough damage as far as I'm concerned."

"I don't think your mother sees it quite that way, hon."

"Did the deputies mention their next move?" Augusta asked.

"They're looking into more details regarding those mechanical instructions that were found under the dead cat in Betsy's yard. Lots of legwork. Should keep them occupied for a while."

I walked to the Keurig and plopped in a K-Cup. "Too bad their safe-hunting expedition with Betsy's ex didn't work out."

"I'm sure they'll come up with other leads. Meantime, I've got to get started on some of our smaller cases, as well as some further interviews with Jared and Holt. One of them might be able to identify a link between Darleen, Luella, and Betsy. Other than the obvious auto restoration club."

"What about Aimee? According to Wayne, she's been quite the Girl Scout."

"Not sure if Darleen will agree. For sisters, they're not on the best terms."

"That's why I'm glad I was an only child," Augusta announced. "Of course, I had to deal with a passel of nincompoop cousins, but at least they went home at the end of the day."

Marshall all but choked. "Good to know. Thanks for sharing."

With a full load of work at my desk, I completely forgot about calling my mother back. Unfortunately, she didn't. She left one message with Augusta while I went out to get us lunch, and another on my cell phone. Both imploring me to attend the "regroup" at Bagels 'n More in the morning.

"That regroup will be more like *re*-gurgitate once I get there," I said to Augusta. "*If* I get there."

"Can't say I blame you, but you always manage to eke out information from those brunches. Besides, who can pass up their apple cinnamon bagels or their double chocolate chip ones?"

"Ugh, I suppose you're right. But do me a favor. Call or text me so I can make an excuse to leave."

"Coward!"

"It's self-preservation."

• • •

The next morning, I found myself once again at Bagels 'n More with my mother's book club. Surprisingly, even my aunt Ina made it because Uncle Louis was sleeping in after a late-night gig in Fountain Hills.

Myrna and Louise studied the well-worn menu while Cecilia used the paper napkins to clean/polish her silverware. First by dipping an end of it into her water glass, and then rubbing the daylights out of the utensils. Meanwhile, my mother and Shirley looked at photos of Streetman and Essie, leaving me to chitchat with Lucinda and my aunt.

Finally, my mother looked up from her cell phone and announced, "Once we place our orders, we'll need to get down to serious business. I take it none of us was able to find anything of importance while we tagged along with the men at the garage."

"I found out Bill turns his socks inside out so he doesn't have to wash them right away," Lucinda said.

I cringed and did a mental eye roll.

Undaunted, my mother kept going. "I suppose it wouldn't be such a bad idea to expound on what we already know."

"What do we know, Harriet?" Myrna asked. "Other than someone tried to murder Aimee, someone did murder Betsy, and someone planted something under a dead cat in Betsy's yard. Probably Betsy."

"We know that Luella was the intended paint booth victim and that Kevelyn most likely staged her own bout with toxic fumes to pull it off, only it was Aimee she nailed, not Luella." Then my mother looked at me. "I hope that was all right telling everyone, Phee. I know you said to keep it between ourselves but honestly, how are we going to get anywhere if everyone is kept in the dark. We're not mushrooms."

"Please," I said, "keep this among yourselves." *In what world?*

In that instant, an obnoxious voice bellowed across the room. "Hey! Harriet! Myrna! Phee! And everyone! Mind if I join you? I've been fishing since five and I'm starved."

Paul shoved Myrna aside, grabbed a chair from the table behind us and wedged it in between Myrna and Cecilia. Cecilia immediately moved her chair as far to the right as possible, nearly colliding with my aunt.

"We were hoping to hold a book club meeting," my mother said, but Paul didn't get the hint.

"I suggest the *New York Times* bestseller *Four Fish*, by Paul Greenberg. Talk about how those slippery buggers are moving our economy. Go figure."

"Maybe another time."

Just then, the waitress appeared and the next six or seven tortuous minutes were spent listening to everyone order. Paul must have forgotten about his fish book because he launched into another topic—Wayne's threatening note.

"Did you ladies hear about the apology Wayne got from Harvey Lankmeyer? He told us last night at Curley's."

"What apology?" Cecilia now started wiping the edge of her water glass with the same napkin.

"Seems Harvey was the one who left that note for Wayne about wanting him to confess so they could get back to work in the auto restoration garage."

"Why? Why would he do something like that?" I asked.

"Because Harvey's wife nagged the daylights out of him to get the men and their automobile oil and grease out of her tandem garage. Apparently, she wanted to use the tandem space for her crafts projects."

"Did Harvey admit this to the deputies?"

"According to Wayne, he was really sorry and said he'd make a full confession. Also offered to help Wayne with his car but Wayne already has Aimee working so he told Harvey no go. Hey, excuse me for a minute, will you? Got to use the men's room."

Paul tromped off, and when he was a few yards away my mother motioned everyone closer. "We can't very well discuss our next move with the 'Voice of the Valley' sitting here. Let's reconvene at my house once we've eaten."

"I have a better idea," my aunt said. "We tell Paul that we have it on good authority that Betsy's murder and the infamous doll are connected."

"Um, they might very well be," I said.

My aunt waved me off. "I'm getting to that. We tell him a psychic was hired and the doll can conjure evil spirits to whoever is in possession of it. Unless it is stored in a leaded or steel and concrete-reinforced vault or a reasonable facsimile. We all know Paul won't be able to keep his mouth shut. Plus, his fishing show will be on the air Monday morning. Dollars to donuts, he blabs it over the airwaves, thus compelling the actual thief and murderer to run to the nearest bank and get a safe deposit box."

And all this time I thought my mother was the sister with the vivid imagination.

"Aunt Ina, that person may already have a safe deposit box."

"I already thought of that. We tell Paul that the doll must be covered in dried thyme and sage. So, that means the culprit will be heading to the bank one way or another. Depositing the doll or covering it in herbs."

"Ina, you're a genius!" Myrna said. "An absolute genius. There are only a handful of banks in Sun City West and we can stake them out Monday after Paul's show airs."

Lucinda used the back of her hand to swipe her hair from her face. "You don't think anyone actually believes in that hooey, do you?"

"You'd be surprised," Louise said.

"Lordy, we're going to catch a thief and a murderer!" Shirley clapped her hands together. "I never thought I'd live to see a day like that."

Me either. I felt the stomach acid make its way up my esophagus. "I'm not so sure this is the best—"

But before I could finish, Paul approached the table and got an earful from the new "liar's club."

CHAPTER 37

My stomach was in knots the entire drive home. I envisioned pairs of book club ladies stalking bank entrances and pouncing on whichever unfortunate person from the auto restoration club entered or exited a bank. Worse yet, I couldn't get that scene from the old Andy Griffith show out of my mind where Gomer Pyle makes a citizen's arrest.

The second I got home, I called my mother and implored her not to do anything rash. "It's bad enough Paul's going to muddy the waters, you and your friends don't need to swim in it," I told her.

She answered, "There's no crime observing people from a parked car."

If only.

I knew I'd never be able to talk them out of it, especially since they all seemed so gung-ho. Well, except for Lucinda. Having little choice, I called the office and Nate picked up.

"How many women and banks?" he asked.

"They haven't quite put it all together. I just left there."

"Okay. Thanks."

"That's it? Aren't you concerned?"

"Actually, I'm flabbergasted. But flabbergasted in a good way. Your mother and those kooky friends of hers may have found a way to speed up this investigation. But I'll need to do a few things first. Enjoy the rest of your day! I know Marshall and I will. And thanks, kiddo."

Stunned didn't even come close to describing my reaction. With little else I could do until Marshall got home, I straightened the house and went food shopping. Then, I prepared the first home-cooked meal I'd made in what seemed like ages—lasagna. To top it off, I got all the fixings for a super salad to go with it, as well as a ready-prepared garlic bread since I already went overboard with the lasagna.

By the time Marshall walked in the door, the pungent aroma of tomato sauce and Italian spices filled the house.

"Did I miss something? Is this a special day?" He inhaled and hugged me.

"We haven't had a home-cooked meal in a while so I thought I'd be a homemaker instead of an amateur sleuth for one day."

"I think your mother took over that sleuth role."

"You know what's scary? Nate liked the idea."

"He was bummed that we didn't think of something similar. He called Rolo, and since Rolo had a list of the auto restoration club members in question, he was able to find out what banks they use. All except one of them does business with the big three—Chase, Bank of America, and Wells

Fargo. Jared's accounts are with BMO."

"If I'm hearing you correctly, you guys are actually going to divulge that info to my mother, who will, in turn, set up her parking lot surveillance accordingly."

"Hey, we're not *that* crazy. Bowman and Ranston are setting it up. They're trying for 'Sting Two' since the first one was such a flop."

"You know this is going to burst my mother's bubble, don't you? Not to mention my aunt Ina, who came up with the idea in the first place."

"Not if we phrase it in a way that gives them and the book club all the credit."

"Now I'm praying Paul will blab about it on the radio. But what if he doesn't?"

"Oh, he will. Trust me. I swung over to the auto garage for a chitchat after the banks closed. In case Paul started sharing the rumor in person."

"And?" I motioned for him to speak faster.

"Jared, Wayne, and Aimee were there and all of them went on and on about some psychic who had a premonition about the doll. I'd say that little tidbit of nonsense will hit the airwaves as soon as Paul picks up the mic on Monday. By the way, do you know what time his show starts?"

"At nine. Thankfully when most people are at work and don't have to listen. Go get comfortable and we'll sit down to a real dinner."

"You don't have to tell me twice."

So many of our meals were interrupted by emergencies, real or otherwise, that I was afraid the same thing would happen with my lasagna. Thankfully, we were spared. At least until the dishes made it to the dishwasher. Then, the long-expected phone call from my mother.

"Your aunt Ina can't stop bragging about her perfect plan to thwart an assassin. Her words. Never mind it's a thief at this point. I suppose you already know what's going on. And again, you should let me know when you know so I don't get blindsided."

If I hear the word "know" one more time, I'll get hives.

"Um, sure. Listen, I imagine Nate told you that our office, along with MCSO, will be handling the situation."

"You mean the surveillance and arrest."

"They can't just stop someone and search them. Not without reasonable cause. Still, I imagine they'll come up with something. At this point, you need to stay out of it."

"The women are going to be devastated. We'll have to console ourselves tomorrow morning at Boyer's Bakery. Cecilia thinks the waitresses at Bagels 'n More need a break from us."

"She's probably right. Oh, and before you ask, Marshall and I will be sleeping in with breakfast at home." *Whether he knows it or not.*

"If anything else happens, call me. Do you want to say good night to Streetman and Essie?"

"Good night! You too, Mom."

"I can only imagine," Marshall said and smiled when I got off the phone.

"I did make it clear to my mother that even if the deputies spy one of those folks bringing in a package to the bank, there's not much they can do. I mean, other than ask them a few generic questions and stall them."

"Intimidation seems to work for Bowman, and annoyance does the same with Ranston, so they might be able to get somewhere."

"Oh, they'll get somewhere, all right. I guarantee my mother and her friends aren't going to let this opportunity slip by. I hate to say it, but I probably should cruise around those banks on Monday and keep an eye out. That is, if the office can spare me."

"It'll be tough, but we'll manage. Besides, you bring half that work home with you all the time."

"That's because I love it. The orderliness, the numbers . . . it's the reasonable part of my day."

Marshall walked over and planted a soft kiss on my forehead. "Let's definitely sleep in tomorrow. Then we'll find a fun breakfast place and let them do all the work."

"As long as it's not in Sun City West or vicinity, I'm all for it."

• • •

My nerves were on high alert come Monday. Even Lyndy told me to keep taking deep breaths and "let the universe unfold" when I spoke to her the night before. It was more like "unravel" to me, but even unravel didn't come close to the debacle I witnessed.

At twenty after eight, I bid Augusta adieu, and with a donut in my hand, drove to the BMO branch on RH Johnson. No Buicks in sight. Went further down the street to Wells Fargo, Bank of America, and finally the Chase Bank branch on the corner of RH Johnson Boulevard and Camino de Sol. So far, nothing.

Drat! I chastised myself for not thinking to get a cup of coffee. The donut was a lead sinker in my stomach and I knew if I didn't wash it down with something, I'd be miserable. Not many options, but there were nearby Starbucks inside the grocery stores. Without wasting any time, I drove to the nearest one. As I pulled out, an MCSO Sheriff's car pulled into the Chase Bank parking lot. I couldn't tell which deputy it was but I'd find out soon enough.

Back ten minutes later with a venti vanilla almond milk cappuccino, I was ready for whatever stunt my mother's entourage would pull. The sheriff's car was parked diagonally across from the walkup ATM and there were only a few other cars in the lot. I chose to park on the other side, but close enough to see if Bowman or Ranston made a move.

After six or seven minutes, I pulled out and perused the other bank parking lots. Bank of America and BMO had posse cars stationed in their lots and Wells Fargo had the other MCSO car. I surmised it would be a long morning. Then, a maroon Buick drove into Chase's lot and I zeroed in.

It had to be Shirley. I watched through the rearview mirror, careful to bend down so as to be nearly inconspicuous. A tall bald man got out of the car and slammed the door shut. False alarm.

The minutes trickled by and I was about to make another loop through the remaining three banks when a gray-haired lady in a golf cart parked alongside of me and stepped out. Her overweight Shih Tzu was sleeping in a comfy dog bed in the passenger seat, oblivious to the world. Unfortunately, that ended abruptly when Gloria Wong, of all people, rounded the building's corner from the ATM machine, with Thor.

Thor immediately spied the Shih Tzu and broke free from Gloria, his retractable leash following him like a curling stone. At the same time, a red-haired woman headed to the side entrance of the bank, carrying a large box.

Before I could open my door and get out, I heard Deputy Bowman yell, "Put the box on the ground and step back!"

Then Gloria screamed, "Is it a bomb?"

The lady with the Shih Tzu spun around to get back inside her golf cart but couldn't because Thor was now in the driver's seat nuzzling the unsuspecting little dog.

The red-haired woman put the box on the ground, put her hands in the air and said, "It's donuts! For a conference meeting!"

No doubt, operation "Sting Two" was not off to a great start. I rubbed my temples and exited the parking lot just as Gloria got ahold of Thor's leash. As for Deputy Bowman and the donut disaster, I figured I'd hear about it later.

My next stop was Wells Fargo. And no surprise there. Since Bowman was at Chase, the other sheriff's deputy had to be Ranston. No action there, but that was short-lived. I saw Myrna's car across from the entrance and thankfully it was Cecilia seated in the passenger seat and not my mother.

I immediately drove to BMO and remained there for fifteen minutes before making a stop at Bank of America. Other than the incident at Chase, the next hour was uneventful. Then, the "universe spun," as Lyndy would say, and for one fleeting second I thought we'd nab the culprit. Then again, how was I to know the universe would be off-kilter?

CHAPTER 38

I should have figured something like this would happen when Paul announced on his radio show that he learned of a major development regarding the "missing museum doll with the soul trapped inside." How this related to fish was anyone's guess, but then again, it was Paul.

As if it was orchestrated, it appeared as if every vehicle within a ten-mile radius suddenly pulled into Bank of America's parking lot. Some with binoculars. Paul must have had lots of morning listeners.

It shouldn't have surprised me when he told listeners that a noted psychic insisted the doll would conjure evil spirits. Then he went ahead to tell them that whoever possessed it would need to conceal the object in a reinforced vault or something similar. Then he made it really obvious by adding, "If that were me, I'd get a safe deposit box at the nearest bank and lock that doll up."

I sipped my remaining cappuccino, now cold, and phoned Augusta after I gave the other banks a swing-through.

"You won't believe this," I said. "I think people want to get a glimpse of whoever may be stashing that doll. Either that or it's a run on the banks. The parking lots are packed to the gills. It's drawing in a bigger and bigger crowd. No way are our guys going to catch the real culprit."

"Mr. Williams already said as much. He called a few minutes before you did. I was about to phone you. The plan is nixed but not DOA."

"What do you mean?"

"At Mr. Williams's suggestion, the deputies met with the bank managers and they'll be notified if anyone opens a new safe deposit box. They'll also get the names of the people who went to their own boxes today."

"It's not the same as nailing them in the act, I suppose, but it's better than nothing. Okay, I'm heading back to the office. Want subs? I'm right across from Subway."

"Sure. Get me the Outlaw with all the toppings."

"You got it."

When I got back to the office, Augusta handed me a fax from Rolo. "Not sure how to interpret this picture, Phee. What do you think?"

"Wow. It's an outdoor Signature Series barbeque with side grills and everything. Marshall and I saw them at the Maricopa County Home Show last year. The cheap models start at four grand. Average cost is seven. And—oh no—we could be looking at the twenty-thousand-dollar model!"

Augusta eyeballed it again and shrugged. "Still not sure."

"Think! Rolo gets paid in kitchen gadgetry. Whatever information he dug up is going to cost our office and MCSO a small fortune. Looks as if we're no longer talking Cuisinart Air Fryers or food processors."

Just then, the fax machine started up and Augusta walked over to retrieve the paper. "Oh, brother. Another one from Rolo. All it says is for Mr. Williams or Mr. Gregory to call him on a burner phone but, and I quote, 'Will take Phee's call if the guys are tied up.'"

"I can only imagine. Where did we put that burner?"

Augusta reached into her top desk drawer and handed me the phone. "This should be good. Better take a piece of paper and a pen. I think you'll need it."

I kept my voice chipper and upbeat. "Hey, Rolo, it's Phee. What's going on? And nice Signature Grill by the way."

"Tell your boss to chill. I'll try to keep expenses down. He's going to want the info I'm giving you so get this on paper."

He better not tell me to chew and swallow it once I read it.

"I'm ready."

"Betsy Sprig is, or *was*, the great-granddaughter of Germaine Webb, the descendent from whence that priceless doll came."

Whence. Must be he's reading a gothic mystery.

"You're saying the doll really belonged to her but was given to the museums before she was born?"

"That's what I just said. Let the guys know that I dug into the family histories of all their auto restoration club members. And their bank accounts."

Ka-ching. Ka-ching.

"There's more. Are you writing this down?"

"Yes." I pressed my fingers to the center of my forehead and took a breath.

"There's a hex on that doll. And here's where it gets interesting."

Not interesting. Expensive.

Rolo continued. "The thief who carved that doll wrote the hex in his last will and testament. I had to track it down through channels I'd rather not mention, but it's sitting somewhere in the National Archives along with other prisoner correspondence dating back to the Civil War."

"What kind of hex? Not that I know about that sort of thing." *And holy cannoli! Paul's fabricated stunt is actually real!*

"The doll needs to be sealed up or buried to prevent the soul inside it from escaping."

"Did the will mention any instructions for the cipher?"

"Nope. Just the hex. Why?"

"Because those mechanical instructions we sent you were found in a box that was buried under another box with a dead cat."

"Maybe whoever dug it didn't want to dig the hole twice when their cat died."

"Not likely. It was the neighbor's cat."

"Ha! And people call me strange. Yeah, those instructions were for a coded locking system. And wood, as well as metal, could have been used. Want my take? Those are the instructions for the doll's cipher. But I wouldn't crack it open any time soon."

"The hex?"

"Hah! No. The chance you'd mess it up."

I told Rolo I'd have Nate or Marshall call him and that I'd be sure to show them the Signature Grill. He ended the call with "Tell them I'm still swimming with the fish in the dark web."

Wonderful. And Paul's swimming with the real ones.

No sooner did I get off the phone with Rolo when Augusta answered the office phone and replied with three words—"I sure will."

"What was that about?" I asked.

That was your husband. Tim Justin, the reporter from channel 10, is on his way over here to speak with him. Told me to tell Mr. Justin that he may be a few minutes late. That's all I know."

"I think I can guess the rest. It has to be an update on that doll theft. Most likely Paul's early morning show set off a firestorm of rumors and channel 10 doesn't want to miss out on the action."

"You're probably right. Hope your husband can spin this one to our advantage."

It was a little after eleven and too early for lunch. I stashed our subs in the fridge and applauded myself for picking up an extra two for Nate and Marshall. I was positive it was going to be one of those days.

No sooner did I delve into the spreadsheets that awaited me when I heard Augusta greet Tim Justin.

"I didn't think the network would want to feature this story, but my producer thought otherwise. His phone line's been off the rails since KSCW aired this morning. Face it, a priceless treasure somewhere in the area with a hex on it to boot? It's a magnet for every treasure hunter, bored housewife, and retiree. Meanwhile, we're sitting on a murder and now that's become the second string."

Just then, I heard Marshall's voice as well as the door to his office open and close. I went back to my own work and waited it out. When Tim finally left the office, I stepped out and watched Marshall go straight to the Keurig with only a "glad that's done."

"You know what this means, don't you?" He watched as the slow liquid dripped into the coffee cup. "Every lunatic with a theory will be calling us or the deputies. And reburying a dead cat? I can't wrap my head around that. Thank goodness that didn't make it to the papers."

I was about to say something when the startup sound from our fax machine took us all by surprise.

"It's the toxicology report on Betsy Sprig from the lab," Augusta announced. "Well, from Ranston it seems, and he sent a copy to us. Hmm, bloodwork appears normal. Procedure was immunoassay. Isn't that the one where they use certain antibodies to look for drugs in the bloodstream?"

Marshall took the paper from her and perused it. "Yes, antibodies. Anything else you'd care to add?"

She shook her head. "Nah, I think you'll figure it out."

"And then some. Unbelievable. Everything in range. Everything! She could've lived another few decades if it wasn't for foul play. Honestly, it substantiates the coroner's report. She died from injuries sustained by the hoist failing and Wayne's car trapping her underneath. And she wasn't drugged prior to the incident."

"If she wasn't drugged or dragged, then wouldn't she have had defensive wounds on her hands, Mr. Gregory? They always have defensive wounds on TV."

"Augusta has a point. Even if Jared told us Betsy never got her nails messed up, maybe this was the exception. Maybe she wanted to tamper with Wayne's car but never got that far. Face it, Aimee would have noticed something. She's worked on the undercarriage."

"Or maybe Jared lied." Augusta rubbed the bridge of her nose, careful not to dislodge her glasses.

"We went back to the original report," Marshall said. "Her nails weren't perfect but they weren't chipped or messed up. And they were natural. Not acrylic."

I bit my lower lip and sighed. "We're back to where we started."

The sound of Augusta slapping the edge of her desk jolted me. "What if Betsy killed the neighbor's cat and the neighbor got even? Happens more than you think. Revenge killing. Been known to happen on farms for chickens, hogs, and livestock."

"You think the neighbor could have been responsible? That's a new twist," I said.

Marshall shook his head. "Not likely. Too far-fetched for the neighbor to murder Betsy and somehow get her body under Wayne's car. Besides, the deputies said the lady was pretty 'long in the tooth' and used a walker."

Augusta shrugged. "Win some, lose some."

With that, Marshall went back to his office and I scurried off to mine. It was approaching our usual lunchtime but a thought popped into my head and refused to vacate.

"I need to run a few errands, Augusta. I'll eat my sub at my desk when I get back."

She furrowed her brow, causing her glasses to slip down a bit. "I've seen that look. Errands, my patootie. I know what you're up to. You're going to pay a visit to Betsy's neighbor, aren't you?"

My cheeks suddenly warmed and I was positive she'd notice a blush. "Shh. Fine. Okay. Maybe she didn't murder her neighbor, but maybe she has information to help us figure out who did. I'll be back in an hour. Too bad I don't have her name, but then again, seeing someone face-to-face is more effective."

"Did you want that detective plaque on your door to read *Kimball, Gregory*, or both?"

CHAPTER 39

I wasn't exactly sure how to approach my impromptu visit to Betsy's neighbor so I kept it short and simple. When the lovely white-haired octogenarian answered the door, I told her who I was, and handed her my business card from Williams Investigations.

"I'm their bookkeeper/accountant," I said, "but sometimes I assist with data-gathering when the detectives are too swamped. I'm afraid this is one of those times."

The woman, Mary Ruth McKay, welcomed me into her house, and as I glanced around, I realized everything was as originally installed in the late eighties. Mauve kitchen cabinets and white overhead fans without lights. I imagined the bathrooms would be similar and that the trim would be in gold.

Nonetheless, the house was impeccable. Even doilies on the coffee table and end tables. The walls had framed photos of various cats and I wondered which one was unearthed at Betsy's place. As I studied the room, I reached the conclusion that whichever one it was, it had been the last of her feline friends.

"I won't take up much of your time," I said, "but I hoped you could give me some information about Betsy. Her death still remains a mystery."

"Not a mystery. A murder. And believe me, I was tempted too. Would you care for anything to drink? I can reheat coffee."

"Thank you, no." *Reheated coffee. Just like my mom.* I smiled. "I've had my fill. I won't keep you long."

She motioned me to a tartan chair in her living room and took the one next to me. "Betsy wasn't exactly the friendliest of neighbors. And if you must know the truth, she was rather surly."

"Um, yes. That's what I've heard."

"I wish I could tell you more about her, but I really don't know much, even though we've lived next door for over a decade."

"Would you have any idea why on earth she would rebury your cat?"

"None whatsoever. The ground is as hard as can be. And the gravel above it is a nightmare to dig up. Funny, but shortly before Precious Kitty passed on, I saw her burying something under her bushes. Maybe even the same bush where they found Precious Kitty. Anyway, I approached her and asked if she had lost a pet. That's when she told me she abhorred cats and dogs, but she did have a parakeet who passed away. That's why she dug the hole. Odd, but I never heard any chirping. Neither did I see a birdcage by a window, and that's where people usually have them."

Unless there really was no parakeet.

"What about friends? Did she have any frequent visitors?"

"Not really. But a red-haired woman did stop by on more than a few occasions. Not that I was spying but I could hear them argue. Voices carry, you know."

"You wouldn't happen to remember what they quarreled about, would you?"

"Not what they argued about, but I did recall what the redhead said the last time. It was rather harsh. She said, 'It's going to take more money than this if you want me to risk it.' I thought it had something to do with casino gambling but I could be wrong. Especially after what she said next."

By now, I was all but salivating for details. "What? What did she say?"

"The redhead said, 'I had to bribe one of the Bobbsey Twins to keep her mouth shut. She must have overheard us.'"

"And then Betsy responded, 'Then she overheard where I hid it. You idiot! You should have denied it.'"

Bobbsey Twins. Has to be Darleen or Aimee.

"Did she say anything else?"

"Not the redhead. But Betsy got really agitated and told the redhead she'd call her later."

"Thanks so much. You've been a big help. Oh, and one more thing. Was the woman's hair a bright red or brunette red?"

"It was all sorts of shades of red. And all different lengths. Sometimes I'd see her with chin-length and other times it was longer. Shoulder-length. On the very next day! Must be nice to afford a matching wig when you have a bad hair day."

I froze and Mary Ruth asked if I was okay. "I hope I didn't offend you," she said. "I mean, if you're wearing a wig."

"Oh, no offense taken and it's my own hair. I was just surprised about the wig. Guess it's more common than I thought."

"Indeed. Especially at my age, with thinning air."

"You look fine. And thank you so much for your time. I appreciate it!" I made a graceful exit out of there and hammered on the gas to get back to spill the news to Augusta.

"Augusta! Augusta!" I shouted her name as I opened the office door. "You won't believe this but I'm positive Kevelyn is our thief and our murderess. Are the guys still in the office?" Then I looked around, hoping there weren't any clients in our small reception area.

"Only me and a half-eaten Hershey bar. But that's about to change." She took a large remaining bite and motioned for me to keep still. "Did the neighbor witness anything? It that what this is about?"

"More or less." I leaned on her desk and proceeded to tell her what I found out from Mary Ruth. "Kevelyn is one diabolically clever woman," I mused. "I'm convinced she orchestrated her own 'near-death' experience in the paint booth and went as far as to switch dolls in the shipping facility the other night. Most likely she left but went back without signing in. This time in a scarf and wig. You know how it is in those places. People sort of recognize you but they're way too busy with their own work to take a close look."

"Hmm, you've got a point."

"It's quite logical really. Betsy knew about the doll. She was a relative of Germaine Webb and that paper she buried had to have been the instructions for working the cipher. It must have been in her family. All she needed was the doll, but it was sold and then gifted to a museum before she could crawl."

"Yep. And when she read that it was going out on loan to the unity council, she made her move."

"Only *she* didn't make the move. Kevelyn did. She and Betsy were in cahoots. That's why Mary Ruth overheard her say it was a risky venture and would cost Betsy more money."

"Pretty convenient that Kevelyn worked for that same company."

"Birds of a feather, I suppose. And it was only a matter of time before the package would appear and Kevelyn would be able to switch it. And make a quick exit out without getting caught."

"Think you can prove any of it?"

"I doubt it. Not until I figure out why she wanted to get Luella out of the way."

"A third party in the get-rich-quick scheme perhaps?"

I shrugged. "Could be, but that'll involve more digging. I'll let Nate and Marshall know what I learned, but it's all hearsay at this point. With some classic analysis on my part."

"Classic analysis, huh?" Augusta grinned.

"Sounds better than theorizing."

"Still doesn't explain why Betsy hid the cipher letter under Mary Ruth's cat."

"She was seen burying her parakeet. Or burying *something.* She had to find a plausible reason for burying something, and that something was the cat. No one in their right mind would keep on digging in that hard soil once they discovered the box with the cat's remains. So . . . her cipher secret was safe. Until my mother decided to bring Streetman to the scene."

"Say no more! But honestly, Phee, you astonish me."

"Too bad the deputies don't concur. Face it, I still need to probe further while I try not to step on Nate's or Marshall's toes."

"I'm afraid to ask. You're beginning to make the book club ladies look mild."

About an hour later, Nate bustled through the door and announced that he read the DNA evidence on the wig and scarf. “I stopped by the posse office to chat with Bowman when the report came in. MCSO put a rush on it.”

“We’re all ears, Mr. Williams,” Augusta said.

Nate nodded. “We know this much—the wearer of the wig is a natural redhead. Found some human hairs attached to the wig. Apparently redheads have certain pigment-producing cells. Melanocytes. That’s not all. The techs were able to pull up some partial fingerprints from the scarf fabric. They’re still going through the database for any matches. Bowman expects results by tomorrow the latest.”

I widened my eyes at Augusta and turned to Nate. “Luella, Kevelyn, and Aimee all have red hair. Even before Aimee dyed hers it was auburn-colored.”

“Still a wide enough playing field. Marshall is following up with Luella and Aimee. Letting them know about the situation at the shipping facility and watching for a reaction. Right now, we’re out of action plans so we’ll need to rely on what Rolo finds out as well as our usual surveillance.”

“Tell him your theory, Phee,” Augusta said. “About Kevelyn. It may be enough to have her arrested on suspicion of attempted murder.”

Nate shifted his gaze my way. “What theory?” Then he returned the look to Augusta. “It’s the evidence that allows for an arrest to be made. Evidence followed by theory. Not the other way around.”

Augusta was steadfast. “It might be. Once you hear what Phee has to say.”

“Okay, kiddo, spill it!”

The next five minutes were spent with me articulating my “very logical theory,” bolstered with the comments from Mary Ruth. Unlike Bowman or Ranston, Nate weighed everything carefully before responding. And when he did, it was to Augusta.

“Better have another plaque made. We may have to change Phee’s title.” Then he winked at me. “Your husband and I had a similar thought about the three redheads. Unfortunately, there are still loose ends. Like the miniature we found in the Thorne Room diorama that was carved from the same piece of wood as the miniature you found at the auto restoration garage. Had to have come from the same person. But who? And even more pressing, how did they get into the museum’s display to leave the first one?”

“Did anyone ever figure out the f minus 1?”

Augusta furrowed her brow. “What f minus 1?”

I explained what it was and she jotted it down. “Hey, I’m no mathematician, but I remember ninth-grade algebra. More than I can say for you two!"

Nate and I looked sheepishly at each other before he motioned for Augusta to tell us.

"It's an inverse equation. If f takes x to y, then f minus 1 takes y to x." Augusta fluffed her hair and stared at us.

"I still don't get it."

"I think I do," Nate said, "but it doesn't have anything to do with algebra. It stands for *inverse*. It's a message. A code. Someone at the museum put in a code for someone else to tell them that a switch was made."

"Oh my gosh! Oh my gosh! Whoever it was told their accomplice that the doll was switched in the shipping office."

"Don't start jumping up and down, Phee. You'll knock over my coffee." Augusta moved it closer to her and took a sip.

"I'm shooting off a text to Marshall and the deputies. Looks like we'll need a new plaque for Augusta as well." Then he gave her a thumbs-up and hightailed it to his office.

CHAPTER 40

When I heard Marshall's voice a short time later, I came close to knocking my chair over as I raced to the outer office. "Did you get Nate's text? Did you find out anything from Luella and Aimee? Do you think one of them did it?"

Marshall darted his eyes back and forth as if to avoid enemy fire. "Yes to Nate's text, yes to your question, and not sure on your other question."

"I lost you after the word *text*." Augusta said. Then she looked at me. "What was it you wanted to know? You spoke too fast."

"I think I can help you ladies, but not before I fortify myself with coffee and whatever snacks are floating around." Marshall plunked a K-Cup in the Keurig and took a chocolate chip cookie from the last sleeve in the bag. "If nothing else, I put Luella and Aimee on notice. If one of them was responsible for any part in this, they'll either keep a low profile or commiserate with whomever they were partnering up with. That means your mother and her merry band of yentas will need to hang out some more at the garage with the men."

"No problem. They live for that stuff. Ugh. If only I could text her but I'm afraid it will sit there until Ground Hog Day. Guess I have no choice but to call."

Augusta snickered. "Be brave, Phee."

"By the way, hon, Nate shared your theory about Kevelyn and Betsy working in tandem." Then he looked at Augusta. "He also went on about your amazing code-breaking."

Augusta straightened her spine as if someone was about to pin a medal on her chest.

"So, now what? Other than my mother's snooping? And by the way, that buy-sell-trade event is still on. The rec center sent out a community email. Looks like Jay Leno will be making his appearance after all."

"What was the date again?"

"Two weeks from this Friday. It's an all-weekend thing. Prizes, refreshments, entertainment . . ."

"Think Wayne's car will be ready by then?"

"He believes so. For some reason, Aimee decided to work on it even though she wasn't part of the original crew. Wayne thinks it's because she has a soft spot for him."

"Harrumph." Augusta couldn't have been any louder. "The only soft spot she has is probably for some of the profit money. How old is that chickee anyway?"

I shrugged. "Sixties maybe. Younger than Wayne, for sure."

"Listen, much as I'd like to hang around and gab about chickees and cars, I've got to get with Nate and the deputies. Our new leads may be the most promising yet."

"You can thank us later," Augusta said as Marshall trotted off to Nate's office.

"I suppose I'd better get this over with and let my mother know she and her crew are still needed at the garage for reconnaissance."

"Interesting word for it."

I grinned and walked into my office. A few seconds later, I had my mother on the phone.

"Did they find out who the woman in the scarf was? Did they catch Betsy's killer? Is that why you called?"

"No, no, and again no. I called because Nate and Marshall need you and the ladies to keep on snooping at the garage. It's only a matter of time before you'll find some tidbit of information that will help unlock the theft, the switch, and the murder."

"Hmm, sounds like a good title for a book. Hold on a second. I need to move the vacuum so I don't trip over it."

A quick pause and she was back. "Streetman has developed a new and annoying habit of moving his dog biscuits all over the place. First in one room, then another. Not hiding them. Just moving them. I must have stepped on a half dozen of them and the crumbs go everywhere. I never used the vacuum as much. You would think he's doing this because he wants to make sure the cat doesn't get them. But Essie's not the least bit interested. In fact—"

In that instant, something clicked in my mind and it was as if fireworks went off. "Moving them from place to place."

"I just said that."

"Give Streetman a kiss from me. He may have broken the missing doll case."

"What?"

"Can't talk right now. I'll call later."

The second I ended the call, I raced out to Augusta. "I think I know where that doll is, or isn't."

"That was a quick revelation. Don't tell me one of the book club ladies figured it out."

"No, Streetman did."

"Now I'm lost."

I took a breath but I still wound up blurting out my words. "There had to be at least two people working together. One at the museum and the other at the auto restoration club. That's why there were two wooden miniatures. The inverse equation you figured out was a message—the switch had been made. And it was made at the shipping facility but the person at the museum needed to know. Are you getting this?"

"I'm trying. Slow down."

"Okay. As far as we know, the only person who would have had access was Darleen, but she no longer works there. Still, she could have made a duplicate key."

"And she could have been the person who wore the wig and scarf that night when the bait was dangled at the shipping place."

"But the DNA said it was a natural redhead."

"Phee, hair darkens. Natural redheads sometimes wind up as reddish brunettes. Didn't you say Darleen fit that description? It was Aimee who had the blue streaks, right?"

"Yes! Holy cannoli! It had to be Darleen. Quick—buzz Nate and Marshall!"

A minute later, Nate's door flew open. "Augusta said you figured out who stole the doll."

"It had to be Darleen," I said. "And I'll tell you how."

Nate and Marshall listened intently as I substantiated my "reasonable and most-likely theory."

"Got to hand it to you, hon," Marshall said. "The pieces fit together, but we have a long way to go proving it. Especially if Darleen was responsible for Betsy's murder. It's a tight-knit little group in that garage."

"That group will unravel if you get under Darleen's skin."

Augusta nodded and gave the men a thumbs-up. "Use Columbo's method. Nag her to death until she cries uncle."

"Got one better." Nate winked at us. "I'm about to sic Bowman and Ranston on her."

Just then, the fax machine buzzed and Augusta jumped to retrieve the paper.

"Incoming from Rolo," she announced as she read it. "He wants one of you to call him on a burner."

Nate held out his hand as she went to the cabinet to retrieve one. "We should order a case from Amazon."

The three of us crowded around Nate as he tapped the number into his phone and spoke. "Do I need to take out a business loan?" Then, a laugh followed by an "Uh-huh" and silence. Then, "That's a new spin" and "You've got more?"

Augusta and I flashed looks at each other like schoolgirls on a field trip. We strained to hear every word that Nate muttered while Marshall shifted his gaze from Nate to us.

Finally, Nate ended the call and exhaled. "Got to hand it to him. The guy lives for this stuff. First off, it's not a map that's concealed in the doll, it's a maze! Someone got their signals crossed on the dark web. Oh, and let me add that the maze isn't concealed, it's the cipher, or puzzle if you will, that's needed to open it. So, no treasure hunt. Whatever's in there *is* the prize."

"Wow. The maze is the coded locking system instructions that Streetman and Thor dug up," I gasped. "We can do it! Um, that is, if we find the doll."

"Thought there was a hex." Augusta lifted her glasses and rubbed her eyes. "Don't like messing with hexes. Never turns out well."

Nate shook his head. "Rolo thinks that soul-trapped-inside thing was fabricated to keep people at arm's length."

"It'll keep the book club ladies away for sure," Marshall said and laughed.

"Anyway," Nate went on, "he said to wave some sage sticks around it if we were that worried. Or better yet, burn them."

"Yikes! He's sounding like my aunt Ina."

"That information was his warm-up. The rest is a bit more definitive. Seems he did quite a bit of research into our auto restoration club members who were on scene and found some rather telling connections."

Augusta looked around as if there were hoards of people waiting to latch on to Nate's every word. "Tell all, Mr. Williams, I'm bracing for it."

Without wasting a second, Nate spit out the details as if it was a grocery list. "Holt worked for the auditing firm that handled the museum. That connects him for sure."

"What else? There's got to be more," I said.

"While he was at it, our buddy reviewed the museum employee names and histories again. The guy gives new meaning to that age-old expression burning the midnight oil. Seems the Turk sisters may have a connection over there."

"I knew it! I knew it! It's Darleen! She had to be the one who left the cryptic message in the diorama because she couldn't risk other means of communication with her partner-in-theft. Face it, nothing is safe. Not emails, text messages, phone calls . . . nothing! In fact, three of the book club ladies stopped using Alexa because they were positive she spied on them."

Augusta literally belched out a laugh. "And find out what? The secret ingredient for chopped liver?"

I looked at the men. "Do you think Bowman and Ranston will be able to eke out a confession?"

"No," they answered in unison. And then the quote that stayed with me all afternoon—"Not without us working the other end. Good thing we have Grub Hub and Door Dash on speed dial, hon."

CHAPTER 41

I was certain I had figured everything out except the location of the doll. Sadly, as the day ended without any major breakthroughs or arrests, I began to question my own logic. As I tossed around the roasted potatoes from a Stouffer's dinner, I wondered if Nate and Marshall were having any better luck revisiting the locations of interest, starting with the museum.

At a little past eight, Marshall phoned. "Never underestimate the power of rooting through papers on their way to be shredded," he said. The exuberance in his voice was unmistakable.

"Huh? Where are you?"

"Right now, back at the garage. Wayne and Aimee are the only ones here, along with Mike, who's busy reorganizing some shelves. Nate had a hunch about correspondence from the museum so when we were there, we back-doored ourselves in and went through their office bins before they reached the shredder. He remembered the curator telling him that shredding only takes place twice a month and papers are stored in a special holding area."

"I know you found out something—what was it?"

"The best part of my night." Then he paused. "So far."

"Tell me, don't keep me in suspense."

"A copy of an email from Betsy to the curator. It said, "'Worth your while to return what's mine.'"

"That's it?"

"Nope. There was a reply. Bank routing numbers. I called Rolo. Sure enough, the curator deposited a substantial amount of money, just under forty grand, in Betsy's account. No red flags went up because it took four separate transactions."

"Is that enough to arrest her?"

"No, but it's a good start. Lots of players and it's a tangled web. We need to work carefully."

"Who's the curator? You and Nate never said."

"Felice Boyd. Rolo's getting us her full name and any prior married names she might have had."

"Funny, but I think Nate was suspicious of her all along. Remember when he was relieved I had copied those files? He was convinced she wouldn't give him the real ones."

"Uh-huh. In this business, it's a good idea not to trust anyone, even if they're the one who hired you."

"I hate being so jaded."

"Comes with the job. Listen, I need to go. We'll talk later. Love you."

Suddenly, my appetite returned and I gobbled up the remaining potatoes. As far as I was concerned, one edge of the puzzle was clearly in place—the curator got a payoff from Betsy to get the doll back to her, but the only way she could do that, without arousing suspicion, would be to have it switched while it was in transit.

That meant they needed another cohort to make the switch at the shipping facility and find a way to leave the cryptic message at the museum that the deed was done. Kevelyn was the only one who worked at the facility and Darleen was the one who had access to a museum key. That meant what? Darleen got into the deal? My gosh, Marshall was right. This was complicated.

As for murdering Betsy, any one of those three could be culpable. The curator, because ultimately, she'd get the doll back, and/or Kevelyn and Darleen because the doll was worth a fortune. Hex or no hex.

It had been a while since I kept Lyndy in the loop and now was as good a time as any, so I phoned her. She apologized for not finding out more about "her assigned suspects," but told me she'd check to see if her aunt heard any new scuttlebutt. She did mention one thing, though, and I was pretty sure Rolo would have checked it out. I made a mental note to get an answer to her question—"What did Kevelyn's and Darleen's bank accounts look like in terms of recent transactions?" Or Aimee's, for that matter. Heck, why not include Holt and Jared as well as Luella?

To my way of thinking, none of them were really off the hook for theft or murder. But I needed to focus on first things first and that meant following the doll's trail. And unlike Streetman's prize, this one wasn't limited to a one-story house in Sun City West.

The best I could figure was that Kevelyn made the switch and got the doll to Betsy, but considering Betsy was found dead under Wayne's car during that time frame, maybe Kevelyn did the nasty deed and, with Darleen's help, moved Betsy under the car. That meant Kevelyn would still be in possession of the doll.

I sent a brief text to Marshall: *Pretty sure Kevelyn's got the doll.*

He texted back: *Keep going, Miss Marple. See you soon.*

I tossed the empty TV dinner plate into the trash, rinsed my fork, and perused my murder map again. About an hour later, Marshall returned, eager to hear my latest spin on the murder-for-doll case, as we had come to call it.

"It makes sense, hon, but Bowman wants to speed things up. You won't believe this but he wants to pull a 'great reveal.'"

"A great what?"

"You know, like the end of the Agatha Christie novels or *Death in*

Paradise where all the suspects are together and the detective expounds on his or her theory until the suspect finally confesses."

"Those are fiction. It'll never work. There must be something we're missing that can pull it all together."

"The only thing I'm missing right now is a good night's sleep. I'm beat. Maybe I'll get an epiphany before dawn."

"We can only hope."

The two of us crawled into bed and watched the local news, followed by the national news until our eyes blurred over. Sleep came fast but it didn't last. At two fifty-three, the landline rang and it was my mother. "Good. You sound more awake than I thought you would be."

"What's going on, Mom? It's almost three in the morning."

"That's what Gloria Wong and I want to know. We're standing across from the auto garage because Gloria lost her cell phone and thought she might have dropped it on the walking track when she was here earlier so we came to look. She didn't realize it was missing until an hour ago when she decided to watch YouTube because she couldn't sleep. She called me because she didn't want to go alone to the rec center complex. Her daughter is working the night shift at the hospital."

Her daughter's the smart one.

"Um, that's more information than I can handle right now. Hold on, I'm putting you on speaker."

Marshall rubbed his eyes and scooched closer to the phone as my mother continued.

"I called you because something's going on in that garage. The lights are on and we can hear shouting."

"Did you call the posse?"

"Yes, they're between shifts. They'll send a car but we didn't want to wait. In case someone else is getting murdered."

"I think that's a bit dramatic, but—Oh, never mind."

"The door opened. A woman's running out!" Then to Gloria, "Can you video this? Oh wait, I forgot. You lost your phone."

I must have rolled my eyes a half dozen times. "Can you see who it is?"

"Now she's being chased by another woman. It's dark. I think one of them is Aimee. She's got something under her arm."

"All right. We're on our way. Don't do anything. You and Gloria stay where you are."

"I heard that," Marshall said. "I'll grab my jeans and a sweatshirt. Ready in five."

"My mother didn't mention the dogs. That's a good thing."

"Good thing? It's a miracle!"

We made it to the auto restoration garage in less than a half hour. No traffic at that time of night. Sure enough, the lights were on and the door was wide open. My mother and Gloria were seated in my mother's car near the walking track and out of view from the garage.

Marshall and I slid into the backseat and he closed the door as quietly as he could. "What's going on, ladies? Did the women take off?"

"No, they went back inside the garage," my mother said. "One of them was Aimee. The other one must be Kevelyn. The lighting is dim but I would have recognized Luella and Darleen."

"Did you hear anything, Mom?"

"And how. Didn't we, Gloria?"

Gloria turned to face us and leaned forward. "One of them said not to be a fool and that it was safer where they stashed it originally. Then the other one yelled, "'Wayne plans to take the car back to his house tomorrow. Then what? We can't sneak over there to get it.' I don't think she meant the car. Shh, listen. They're still arguing."

Sure enough, when we stopped talking to each other, we heard voices. And they got louder.

Suddenly, something jumped up from between my mother and Gloria, and I nearly screamed.

"It's only Streetman," my mother said. "He was sleeping in his tote."

"Some miracle," I whispered to Marshall, but no one heard because the next voice I heard yelled, "Forget the stupid hex and put it back. We'll deal with it later. And if we have to deal with Wayne, we will!"

Then Aimee's voice, "I didn't like cleaning up your dirty work the last time. You got too greedy and what was I supposed to do? By the way, Betsy was dead weight. Good thing there was a heavy-duty dolly in here."

"You didn't mind the payoff, did you? Or leaving the signal at the museum. So don't point a finger at me. Besides, what choice did I have? Betsy threatened to call the sheriff's office. I panicked. It wasn't as if it was premeditated. We were in her kitchen and she had one of those huge skillets on the stove. I swung it at her in anger. The fact that it killed her shocked me as well!"

"My gosh—it was Kevelyn. She killed Betsy." I tried to process the sequence of events but my mind was in a fog. "And Aimee was the one who carved those miniatures. Go figure."

My mother leaned over the edge of the driver's seat and grabbed Marshall's elbow. "They have the doll! What else carries a hex? Oh no! Does that mean they'll kill Wayne?"

"Calm down, Harriet. Don't take things out of context."

"Context? One of those hussies is Betsy's killer!" With that, my mother handed Gloria her tote bag and pointed to the garage. "Those two will bolt out of there any second. Marshall, you have a gun. Don't be afraid to use it!

Phee and I will be right behind you." Then to Gloria, "You stay here and protect my little man."

"All of you, stay here!" Marshall directed. "And don't make a move."

With that, he stepped out of the car and crept toward the garage. That's when bright car lights illuminated his back as a sleek Mercedes rolled into the driveway.

"Did the posse get new vehicles?" Gloria asked. "That car looks larger."

"Not as large as the gun that woman is holding," my mother replied. "And no, Gloria, it's not the posse."

CHAPTER 42

Marshall slipped to the rear of the garage and I prayed whoever it was with the gun hadn't noticed him off to the side. My hands shook as I texted MCSO and Nate. It would be at least twenty minutes before one of the deputies arrived. And Nate lived even further away.

A sudden ping and a text message appeared from Marshall: *That's the curator—Felice Boyd. Stay where you are.*

I texted back: *I SOS'd N, B & R.*

Then, from Marshall: *Me, too. Don't make a move.*

And while I wasn't about to make a move, Streetman sure was.

"He has to potty, Phee. He's pawing at me. No one will notice. The gunslinger over there just went inside the garage. We'll only be a minute."

Then, before I could stop her, she and Streetman were already on the sidewalk across from the garage.

"Oh dear," Gloria said. "Thor might have to go, too."

"Thor? Isn't he home?"

"No, I brought him with me. He's waiting in my car. It's the gray one over there."

This night cannot possibly get any worse.

"Okay," I found myself saying, "let's get my mother and we'll let Thor out. We can walk in the opposite direction from the front of the garage." *And keep walking until the posse gets here.*

As Gloria and I headed to her car, the electric garage door lifted and we hustled to get out of view. Plastered against the side wall, I heard Felice say, "You sneaky little double-crosser. You had this planned all along. Well, you're not about to ruin everything."

Then another voice. Aimee's. "I'm holding a Bernzomatic Blow Torch with a far reach. Fire that gun and you'll be engulfed in flames. You got paid. You're not in this deal. Even *if* Kevelyn is your sister. And you're not getting your hands on that doll. Unless, of course, you want to go into the paint booth where Wayne's car is."

My mind worked overtime as the puzzle pieces came together. Kevelyn and the curator were sisters. But how did Aimee fit in? And where was Darleen? Then my brain flashed back to a conversation I heard when I first met the Turk sisters. Aimee said she inadvertently took Darleen's keys and later returned them.

Inadvertently, my foot! Aimee had to have known Darleen kept a stolen key to the museum on her key chain from when she worked security there. It was a no-brainer. Given Aimee's mechanical skills, she was able to leave a clue for Felice that the switch was made by Kevelyn.

So much for my finger-pointing at Darleen. And it had to be Aimee in the wig and scarf. Not her sister! Red hair is red hair. I could have kicked myself for putting the wrong pieces together.

Not that it mattered. Not with Felice holding a gun, Aimee holding Wayne's car as a hostage, and my mother traipsing around in the dark with Streetman. I only prayed Marshall had a plan. Meanwhile, Thor yanked on his leash and Gloria had no choice but to skirt around the building.

Then, without warning, a maroon Buick pulled into the far side of the parking lot and Shirley, Lucinda, and Cecilia got out. All of them dressed in heavy parkas over long nightdresses. Next thing I knew, Myrna's car pulled up, followed by Louise's. At least those two took the time to put on long pants and sweatshirts.

"Have you found Gloria?" Myrna bellowed as soon as she spotted me. "Her daughter, Lydia, phoned Lucinda since she was first on their phone tree. Lydia got home from her twelve-hour shift at the hospital and when Thor didn't greet her at the door, she looked around for him. That's when she realized her mother was gone. At first, she thought Gloria might have taken the dog out back but they weren't there. And Gloria never walks him after dark. She tried her mom's cell phone but no answer. So she used the Find My Phone app and saw that Gloria was across from the auto garage. She thought the worst and called the posse but they were between shifts."

"Where's Lydia now?" I whispered, hoping Myrna would get the point to speak softly.

She didn't. "She's on her way over here."

"Shh!" I held my finger to my lips but Myrna paid no attention and kept talking. "Gloria could have been abducted, you know. And by the way, your mother's phone went to voicemail."

"Shh! Quiet! Gloria is on the other side of the building and my mother is nearby. Go back to your cars. Betsy's killer is in the garage. Marshall is dealing with it."

"Did the killer kidnap Gloria?" Louise asked.

It was a miracle my eyeballs remained in their sockets. "No, Gloria lost her cell phone around here and got my mother to help her look. Then they heard a ruckus in the garage."

"What did you say, Phee?" It was Shirley. "I couldn't make it out."

Just then, Marshall texted: *Deputies on their way. Nate, too. Can see Aimee and Kevelyn. Can't see woman with gun from this angle. No one is making a move.*

Well, no one that Marshall was aware of. Before I could stop them, Shirley, Lucinda, and Cecilia rushed to the garage door and flung it open. "We're here, Gloria!" Shirley shouted. At the sound of her voice, Thor, who forged a bond with Shirley while she babysat him from time to time, broke loose from Gloria in the parking lot and thundered into the garage, taking Aimee and Kevelyn by surprise.

Thor immediately stood on his hind legs, placing his huge front paws on Shirley's chest. Caught off guard, Shirley fell backward onto Felice, who stumbled over the Media Blaster cleaning booth for small automotive parts. She dropped her gun and bent down to retrieve it, but not before Cecilia shrieked, "Is that a gun?"

Then Shirley caught her footing and grabbed a fireproof blanket from a nearby shelf and tossed it over the gun.

"It's not a grenade," Myrna yelled. "It'll only go off if someone fires it." At that moment, Felice grasped the gun in her hand and Myrna responded with her Screamer. It was like a seventies disco party that featured an air-raid drill. Only Myrna's device was louder and the strobes were faster and more annoying.

That sent poor Thor heaving all over the place. And a somewhat hysterical Gloria.

Her voice resonated across the garage. "Quick, someone—find some towels before the place becomes unrecognizable."

As if the catastrophe wasn't bad enough, my mother made her grand entrance with Streetman tucked under her arm. *Please keep a tight grip on him.*

Marshall rushed in and managed to elbow through the women, grabbing Felice by the wrist and knocking the gun to the ground again.

"I wouldn't move if I were you," he said to her, "or it will make things worse."

I wasn't sure exactly how, but still, it did put her on notice for all of thirty seconds. She crossed her arms and glared at Marshall. "Aimee Turk's the one you need to be arresting. I only showed up to retrieve museum property."

"You can talk arrest with MCSO, not me."

Suddenly, the sound of a car engine broke through the noise from the Screamer. All heads turned to the rear garage door as Aimee took Sally Stang from the paint booth bay and drove out the door. With the window rolled down, she yelled, "Now it's grand-theft auto!"

Chapter 43

"She'll be back," Kevelyn said. "Same as last time, but the car will be a few pounds lighter."

"You better not be saying what I think you are," Felice said as she struggled to free her arm from Marshall's grip. "Seems our sweet little accomplice wanted to keep the treasure all to herself."

Within seconds, a siren roared and I knew that Bowman and/or Ranston had arrived. As I looked around, I was hard-pressed to make sense of what I saw.

My mother and Gloria had grabbed rags and towels and were frantically cleaning up after Thor while Streetman remained tucked under my mother's arm, growling at anyone within three feet of him.

Lucinda and Shirley managed to talk Myrna into turning off the Screamer, but only after they agreed to let her brandish her can of bear spray. Cecilia and Louise, in the meantime, stood in front of Kevelyn, making it nearly impossible for her to move since one step backward would have put her in the large primer booth. Meanwhile, Marshall remained still with an unhappy Felice at his side.

"All of this over a doll?" he asked her.

"Not any doll, the fortune of a lifetime."

"But you didn't want it back for the museum, did you? It was your intent all along to keep it with the hope of figuring out the cipher."

"I waited a long time for an opportunity like this and it finally came, thanks to Betsy Sprig's money problems. In fact, it landed in my lap. How could I refuse? Betsy came to me, wanting what was hers, even though the artifact had been donated to one museum or another before we acquired it."

"So you made a deal?"

"It's not as if I made it with the devil, even though that doll carried a nasty little pox on it."

"I'm listening," Marshall said.

"I want to hear this, too," Cecilia added. "Myrna, put that spray bottle down. She's not going anywhere."

Then, from across the room—"Phee! Can you please take Streetman? He's getting antsy and I have to help poor Gloria. Thor is upchucking everywhere."

Just then, Shirley broke in. "I'll take Thor. He'll calm down."

No doubt Shirley got the better end of the deal as Streetman squirmed, wriggled and wrangled in my arms.

"Can't you control him?" a voice bellowed from the door. I turned and it was Bowman. He strode toward Marshall and Felice like a gunslinger ready for a shootout. "By the way," he said to Marshall, "Nate saw Wayne's Mustang speeding down Spanish Garden. He's on it. Good thing you shot off that text to all of us. Got a BOLO on the vehicle."

"Better hope she doesn't wreck it," Felice said. "And I'm not talking about the car."

"At least Wayne doesn't know. This will put him over the edge."

As if on cue, Myrna replied, "Uh-oh. Look behind you."

A terrified Wayne, accompanied by Herb, Kevin and Bill, rushed in. "My neighbor woke me up! Once a fireman, always a fireman. Keeps his scanner on all night. He heard there was a BOLO out for my car and thought someone stole it. Figured he better not wait to call me."

"Yeah," Herb said. "So Wayne called us. Kenny couldn't get away from his wife or she'd divorce him."

"I'm sure we'll recover your vehicle," Bowman muttered as he surveyed the room.

Streetman was still growling, my mother and Gloria were still cleaning, and the rest of the book club ladies were still elbowing and straining to see what would happen next.

"Recover my vehicle? What happened?"

Before Bowman could answer, a voice I didn't recognize called out, "I'm looking for my mother." I turned to see a slender Asian woman in her late twenties or early thirties. Sleek chin-length hair and absolutely stunning. Especially in the middle of the night. She wore black scrubs that identified her as a technician at the local hospital.

Within seconds, Thor was all over her and Gloria called out, "Over here, Lydia!"

She went straight to Gloria, but not without surveying the situation. Especially Marshall pointing to Felice's gun on the floor. "Mom! What's going on? I was frantic when I didn't find you at home."

"I'm frantic now!" Wayne announced. "What happened to Sally?"

"Is that one of your friends?" Lydia asked her mother.

Then everyone tried to answer at once, creating a cacophony that will most likely linger in my brain for weeks. As I tried to make sense of the events cascading around me, the random thoughts in my head mobilized and I was struck with something—I knew where Aimee was headed.

"She's going to Irvin Feldstein's house," I shouted. "She must have welded a spot for that doll to be hidden in the undercarriage of Wayne's car. That's why she was so helpful all of sudden. My gosh—does anyone know where Irvin lives?"

"Yeah," Kevin replied. "Corner of West Hyacinth and Spanish Garden. I had to give him a ride home from Putter's Paradise once when his car broke down."

"That's close." I looked at Bowman and Marshall. "We can be there in five minutes. Nate should be on the scene already."

"Go!" Bowman growled at Marshall and me. "I'll call for backup at Irvin's and keep this lovely redhead in custody. Darn it! What's keeping Ranston? He better not have pulled into Quik Stop for a donut."

I looked around for my mother in order to return Streetman to her, but I couldn't spot her. With no time to waste, I gripped tighter to the little snapping turtle and flew out the door alongside Marshall.

"It's a madhouse in there," Marshall said. "Glad to turn the reins over to Bowman. And Ranston if he ever makes it there. Boy, you've got a good memory. About a hoist at Irvin's."

"I only pray I'm right, but I'm pretty sure I am."

Less than three minutes later, Marshall turned off of RH Johnson onto Spanish Garden. That's when he got the text from Nate: *Flat tire. Pulled into first driveway. You passed me.*

"Nate got a flat. We need to keep going. Over there! On your left. Garage lights are on. She must have pulled in. Come on, I doubt she's armed, but that doesn't mean she isn't dangerous. All we need to do is watch and take photos. No moves until the MCSO deputies arrive."

Fortunately for us, Irvin's garage had a side door and small window. We snuck over and peered in. My hunch was right. Aimee had gotten the QuickJack in place and was already under the car.

"Whoa, that woman moved fast," Marshall said. "By the looks of things, she's pretty adroit with those tools."

"Yeah, years of being an aircraft mechanic."

"I wonder what's taking those deputies so long? They don't have posse shift changes."

"No, but they wind up with other distractions like accidents or shootings. It's Phoenix, remember?"

"At least we're out here in the bubble."

"The bubble?"

"That's my mother's new term for Sun City West."

Streetman's ears perked up and next thing I knew, he wrangled about with a new intensity. I couldn't imagine what had provoked him, but knowing that little chiweenie, it could have been a leaf blowing.

Unfortunately, it wasn't. Two menacing-looking coyotes headed toward us. Usually they scurry off if humans yell or make noise, but the last thing we wanted to do was alert Aimee of our presence. We even parked across the street and one house down.

"Just stay still," Marshall whispered.

Too bad Streetman didn't concur. That brazen little dog sat up and barked with a high-pitched sound that I feared would pierce my eardrums. The coyotes turned and headed in the opposite direction, but Aimee opened the garage door to see what was going on. She also saw us.

With the wooden doll in her hand, and a cold, fixed stare, she said, "If you don't want me to crack this thing wide open as if it was a chestnut, you'd stay put and let me leave."

"I have no problem with that," Marshall replied, "but I think the crew coming down the block may have a different opinion."

I turned, expecting it to be the deputies, but instead it was Wayne, Herb, and Kevin. It was like a scene from an old Clint Eastwood movie only no one carried a gun.

Terrific. This is all we need.

"Give me the car keys," Wayne shouted to Aimee.

"You know I can't do that. Not now, anyway. And if all of you want to see this priceless piece of history remain that way, you'll wait until I remove the QuickJack and be on my way."

"Not so fast," I said. *Oh my gosh. What am I saying? Not like I have a plan.*

As if Streetman could read my mind, he leapt from my arms, charged at her and tore into her pant leg. The suddenness of it all took everyone but Marshall by surprise. He seized on that moment to race over and snatch the doll from Aimee.

Then, as she lashed out to get it back, Herb and Kevin restrained her. As for Wayne, he was too preoccupied fawning over his Mustang. Worse than my mother with Streetman.

I bent down and picked up the dog, who still had a vested interest in tearing Aimee's pant leg into shreds.

"He doesn't like some fabrics. Can smell them a yard away." Why had I forgotten that tidbit of information about the dog?

Then, reinforcements arrived. First the blaring sirens that sent Irvin and his wife out of the house. Then, four county deputies who charged the scene as if it was Bunker Hill. I don't remember how long we were there, but when Marshall and I headed back to the auto garage, we were in possession of Streetman and the priceless hexed doll that I never wanted to see again.

"Not bad for the relaxing sleep we were supposed to have," Marshall said and grinned. "And brace yourself, it's going to get even longer once Bowman and Ranston decide to take notes."

CHAPTER 44

"My precious little stormtrooper," my mother gushed at the dog the second Marshall and I walked back into the auto restoration garage. It was a worse "homecoming" than the lake incident.

Gloria, Shirley and Thor raced over to us, along with Lydia, who looked absolutely shell-shocked.

"Did they catch Aimee? What about Wayne's car?"

"I can only answer one question at a time, Mom. Yes, they got Aimee. Yes, Wayne got his car, and finally—we are in possession of that doll. Marshall's got it under an old towel we had in the car. We didn't want to leave it there."

"He's holding the doll? The hexed doll with the trapped soul? Everyone! Step away! Step away!"

"Lordy! Not the hexed doll!" If Shirley could have moved to the next county, she would have. Instead, she backed as far away from us as she could.

Then Cecilia turned to Lucinda. "I told you we should have snuck out some Holy Water from the church when we had the chance, but no, you were too afraid we'd be caught."

"That doll isn't going to curse anyone," I said, my voice louder and more deliberate than usual. "I'm positive it was a ruse to keep people at bay."

"That doll is evidence," Ranston announced. They were the first words he'd said to us since we walked into the garage.

"Here, take it." Marshall held out the towel with the doll inside. Ranston recoiled and motioned for a deputy. "Call the lab. Get a forensics guy over here." Then he looked at me and continued. "Or a gal. Don't care as long as I don't have to go near it. And tell them to bring a heavy-duty evidence bag."

I tried not to laugh and as a result, tears streamed down my face.

"Are you all right, Phee?" my mother asked. "Don't tell me that hex has gotten to you."

Not any more than the dog, the book club ladies, Herb's pinochle crew and you.

"No, it's allergies."

At that moment, Bowman approached us. "Too bad your boss missed all the fun. Wait! Here he comes now."

I turned and Nate straggled in. "Talk about nightmares. I never want to see another tire donut ever again!"

Bowman chuckled. "Understood. Your team can fill you in. No reason to keep everyone here. We'll get complete statements in the morning. By the way, it was Miss Viviani who trashed Betsy Sprig's house while trying to find the doll that Miss Turk had hidden. Needless to say, Miss Viviani and Miss Boyd are on their way to county lockup for the night. Got a text from MCSO. Miss Turk will be joining them. Nice work, Marshall." Then he looked at me. "You too, Mrs. Kimball. Gregory. Whatever."

I finally took a relaxing breath but it was short-lived. Next thing I knew, my aunt and uncle charged into the garage, my aunt's long braids bouncing off her chest and my uncle's sleep mask sitting on top of his head.

"Louis accidently unplugged the phone. Just heard the message from the phone tree and we got here as fast as we could. What did I miss?"

Only the opening and closing acts of a Broadway production.

"Come on, Ina," my mother said, "we'll go back to my place and I'll make coffee. Still have those frozen holiday treats from December."

I grabbed Marshall's arm, said good night to everyone and told Lydia how nice it was to finally meet her. She nodded, still in shock.

"You know this isn't over, don't you?" I said to Marshall when we crept into bed for the second time.

"Betsy's killer and the collaborators confessed and the doll was returned. I'd say it's over."

"Not that, the endless brunches at Bagels 'n More to revisit the entire thing. And what about the doll? Won't someone want to use the cipher and see what's in it?"

"That will be up to the museum. It's their property. They refused to X-ray it when they first got it for fear it would damage the contents. This, however, may be different. But still, it's hard to say."

"Maybe so, but it's a historical mystery and Tim Justin isn't going to let it ride. Come on, let's get some sleep. But first, one of us should text Augusta with the news. Don't want her to find out from the TV, or worse yet, social media."

"No worries. Nate already shot off a text. He also asked her to pick up chocolate donuts tomorrow."

"To celebrate?"

"Nah, he just likes them."

• • •

At a little after six, Augusta sent all three of us the same text: *Williams Investigations was just on channel 10.* It was followed with a thumbs-up.

I flipped on the TV and hoped they'd replay whatever it was she'd watched. Eventually, they did, but it was forty or so minutes later when the re-loop of stories came on. I had the TV cranked up so loud, I was afraid the entire block would hear it.

"A number of arrests have been made in the Betsy Sprig murder case, thanks to the comprehensive work from the Maricopa County Sheriff's Office in conjunction with Williams Investigations out of Glendale."

"Did you hear that?" I called out from the kitchen. "We finally got credited for our work."

"Helps when you know the reporter."

"You called Tim Justin in the middle of the night?"

"More like predawn, and believe me, he scurried to get that early-bird story on the air."

"It was like unraveling spaghetti. All those people connected to each other by happenstance and greed. At least it didn't deter that buy-sell-trade event. Or Jay Leno's appearance."

"Until he gets wind of your mother, Myrna, and Paul doing the MCing."

"Don't remind me. And speaking of which, the entire senior rumor club is having brunch this Saturday at their usual haunt. You weren't the only one texting at an ungodly hour. My mother sent me that invite sometime after five. They need to 'flush out' the details."

"Why?"

"Because that's what they do. Beat something to death until the next drama wafts their way. And in this case, it'll be that doll's cipher. Mark my words. I honestly wished Thor would have latched on to it like a dog toy and chewed through it."

"The museum may choose not to tamper with it."

"Then they'll be tampering with something far worse—the Booked 4 Murder book club. Boy, I can't wait to share this with Lyndy!"

• • •

And while we spent the next few days wrapping up the investigation and touching base with Rolo, Wayne spent it at the garage prepping his car for the event. This time with the help of Bill and Kevin. Paul stopped in a few times as well to offer Wayne large decals of trout for the vehicle, but it was a no-go.

Rolo was insistent that *if* and *when* the museum decided to crack open the heirloom doll, he needed to be the one to guide them. "Those code-locking devices are tricky. One wrong move and it'll be kaput."

And while the murder investigation was over, the mystery of what was inside that doll was not. Endless letters to the newspaper appeared along with never-ending threads on Next Door Neighbor, Buzz About Town, and Sun City West Chit-Chatters. The pressure reached the museum board because next thing we knew, my aunt Ina called the office. Augusta was only too thrilled to hand her over to me.

"Phee! The art museum held a special board meeting last night to discuss the priceless doll. The sheriff's office no longer needed it for evidence and it was returned to us by courier. We voted unanimously to use the cipher and unlock the treasure. After all, it could turn out to be an even more priceless bit of history that we could display."

Or a Cracker Jack prize.

"Unanimous, huh?"

"That's right. Let your boss know. This has to be done with the utmost discretion. Can't very well have a circus going on."

"Then be sure not to breathe a word of it to my mother or the book club."

"My lips are sealed."

And while Aunt Ina's lips were sealed, Uncle Louis's were not. He ran into Herb at Costco and blurted it out. That's why it came as no surprise a week later when Nate, Marshall, and I drove to the art museum after hours to unlock the code, when we spied the book club ladies and Herb's cronies alongside the building.

"Unbelievable," I muttered. "Totally unbelievable. Worse yet, my mother never said a word to me."

"Probably because she knew what you would say." Marshall squeezed my shoulder as I exited Nate's car.

"No harm, no foul. The museum has a large demonstration room. We'll seat them there. I'll let the assistant director know. It will be a while until they find a curator."

"She better not have the dog with her."

Nate glanced at the women as they ambled toward us. "No tote bag in sight. You may have lucked out."

"You should have told me, Phee," my mother called out. "I had to hear it from Herb."

I spun around and walked toward her. "You weren't supposed to hear it from anyone. It's a covert operation."

"This isn't the Cold War."

"Fine. Just lay low. Nate will get everyone set up in the demonstration room."

I glanced at the ladies and tried not to laugh. With the exception of Myrna, they all wore masks left over from the pandemic a couple of years ago, as if that could prevent them from inhaling a hex.

"This way," Marshall said. "Nice to see all of you."

Thankfully they were on their best behavior. A security guard ushered them into the horseshoe-shaped demonstration room on the ground floor, only yards away from where my mother and my aunt got trapped, and I prayed all would go well. Two other guards flanked the demo table, giving me some peace of mind.

The board members sat in the first row along with Marshall and me. Nate, with a burner phone in hand, secured the doll from the assistant director and called Rolo. The tension was palpable as if someone was about to diffuse a bomb.

Had it not been for Nate repeating everything Rolo said, I wouldn't have known what was going on.

With doll facing up, lift left arm. Roll it three times.

Move to right arm. Roll it twice.

Listen for light audible click.

Seam should open beneath the neck.

Carefully twist to the left until you hear another click.

I whispered to Marshall, "Sounds like a combination lock from high school."

Then, chest should split open.

This was followed by Nate, "It did."

Then, look at the puzzle. It should resemble a labyrinth.

Then, "It does."

All of a sudden, Shirley poked me from the row behind. "You don't think he's letting the evil spirits out, do you?"

I shook my head. "It's not Pandora's box."

Next came the really complicated part. It took Nate over fifteen minutes to weave his way around the puzzle layers. Just as one layer was mastered, it revealed another one. Even Russian Matryoshka dolls had their limit.

At last I heard Nate ask Rolo, "Is this it?"

I gripped Marshall's hand and closed my eyes. Apparently, I wasn't the only one, because I heard Lucinda say, "How can we see if we keep our eyes closed?"

Deafening silence sucked the air from the room and I heard Nate gasp. I sat bolt upright and kept my grip on Marshall's hand.

"Either we hit pay dirt, folks, or someone played a huge trick on us," he said.

My aunt clasped her chest and shouted, "What? What is it?"

Nate responded, "Someone's heirloom jewelry. Rings, brooches, and gem-laden bracelets."

In a matter of minutes, the museum staff took photos and the director, accompanied by the security guards, heralded the doll and its contents into their safe.

"That's it?" my mother asked. "I expected something a tad more dramatic."

I furrowed my brow. "Like what?"

"I don't know. But something more dramatic."

The drama came all right, but it took another week and a half. Our office got a call from the museum, telling us that their authentication process resulted in an outstanding find—all the pieces had been stolen from the British House of Hanover between 1760 and 1775.

Augusta, upon hearing the news, remarked, "And to think the high point of my week was finding chicken on special at the supermarket."

Epilogue

Sun City West was the center of attention for at least three weeks until someone proposed a billboard on Route 303 and Vistancia, along with the Corte Bella community, went ballistic. Yep, winners and losers for sure.

Rolo got his dream backyard barbeque and Williams Investigations got the bill.

The Phoenix Art Museum was compelled to return the jewelry to the British royal family but an agreement was reached and the museum was able to keep the pieces on permanent loan. Not only that, but an entire exhibit, featuring the murder that led up to the finding, was devoted to that acquisition.

The buy-sell-trade event was a tremendous success but not as tremendous as the one Wayne enjoyed. It seemed Jay Leno had been looking for a 1965 hardtop Ford Mustang and offered Wayne a pretty penny for the car.

So much for love. Wayne kissed Sally Stang goodbye and pocketed his "bucket list" money.

The automotive restoration club elected a new president—Jared Loundsby—and a new secretary—Darleen Turk.

Aimee, Kevelyn, and Felice were still being held at the Fourth Avenue Jail awaiting trial.

Oh, and Lydia Wong was also compelled to join her mother and the book club ladies for Saturday brunches at Bagels 'n More when she wasn't working. Last I heard, Lydia signed up for every Saturday shift.

If only I could be so lucky.

About the Author

Ann I. Goldfarb

New York native Ann I. Goldfarb spent most of her life in education, first as a classroom teacher and later as a middle school principal and professional staff developer. Writing as J. C. Eaton, along with her husband, James Clapp, she has authored the Sophie Kimball Mysteries, the Wine Trail Mysteries, the Charcuterie Shop Mysteries, and the Marcie Rayner Mysteries. In addition, Ann has nine published YA time travel mysteries under her own name. Visit the websites at: www.jceatonmysteries.com and www.timetravelmysteries.com

James E. Clapp

When James E. Clapp retired as the tasting room manager for a large upstate New York winery, he never imagined he'd be coauthoring cozy mysteries with his wife, Ann I. Goldfarb. His first novel, *Booked 4 Murder*, was released in June 2017, followed by nine other books in the series and three other series. Nonfiction in the form of informational brochures and workshop materials treating the winery industry were his forte, along with an extensive background and experience in construction that started with his service in the U.S. Navy and included vocational school classroom teaching. Visit the website at www.jceatonmysteries.com.

Made in the USA
Las Vegas, NV
15 March 2024